The Ark

The Ark

Christopher Coates

Published 2018 by Creativia
Cover art by Cover Mint
Edited by D.S. Williams

Prologue

The comfortable looking home sat on a large open lot with a majestic oak tree in the front yard. The siding was faded, but the paint on the trim looked new. The windows all had curtains, and there was smoke drifting from the chimney. The house was located about three miles outside the village limit. That was not uncommon anymore, people had been willing to move out from the safety of the towns for about the last twenty years.

Without warning, the front door flew open, and a young girl raced out of the house and into the morning air. The summer sun was only starting to rise, but the temperature was already in the mid-seventies. Several birds were searching the lawn for food and they took flight as the intruder disrupted their quest. The girl paused briefly to stare at the birds since they were still such an unusual sight. She looked to be about nine years old and wore faded jeans and a plain red tee shirt. Her long blond hair was braided and almost reached the top of her jeans. She wore a small backpack and a cell phone was clipped to the thin belt around her waist. With excitement in her step, she moved quickly to the side of the house and grabbed her bike. Jumping onto it, she tore off down the road. The bike was red, like her shirt, red being her favorite color. The paint on the bike was new, however, if you looked carefully, you could see that the bike had been welded together in several places, clearly the metamorphosis of several cannibalized bicycles. Michelle wasn't bothered that her bike was not new. She'd never seen a new bicycle, and neither had any of her friends. It was generally assumed that there hadn't been a new bike made in the last hundred years.

The road she traveled was compact dirt with hazardous patches of broken asphalt which stuck up frequently. Michelle loved to ride her bike into town. She would usually go a half hour out of her way to ride down Bell Street, the one street on her side of town that had recently been resurfaced, and the first one Michelle had ever seen made of new concrete. Her parents told her that in time all the streets would be like that. Michelle loved to ride on it because it was smooth, and she could go much faster. Her grandma had told her how all the roads had once been made of cement, but that had been before everyone died. Today though, she took the quick route to town and sacrificed the ride down Bell Street. Today was her grandmother's birthday, and she was determined to be the first one to tell her happy birthday. She could have called, but she wanted to do this in person. Even at her advanced age, Grandma Amy had made sure to come and see Michelle on all nine of her birthdays.

When she got to the house, Michelle raced up the stairs and without knocking raced inside. "Grandma, it's me!" she gleefully exclaimed.

Her grandmother was in her chair, reclined with her feet up listening to music coming from a small stereo. The music originated from one of the two radio stations that were broadcasting. "Michelle, come give Grandma a hug," the elderly woman said, holding out her arms. In truth, the term 'grandma' was not wholly accurate. Michelle was Amy's great-granddaughter.

The young girl gently approached and said, "Happy Birthday, Grandma."

"Thank you, sweetie. You're the best for remembering."

"Was I the first?"

"The first what?"

"The first one to tell you happy birthday," the girl stated with some sarcasm in her voice.

Laughing, Amy replied, "Yes you were."

"Good. I wanted mom to help me make you a cake today, but she said we wouldn't find one hundred and forty-five candles," Michelle said.

"Even if you had, you wouldn't have had enough. I'm one hundred and forty-six now."

"That's old."

"It sure is." the old woman admitted.

"Is it true back when you were young, people didn't live that long?"

That's true. Typically, people only lived to be about eighty. That's how it was then, and how it'll be for you too. Other than the few of us that are left, there won't be anyone else living this long."

"So I won't be able to be as old as you are? I only get about eighty years?"

"Why? Eighty isn't bad, I was just over eighty when I had my first baby, your mom." Together they giggled at the crazy sounding fact.

Michelle rested her head on her grandma's shoulder. She missed the days where she could climb up into that same chair and sit together, but she had gotten too big for the frail old woman to hold. As they sat now, Michelle's eyes moved to the shelves with the photos on them. There were pictures of her mom and dad, and some of her great-grandfather and her grandma. Most of them were photos of Michelle and her brothers and sisters and their many cousins. As much as she loved her family, these weren't the pictures that Michelle enjoyed when she visited. The ones she was interested in were the ones from long ago, the ones of her great-grandmother. She especially liked the one of her sitting in the pilot seat of the powerful military helicopter, dressed in her flight suit.

Michelle's favorite thing in the world was to sit with this woman and listen to Grandma's stories from another time. Even the pictures in books and on computers couldn't compare with hearing her grandma describe how people had lived a hundred and thirty years ago.

Grandma was great at telling about the busy cities, dangerous freeways, amusement parks, and traveling to exotic locations. It seemed these ideas were as crazy as some of the outer space TV programs about aliens invading Earth.

Michelle's parents had taken her to Denver last year, but it wasn't the same as her grandmother's descriptions of the city had been. Denver had a cold and empty feeling, the tall and once magnificent buildings seemed dead in this ghost town. There had been no life except for a handful of people, scavenging for useable items. The only other evidence of people she saw were the thousands of skeletons which seemed to be behind every door they opened.

The trip to Denver had been fascinating, and it certainly had made the global destruction seem more real. She was just glad to get home and hopefully would never visit a city ever again.

Chapter 1 – Day 1075

The ceiling must have been twenty feet high, and the square room had walls that were all about fifty feet in length. One wall was completely covered with computer equipment and medical monitors. On the opposite wall was a large steel door, which resembled a giant airlock. There were no windows in the room, but there were twelve video cameras suspended from the ceiling that together covered every inch of the room.

Through the dim glow of red auxiliary lights, one could just make out the shapes of the dozen coffin-sized capsules lined up in four neat rows. The capsules were black, their sides rounded and smooth. Topping each capsule were two transparent sections, surrounded by a black frame, a lid assembly that fit perfectly on top of the capsules. It was almost impossible to see where the sides ended, and the top began. Each capsule was numbered with a three-inch-high red adhesive label on the front. There were also several rows of indicator lights and LED displays at the end of each capsule.

At one end of each row was a console of complex computer equipment. The capsules had several small monitor screens, displaying what appeared to be an EKG readout. Anyone with medical knowledge would have been concerned by the extremely slow heart rate visible on the screens. Ten of the capsules had multiple rows of green lights, some flashing and others glowing continuously. On the capsule numbered 'Ten', two lights weren't green. One was yellow, and the second glowed an ominous red. On capsule Three, there were no lights at all.

Through the transparent lid of each capsule, the form of a nude human was visible. The people were a mixture of males and females from several different races. They all looked to be in good physical condition and appeared to be between twenty and forty years old.

An unusual mask covered the mouth and nose of each person. It resembled a standard oxygen mask but was constructed of heavier material, off-white in color. The masks fastened behind the head and two tubes connected to them. The ends of the tubes connected to ports attached to the wall of each capsule. The masks, along with an odd mix of tubes and wires running in and out of different orifices, made the occupants of each capsule appear almost mechanical. In the available light, it wasn't possible to tell if the people were dead or alive.

Without warning six banks of overhead fluorescent lights snapped on. Though the change in lighting was extreme, no apparent reaction came from the occupants of the capsules. Seconds later, a bright yellow strobe light began flashing above the long-sealed door, and the activity on several of the computer panels increased.

Following a brief pause, a barely audible hissing sound was heard, and the eleven-hundred-pound door slowly began to open. Four people in yellow biohazard suits walked into the spacious chamber. They'd been packed tightly into the tiny space the airlock afforded and almost struggled to get out. Their movements were slow, and they glanced from one side of the room to the other. From the way they moved it was evident there was a high level of uncertainty being experienced by them all. As soon as they'd walked into the room, the door behind them swung shut, and within thirty seconds, the yellow strobe stopped flashing.

The four new arrivals each moved to one of the rows of capsules and started assessing the terminals. Each team member glanced up briefly when the strobe light began flashing again, before returning to their assessments. Three similarly dressed people joined them, and these three went directly across the chamber to the wall of monitoring equipment, inputting commands into the futuristic-looking systems.

A curse erupted from the person who'd started examining the row of capsules to the far right. "Major system failure, Capsule Three," an agitated female voice announced. There was a slightly mechanical tone to her voice, the result of the positive pressure breathing devices in the masks of each team member.

Another voice stated, "Capsule Three – that would've been Miller."

"Any idea when it occurred?" a third voice asked. This voice sounded different, coming over the headsets, but without echo. Whoever was speaking was not wearing a facemask.

The female had moved to the third capsule in her row and was peering in through the top. The person inside's skin had dried out, and the face was leathery and shrunken, although the mask was still in place. The long blond hair indicated it had been a woman.

"It looks like it was a long time ago, Sir." A slight quiver was evident in the technician's voice.

Before anyone could comment another female voice, this one with a slight New England accent, called out. "Sir, we also have a minor system failure in Capsule Ten."

"How minor?" The natural sounding voice rapidly asked.

From the area with wall-mounted systems, a male voice called out, "All vital signs, core temp, and EKG are within normal limits. It seems the primary cooling system failed, but backup systems are at one hundred percent efficiency."

"Okay," growled the voice from the headset, "give me a report on the rest of the capsules."

"Group A, no additional failures."

"Group B, no failures."

"Group C, no failures."

"Group D, no additional failures."

"Okay, activate the data link so you can get out of there. Then start the bio-contamination scanners. I want a full report in an hour."

Within ten minutes, the room was again empty. Two minutes later, the lights went out.

Chapter 2 – Day 1075

The large conference table in the center of the room was covered with papers and laptop computers, coffee cups and not just a few soda bottles. Fourteen people were seated around the table, discussing the events of the morning. At the front of the room, a door opened, and a tall man entered. He strode in with authority, dressed in a US Army dress uniform. On his shoulder boards were the silver eagles which denoted his rank as an Army Colonel.

The Colonel appeared to be in his late fifties and stood just over six feet tall. He was quite thin and his brown hair was well on its way to being gray. The nametag above his right breast pocket read 'Fitch'.

Following behind him was a stocky man of medium height who was in his mid-forties; he wore a lab coat, the name 'J. Cowan' embroidered onto the breast pocket. Cowan walked with a mild limp and was slightly shorter than the Colonel.

No sooner had they entered the room than everyone seated at the table got to their feet. Half the room stood at attention, and the rest stood casually, revealing the civilian workers and their military counterparts. A faint nod of the Colonel's head was all they needed to sit down and return to work.

Fitch took out a pair of glasses, slipped them on, and quickly scanned the clipboard he held. "Okay, tell me what went wrong with those two systems," he demanded. Again requesting the information he had asked for over the intercom when his team had been suited up in the chamber.

After a brief pause, a short-haired Asian man in a lab coat spoke up, a slight quiver in his voice when he spoke. "Sir, I've been reviewing the data from Capsule Ten. Sometime last year an unexpected hardware failure occurred in the primary cooling system. Three seconds after the failure, the backup system engaged. Since then it has been running without a problem. Just to remind everyone, there is also a third tier in this system, an auxiliary cooling system that comes online if the two other systems failed. This auxiliary system has never engaged and appears to be completely functional. It looks like the built-in fault tolerance worked exactly as we had hoped."

"No, Lieutenant," Cowan snapped, "that isn't how we had hoped it would work. That primary cooling system was supposed to be able to operate, unsupervised for twenty years. Now you're telling me that it only lasted four years into this five-year test."

Colonel Fitch nodded in agreement.

The Lieutenant opened his mouth to respond but seeing the look on his superiors' faces, decided against it.

"Now will someone tell me what killed Miller?" the Colonel demanded. There was more frustration in his voice than anger.

A woman of medium height, with long brown hair, stood up. She wore a US Army dress uniform with Captain's bars on her shoulders and spoke with a slight New England accent. "Colonel, something shorted out her primary life support computer. Until we get her out and can get to the computer, we won't have all the details. However, the monitors indicate that she suffered some form of a seizure about a year ago. And that she was alive for almost two hours afterward. At that point, for reasons still unknown, her life support computer shorted out. When this happened, there was a sudden increase in temperature in the electronics compartment that houses the bio-computer. Apparently, the temperature was in excess of five hundred degrees for about thirty seconds. The main computer cut power to the electronics compartment in her capsule, due to the threat of a possible fire. At this point, the temperature rapidly decreased. The main computer was seconds away from terminating the entire experiment and sounding a general fire detection alarm. Even though the results were tragic, it looks like most of the systems responded as designed."

Colonel Fitch's initial reaction had been a cold stare which slowly melted away as he listened to the facts. He nodded slowly.

Cowan, in a more relaxed tone, asked, "Captain Travers, when will we know the cause of the seizure and what created the short circuit?" As frustrated as James Cowan felt regarding the failure, he wouldn't vent that frustration on Amy Travers. She'd been his right-hand person on this project for several years, quickly gaining expertise in this science. She was the only one who understood the artificial sleep processes well enough to continue this work, if he should ever decide to move on. He'd been offered more lucrative positions recently, but he was committed to seeing this project through.

Travers replied. "We won't know the cause of the seizure before the autopsy. Until Miller is removed from the capsule, we won't be able to get under it to see the electronics compartment."

"When will we be able to go back in the chamber without the biohazard suits?" Cowan asked.

A short, balding man spoke up. "Bio-contamination scanning is just finishing now. If the computers found no problems, we should be able to re-enter within the hour."

"Sir, what about the wake-up?" Travers said.

"That should probably wait until we get the body out," a voice from the back of the room suggested.

"I agree, let's hold off and see what we find with Miller, and his capsule and then we'll start working on Group One," Fitch instructed. With a nod to those around the table, Fitch and Cowan left the room together.

Fitch could feel his head pounding from the stress and frustration of the morning. He'd been serving as the Project Director for the past several years and he'd planned on this being his final assignment before he slipped away to a quiet retirement.

Matt Fitch began his Army career as an infantry officer fresh out of the military academy at West Point. His career moved quickly, and he'd been posted to various locations all over the world. He'd even seen some combat during those years.

He'd developed a reputation for his organizational skills and been promoted to the position of Operations Officer in his unit. Within weeks of reporting for his new duty, a medium-sized mass had been detected in his right lung. Two-thirds of the lung had to be removed, to ensure the cancer didn't spread. Nowadays, he was minimally aware of the decreased respiratory function, and it was only annoying when he exerted himself. However, the impairment was enough to keep him from ever serving again in a combat unit.

Fortunately, Fitch had made the right connections over the years, and one of those connections got him the assignment he currently held, as a Project Director in Deep Sleep Research.

* * *

About an hour later, the massive steel doors started to move again, only the second occurrence in the last five years. Now the technicians and a pair of physicians weren't encumbered by heavy air tanks and containment suits. They brought in medical equipment, including drug kits, portable oxygen tanks, and heart monitors, rolled in on four-wheeled stretchers.

While the medical staff began setting up the equipment, a fifth stretcher was rolled up to the third capsule in the first row. A black, heavy vinyl bag, seven feet in length was unrolled and laid on the stretcher with the zipper facing the capsule.

At the beginning of the first row, a technician began inputting commands into the console. "I can't open it from here. All the automatic systems are down for this capsule." He stepped over to the side of the capsule and crouched down, removing two small hatch covers using a flat head screwdriver to pry them off.

Both openings were barely large enough to insert a hand. The technician reached into the first, and after a moment a slight movement of the transparent lid could be detected, followed by an audible hiss as the pressure changed within the capsule. He withdrew his hand and reached into the second opening. After a slightly longer delay, a loud popping sound echoed in the room, and the lid jumped up about an inch.

"Okay, we should be able to lift it now," the technician announced.

He slowly rose to his feet, and with the help of one of the physicians lifted the lid. The smell of death wasn't as bad as they'd feared, but it was still noticeable. After the facemask was removed and the tubes and wires cut loose, the body of Rhonda Miller was gently lifted from the capsule. The irony of the dead woman being lifted from a coffin-shaped container was not lost on any of them.

Miller was laid flat on the stretcher, and the black body bag was zipped shut. Two safety straps went over the bag and were fastened to keep it firmly secured to the stretcher, and Captain Amy Travers and a physician left with the body to begin the autopsy.

Once the body was gone, James Cowan moved in to begin investigating the cause of the fatal failure of capsule three.

Chapter 3

James Cowan was, by far, the most knowledgeable person when it came to the inner workings of the sleep program. Fourteen years before he'd signed on to assist Dr. Henry Sullivan who was the world's leading expert in the concept of long-term sleep programs at the time.

Over the years, they'd had many successes and only minimal failures. Eventually, their experiments led to a need to progress from animal experiments to placing humans in a sleep state for long durations. The original idea had been to use this technology for lengthy space exploration. As the project progressed, other suggestions for the technology were discovered, including possibly putting a person to sleep until a cure for a specific disease they were afflicted with could be found.

The subject of the first human experiment had been a graduate student, named Randy Rominski. He and eight other students answered an ad, offering them one thousand dollars to take part in an unusual sleep experiment. After physical and psychological examinations were complete, Randy was selected, and the test began.

This first human experiment involved a simple sleep capsule and a crude version of the sleep-inducing formula (SIF) which was continuously infused into the sleeper's body through IV lines. A unique mix of gasses was administered by facemask, while the subject remained asleep. The breathing gas, in conjunction with the SIF formula, created what was known as the Sleep Effect. During this experiment, continual monitoring and adjustments to the dosage of SIF were required. A physician or specially trained nurse needed to be on duty twenty-four hours a day, prepared to make the necessary adjustments. That first human experiment lasted two weeks and was considered by most to be a success, even though it took almost twelve hours for the young volunteer to regain consciousness.

Randy Rominski began forceful vomiting six hours into the waking process. While vomiting, he aspirated and later developed a severe case of pneumonia and after regaining full consciousness, Randy remained delirious for the next twenty-four hours and needed to be restrained. It took a full week before he was back to what could be considered 'normal'.

Further test results showed nearly all body processes had stopped during the sleep cycle. Food he'd ingested before the experiment remained undigested in his stomach. There was also evidence that skin and blood cells hadn't died off as they usually would have had the subject been awake.

These facts and others led Sullivan and Cowan to believe they were on track to find a method for stopping the aging process in a controlled sleep. However, the side effects of the SIF were considered a significant problem. Randy later made it clear he would never agree to being given SIF or being placed in a sleep capsule again.

After several years, after additional work on the SIF formula and with the introduction of a new drug that was administered at the time of awakening, most of the side effects had been eliminated.

The subsequent two-week-long test went much better; the test subject woke swiftly but was still briefly confused. He experienced two episodes of vomiting but was free of symptoms within two hours.

Additional tests further indicated the severity of the symptoms increased as time subjected to the SIF increased.

Longer duration tests came next and it became necessary for anticoagulant to be added to the SIF formula. This was required to prevent blood clots from forming in the extremities while the sleeper was immobile for several years.

At this juncture, the team agreed it was time for more extensive tests of the system. Under Sullivan's supervision, Cowan re-engineered the sleep capsule so that urinary catheters were built in and tied into a central waste disposal system. A positive pressure facemask replaced the standard oxygen mask which had been used up until this point. The new mask was designed to increase the depth of respirations, which had been almost non-existent with the SIF in the occupant's system. By increasing the depth of respirations, it was hoped the pneumonia that often set in with poor ventilation could be avoided.

The plan had been to put four occupants to sleep for one year, using a central source of SIF for all test subjects, and have all systems monitored and controlled by computers. A twenty-four watch was established once the occupants were placed into the capsules.

The experiment proceeded as planned for the first two months, until early one afternoon when an alarm was sounded by one of the medical computers. The blood pressure of the subject in Capsule Four had suddenly crossed beneath the safe limits. The decision was made to remove the subject from the experiment, but before his capsule could be opened another alarm sounded because he'd gone into cardiac arrest. He was swiftly removed from the capsule, and resuscitation efforts continued for half an hour, but they were unsuccessful.

The autopsy which followed showed he'd died from a massive infection. By nightfall, the occupants of Capsules One and Three were also dead, passing in the same fashion. The experiment was immediately terminated, and the female subject in Capsule Two was rapidly removed from the capsule and awoken.

The woman woke up slowly but remained confused. Twenty minutes after awakening, she developed a fever which rose to 105 degrees Fahrenheit. Intravenous antibiotics were administered, and she was diagnosed with a massive systemic infection. Two days later, she too, was dead.

The subsequent investigation showed the shared supply of SIF had become contaminated with a common and usually harmless bacterium. While in a sleep-like state, the body systems which would typically combat such a minor problem were inactive, and by the time anyone was able to intervene, it had been too late.

Questions were also raised regarding the competence of the medical staff in their handling of the crisis. Due to massive public pressure and the threat of legal action, the private funding for the project rapidly dried up.

While devastated by the failure and loss of life, Sullivan was encouraged because one thing was clear – almost all body processes were suspended during the sleep period.

After a year of failed efforts to obtain new funding, Henry Sullivan was contacted by the Department of Defense and given the opportunity to continue his work under the auspices of the US Army Research Laboratory.

Working for the military wasn't the ideal situation for Sullivan, because he'd wanted to avoid the political issues related to working for the government. He'd also been concerned about how much control over the project he would lose. In the end, agreements were made, and he'd accepted. The only demand Sullivan did insist on was that his assistant, James Cowan, be allowed to come along as his partner.

Once arrangement had been finalized, Sullivan and Cowan set to work immediately. Now they were armed with a budget many times larger than what they'd been working with before and they quickly began making improvements to their systems. After a year, they were ready to repeat the test which had gone so terribly wrong.

Four volunteer subjects were placed in the sleep capsules, with the plan of keeping them asleep for a year. It had been decided to continue using a shared source of SIF, purely for manageability reasons –this time, however, it would be better monitored and frequently exposed to specific low doses of radiation to kill any intrusive organisms.

The following night, a large blood vessel in the base of Henry Sullivan's brain ruptured, the hemorrhagic stroke leaving the brilliant scientist in a vegetative state. A ventilator was needed because the part of his brain which controls respiration was dead from the moment the blood vessel ruptured. Two weeks later, with his children and grandchildren at his bedside, the life support system was disconnected. Henry Sullivan was pronounced dead ten minutes later.

James Cowan suddenly found himself in charge of the project. He was almost as knowledgeable as Sullivan, and after some debate, it was decided the experiment would continue. By the end of the year, all four volunteers were awakened and experienced minimal effects from the SIF. That had been six and a half years ago.

Now in its sixteenth variation, SIF had officially been renamed SF016. From the moment when James Cowan took over responsibility for the program, efforts had been made to further automate the systems, in hopes of creating an entirely automated sleep process.

There had been no further failures – until today.

Chapter 4 – Day 1075

Cowan stared into the now-empty capsule, noticing a large, light brown stain on the right side of the capsule. The dried stain darkened the sheet covering the gel-filled mattress Rhonda Miller had slept on and further investigation revealed residue under the sheet had also spread onto the mattress, making it appear as if something had been spilled onto the sheet.

"Mr. Cowan, what's that on the sheet?" asked one of the technicians.

"I'm not sure yet. It certainly wasn't like this when the experiment started," Cowan answered.

The sheet and mattress were removed and sent to the lab for testing, while the rest of the capsule was carefully examined. On the flat surface inside the capsule, where the mattress had rested, was a detachable door. This led to the electronics compartment where much of the medical monitoring equipment, and the capsule's life support computers were installed. There was evidence of the same contaminant all around the door to the electronics bay and when the door was removed, there was a strong smell of burnt electronics. The life support computer rested just inside the compartment. Clearly, there'd been a serious short circuit and a small fire inside the compartment.

"Well, this appears to be where it all went wrong," the technician said. "It seems the same contaminant that was under the mattress got in here and shorted it out."

Cowan got up to leave. "Get the computer to the lab and have it checked, I want to know exactly what caused this. I'm heading to the infirmary. I think I know what happened here."

"What are you thinking?" asked the technician.

Cowan turned back to glance at the other man. "I think that stuff is blood."

* * *

Two hours later, James Cowan stepped into Colonel Fitch's office. "Hey Matt, have you got a minute? I want to give you the preliminary report." He was the only one in the center who would even consider calling Colonel Fitch by his first name while in the office.

"Sure James, come in. What a crazy morning. I was so sure there would be no problems, and now this. Please tell me you've got good news."

"As good as we can hope for. I just came from the computer lab, before that, I was in the infirmary observing the autopsy. The first assessment was correct – Miller suffered a seizure during the experiment. During the seizure, the IV catheter that supplies the SF016 was ripped out of her arm. A mix of blood and SF016 leaked out and ran off onto the mattress. Because of the anticoagulant we have in the formula, she bled a bit more than usual. It leaked through the door and directly into the power supply for the life support systems. It shorted out and started a fire."

Cowan paused to make sure Matt was following the chain of events and when he saw the man nod his head, he continued. "The main computers for the chamber detected the heat and cut power to the capsule, including the computer. Then the fire burned itself out. With the power out to the capsule, the SF016 pump stopped. With the life support off Miller died quickly." concluded Cowan.

"So, why the seizure?" asked the Colonel. "They all had physicals, and I re-checked her medical history after our meeting this morning. There was no history of seizures." Anxiety was evident in the Colonel's voice and Cowan could understand why If the seizure was a result of something to do with the Sleep Process, it could be disastrous for the entire project.

"When the infirmary notified her next of kin, they spoke to her mother. Apparently, she experienced a seizure three days before the experiment. The first seizure she'd ever had. Rhonda didn't say anything to us, because she didn't want to get kicked out of the program. During the autopsy, they removed a golf ball size mass from her brain," Cowan explained.

Matt lifted an eyebrow. "A brain tumor? So if she hadn't had this tumor, she'd still be alive?"

"There are no indications of malfunctions or failures in the system which led to this problem. The only system failure occurred after her IV was ripped out and her blood and the SF016 shorted out the computer. I already have the team working on a redesign of the interior access door to the electronics bay, to prevent things from leaking into the electronics. This is something we never anticipated. A leak in a urinary catheter could lead to the same thing," explained Cowan.

"All right," Fitch said. "I feel better now that I understand the details. With this information in mind, how would you rate the outcome of this experiment?"

"In all honesty, it was a huge success. We expected minor issues would need to be addressed, and that's what we have," Cowan said.

"Even though we have a fatality?"

"Absolutely!" Cowan said defensively. "Miller failed to disclose that there was a medical issue. The experiment didn't worsen her situation! You can't blame the sleep project because she screwed up. The drugs and the hardware performed as designed."

"Easy, James," said Fitch calmly, "I completely agree, I just need to be sure that we're on the same page here."

Cowan took a deep breath. "Okay. Sorry, I got a bit excited. I kinda feel like an overprotective parent when it comes to this project. In my opinion, there were far fewer issues than I'd expected. Though we've yet to wake any of the others."

"True, and I know how eager we all are to do that. With all that's happened today, I think we should hold off until tomorrow to begin the wake-up. Do you agree?" asked Fitch.

Cowan glanced at his watch, surprised to see that it was already 1645 hours. Usually, he would be heading home now, and the whole wake up procedure could easily take four hours. Reluctantly, Cowan admitted to himself that waiting would be best. Especially since if problems arose, he would need everyone quick and alert.

"Well, I'm quite eager to begin, and I know the whole team will be unhappy about waiting. But considering how late it is now, that would be the best decision," admitted Cowan.

"Good," said the Colonel, "I'm eager to see this through, too. But there's no reason we can't wait until morning. Do you want to make the announcement?"

"Yeah, I'll take care of it and then head out," said Cowan, and he turned to leave.

Chapter 5 – Day 1074

Several weeks before anyone outside the Sleeper Team knew of the unfortunate fate of Rhonda Miller, and over a thousand miles away, the Hubble Space Telescope was just completing a study of a distant comet. The Hubble and several land-based radio telescopes had been assigned this task after a West Coast University requested the government to confirm the results of studies they'd recently completed. The results of those studies had been so shocking and unbelievable, they wanted confirmation from agencies with more powerful equipment available.

The data had been collected over time, and sophisticated computer algorithms applied. After years of testing, these methods have proven their ability to accurately chart the path and determine many attributes of objects that moved through space.

Thomas Williams was the current Administrator of NASA, a position he'd held for the last six years and a role he took great pride in. Having come from an unstable family background, Thomas was not only the first person in his family to graduate college, but also the first to graduate high school. No one was sure who his father was. The best answer he'd ever gotten from his mother was that he was 'gone'.

His mother had worked as a waitress in a dark, dingy bar for many years. When Thomas was a freshman in high school, she'd met Darryl, a drummer in a small band. Not long after meeting him, Thomas' mother went on the road with the band and she'd never returned.

Fortunately, Thomas had grown up close friends with Andrew King, a boy he attended school with and whose parents were both financially stable and sympathetic to Thomas' plight. When they found out that he'd been abandoned the King Family took Thomas in, with only one stipulation – he was to excel in school and break the chain of failure that bound his family history.

With only the briefest of hesitations Thomas agreed, and seven years later graduated with honors from the University of Michigan.

Now he was married with three adult children of his own, who'd all excelled in school and gone on to graduate from college. Thomas was satisfied he'd kept his promise to the late Mr. and Mrs. King, and had in fact broken the chain of failure which had blighted his family's history.

Thomas was a little confused this particular morning. It was unusual for a deputy director to request an urgent meeting with him. It was even more uncommon that anyone other than his wife would insist he cancel something as important as his lunch meeting with the two senators from New Mexico.

This appointment had been scheduled weeks before and the senators were no doubt expecting the royal treatment. He was sure he'd be asked the same questions every up and coming junior congressman enquires about, and with any luck, they'd go back to Congress proud of themselves for being knowledgeable about what was going on at NASA.

Ditching the lunch meeting wasn't the problem; he'd been trying to think of a way out of having to deal with them ever since he found out they were on his schedule. The problem was, there was never anything so urgent that he'd be expected to change his plans. After all, the next major launch was five weeks out. There were no problems reported on the International Space Station, and the Orion project was on track. Of course, there was the possibility of an alien spacecraft suddenly entering orbit. But even though he personally believed there was some form of life out in space, he didn't think for a moment they'd decide to arrive for their first real visit just half an hour before his lunch meeting.

"Stan, what can be so urgent that you insist I rearrange MY schedule for this meeting?" asked the overweight Administrator as he stomped into the office.

Stanley Waldorf was the deputy director in charge of the Department of Space Science at NASA, and Administrator Williams had never cared much for Waldorf. Waldorf did his job and did it reasonably well, but he had no concept of how to follow protocol, and his manner of dress left much to be desired. He reeked of an 'I don't care what you think' attitude.

Williams on the other hand, while overweight, was always dressed perfectly. He knew who to talk to and what to say. He'd gotten this far by playing the game and had come to dislike those who didn't want to follow the rules.

"You remember that request we got to confirm that data from the University of Washington?" Waldorf asked.

"Yeah. If I remember, you said we were going to have to check it out but it was probably just a bunch of overeager university types who got their calculations all screwed up," replied Williams.

"Well, that isn't exactly how I said it, but that's what I thought. I was sure it was a huge waste of time and resources. In fact, I considered trying to find a way to ignore the request. The only reason I didn't, was the fact that the people making the request were the same ones who control next year's budget. I mean these weren't the young pups you're supposed to be dining with now, if you know what I mean," explained Waldorf.

"Okay, okay, so what's new?" said Williams, his irritation starting to show.

"It seems those university types didn't screw up their calculations – in fact, they were right on. Their readings were exactly the same as the ones we got. Their discovery was accidental, and we probably would have never noticed unless we were intentionally looking for that type of radiation, which we'd have no reason to do," said Waldorf.

"Has this been confirmed?" Thomas snapped.

"Yes, Tony Jackson and I are working on the details. But there's no doubt that the comet we've been tracking is emitting hard radiation, and it'll pass way too close," said Waldorf.

"How is this possible? Comets are never radioactive." Thomas cringed, knowing he hadn't managed to hide the fear in his voice.

"Don't know. We've never seen anything like this before, but the radiation is clearly present and detectable, even at this range. As of now it still looks like it'll pass between the Earth and the moon."

"I want this kept quiet. There have been many false reports like this over the years, and the last thing I need is one which can be traced back to this office." Thomas warned.

"How long are we going to keep this quiet? This needs to be reported. Also, there might be others who happen to figure it out. The Europeans and Japanese, as well as half a dozen other nations, will eventually detect this and then word will get out fast," argued Waldorf, with concern in his voice.

"I want it kept quiet until we have all the details. Remember, those University of Washington kids found this by accident. It was a fluke that they even detected it, and it took us over two weeks to verify it. We have some time. When I take this up the ladder, I want to have all the answers ready. We'll let them release it as they see fit."

Waldorf nodded abruptly and left the room, and Williams' eyes were drawn to a picture of his twin granddaughters, dressed in the uniform of their community soccer program. Neither was old enough to understand what a comet was.

Williams knew all about comets, and he knew where this one was heading and the danger it posed. As he held the picture, a single tear formed at the corner of his left eye.

Chapter 6 – Day 1074

Usually, James Cowan arrived to work at 0700. Cowan was someone who believed in being prompt, and as the director of the team, he held the others to his standards.

Today the clock showed 0700, and James Cowan had already been there for an hour and a half.

Unable to sleep, he'd slipped out of bed early, careful not to disturb his sleeping wife, and headed into work.

He felt like a kid on Christmas morning. The anticipation of the awakening was so intense, he found himself pacing in and out of the rows of capsules. As he walked, he thought of Sullivan. He would have done almost anything to have his old friend and mentor here with him for this fantastic day.

He noticed the dismantled remains of Miller's capsule in his peripheral vision and experienced a wave of anger. He found he was, in fact, angry with the dead woman. No matter what happened, the fact that Miller died would prevent the experiment from being one hundred percent successful, and it was her fault. The woman's irresponsibility had jeopardized the research and years of work.

Twenty minutes later, the rest of the team was in place, including Colonel Matt Fitch. Since most of the team was civilian, working under the Department of Defense, there tended to be an 'us versus them' mentality, tangible on both sides, but this morning it was nonexistent.

So much work and time had been committed by everyone, and this was their big moment.

Cowan slowly walked to the front of the room, "I know most of us expected yesterday to be the big day, the day when we would wake up our test subjects. Unfortunately, that didn't happen, but don't let yourselves feel down because of the problems we experienced yesterday. Those events are in no way an indication of failure on our part. Our plans and systems worked exactly as they were designed to operate, in fact, the most significant problem, in my opinion, was the primary cooling system failure in Capsule Ten.

"We've reviewed the vital signs and equipment readings for the remaining sleepers and their capsules, and there's no indication any of them are experiencing any problems.

"We'll start with Capsule One, and after she's awake and everything is looking good, we'll start work on the second one. If things are going well after the first two, we'll pick up the pace and start waking them two at a time. Are there any questions?" Cowan asked.

After a moment of complete silence, Cowan continued, "Colonel Fitch, is there anything you want to add?"

Fitch stepped forward. "I know how much work has gone into this project, and the five-year wait has been difficult for everyone. Let's get them awake, so we can finally see the results of our work and officially call this project a success," he stated with more than a little enthusiasm in his voice.

Cowan and Captain Amy Travers, along with one of the physicians, strode across to Capsule One. "Begin wake-up sequence on Capsule One," Cowan ordered.

A technician at the beginning of the first row entered the wake-up sequence into the computer keyboard. Cowan could visualize what happened next. The computer immediately stopped the flow of SF016 through the IV line, and a bolus of two different medications started to be infused instead. Concurrently, the flow of gas into the facemask was replaced by pure oxygen.

Three minutes later, the young Army Lieutenant standing by the row of medical monitors called out. "Pulse rate and respirations are increasing. I'll start depressurizing the capsule."

As the capsule depressurized, a faint groan emitted from the structure. The depressurization process took three full minutes and during that time, Cowan observed that the subject's breathing increased from about four breaths per minute to almost twelve.

"Depressurization complete, activating door mechanism," the technician announced.

The sound of a mechanical device operating echoed through the room, and the heavy, pressurized cover slowly started lifting.

"Door locked and in position, vital signs within normal limits," the technician called out.

The physician and Travers immediately started to work. They removed the facemask and replaced it with a standard oxygen mask. The urinary catheter was gently removed, and the internal IV system was replaced with a saline IV bag hanging from a stand beside the capsule.

Cowan commenced shutting down the many individual systems and backup systems within Capsule one, the life support systems, pumps, and monitors were all powered off. The only thing left operational was the primary computer, and he started dumping all the data it had gathered over the last five years. This data was rapidly transferred across fiber optic cable to the complex's central computer database and by the end of the day, the database would contain every conceivable detail of what had occurred during the study. Over the next few months, all this information would be sorted and carefully examined, in hopes of learning everything that had occurred.

After the subject was unhooked, a sheet was used to cover most of her body, and then four team members lifted Tasha Sanjourn from the capsule and placed her on a waiting stretcher.

When they lifted her, they felt her body start to move, and with a soft moan, she opened her eyes. "Tasha, how are you feeling?" the physician asked.

Her voice was weak and difficult to hear through the oxygen mask when she responded. "Feel like I might barf."

"That feeling is normal, it should pass soon," explained the physician.

Tasha slowly turned her head and noticed Cowan. "You got a little gray in the last five years, Cowan," she said weakly, and with a slight smile.

Her gaze slipped across to the dismantled remains of Capsule Three and the smile vanished, replaced with a mix of confusion and fear. Her blonde hair half covered her face when she quickly turned back to Cowan, the obvious question in her eyes. Cowan closed his own eyes and slowly shook his head, answering the question. Tasha squeezed her eyes tightly shut and Cowan watched as she was wheeled to the infirmary.

"So far so good," Cowan announced, drawing himself back to the present once Tasha was out of the room. "Let's move on to Capsule Two."

* * *

The team gathered around the conference table, seated almost in the same arrangement as they'd been the day before. Colonel Fitch stood at the head of the room, with Cowan at his side.

"As most of you are aware, things have gone as well as can be expected today. I just heard that Number Twelve has been out of bed and walking a little," Cowan began.

"We only had two issues today, and both were minor. There was a capsule door mechanism failure on Capsule Eight, but we were able to gain access rapidly using the manual release. This brings up the point that in the future, we'll have to design a release on the inside of the capsule," There were nods of agreement and Cowan continued. "The other incident involved Subject Four, who did vomit. Fortunately, Captain Travers was quick and sacrificed her dress uniform in order to help contain the rather unpleasant five-year-old stomach contents."

Loud laughter erupted in the room and some embarrassment was evident on Travers' face, sitting at the table in generic medical scrubs instead of the uniform everyone was accustomed to seeing.

"The good news," he continued, "is Number Four was the only one to experience vomiting, which means we've come a long way with the SF016 formula. It wasn't that long ago when they all vomited repeatedly. Also, they're all up and on their feet. This is by far the fastest recovery we've seen, even though the experiment lasted five times longer than ever before. I believe this relates directly to the combination of medications we're giving them at the beginning of the wake-up process. Now, Colonel Fitch has a comment about some of the problems we faced," Cowan concluded.

"Before I start discussing the problems we've had, I want you to know I couldn't be more pleased with today's success. I do feel, however, that we need to bring up the areas we'll need to investigate while they're still fresh in our minds. As we review the computer data over the next few months, I've got no doubt there will be other issues that come to our attention, but these are the initial findings. First, the primary cooling units were designed to last a minimum of twenty years under a much heavier load than we've placed on them. I understand that it's possible to experience occasional failures, but lives are depending on them and even a single failure in five years is a major problem. I want the system dissected and the cause of the failure located. After that, we'll be visiting the manufacturer. The same goes for the door mechanism failure; let's locate the exact cause and determine if a redesign is needed.

"We've made massive improvements in the SF016 formula, but further refining is still a goal. In an automated wake-up scenario, such as a long space journey, we don't want to have anyone puking during a wake-up," the Colonel finished.

"Also, we've added a mix of medications given intravenously at the start of a wake-up to decrease the side effects of the awakening. We've proven their success and need to have the administration of them automated," Cowan added.

"Does anyone have any further observations at this time?" asked Fitch. There was a pause and when no one said anything, Fitch continued, "Good. We had a great day, now get back to work! Everyone laughed as the Colonel left the room.

Chapter 7 – Day 1001

Several months later, NASA Administrator Thomas Williams and his data were heading early one morning for a scheduled meeting at the Pentagon, to discuss their ominous findings.

On arrival, he was escorted to a conference room on the second level in the outer ring. Coffee was delivered by a petite young female in a Navy uniform. Thomas immediately began getting documentation ready, he'd prepared an in-depth report for everyone he'd be meeting with. His laptop was powered up, and many times the data in the reports was readily at his fingertips if there were questions he hadn't anticipated. The laptop was hooked up to a small projector, which he pointed towards a whiteboard mounted on the wall.

Ten minutes later, four-star Army General Lee Draper entered the room, followed closely behind by Navy Admiral Nathanial Atkins and the President's National Security advisor, Jeremiah Baker.

General Draper was the acting Chairman of the Joint Chiefs. The sixty-two-year-old General stood about six four and was quite thin. His receding hairline left a large scar on his forehead visible.

The National security advisor, a sixty-year-old African American man and former senator from Virginia had extensive experience in areas of national defense and politics. He'd spent twenty years as an officer in the Marine Corps, and later another eight years in the Senate, part of that time as the Chairman of the Senate Armed Services Committee.

It was widely accepted that if he'd decided to run in the last presidential race, he'd be sitting in the oval office instead of reporting to the current President. Fortunately for his good friend President Daniel Anson, Jeremiah Baker had no interest in the Presidency. He did, however, have every interest in doing all he possibly could to help the current administration succeed.

Navy Admiral Atkins, also of the Joint Chiefs, began the introductions.

"Administrator Williams, I can say that this is the first time I know of when NASA has come here with a problem related to national security," began Admiral Atkins.

"I wish I didn't need to, but unfortunately that isn't the case. I want to begin by letting you all know that the information I've collected has been triple-checked and we've been trying to disprove our own findings for a couple of months now," stated Williams, as he handed out the documentation he'd prepared. "The basic fact is this; there's a comet heading towards Earth, and there's nothing we can do about it. It's still several hundred million miles away, but it's moving extremely fast."

A look of bewilderment flashed across the other men's faces before Admiral Atkins spoke up. "Don't take this wrong, but we've all heard this before. In a few months, after word leaks out, someone will realize there's been a mistake in a calculation and—"

"Not this time Admiral," interrupted Williams. "The whole reason we've waited this long to say something is because we wanted to make sure this is absolutely certain. There are no doubts; this has been verified by three different teams."

"Please excuse my ignorance, Mr. Williams," the Admiral began, "but like I said, there have been similar stories about asteroids and meteors in the past. While I have some knowledge of comets, asteroids, and meteors, could you give us some background?"

"Absolutely, Admiral," Williams said as he started typing on his laptop. The projector lit up, and a video presentation appeared on the whiteboard. As the slides started flashing, Williams narrated. "Gentlemen comets are irregularly shaped bodies that are composed of mostly of ice, but there usually are other materials as well including, dust, iron, and other minerals. Comets typically travel at speeds around 20,000 MPH. However, as a comet nears its closest point to the sun, and it's more dramatically affected by the sun's gravitational pull it can be traveling at thousands of kilometers a minute. Like the planets, each comet travels on a regular orbit. Planets' orbits are very nearly circular, but not entirely so. Comets have highly elongated orbits that bring them very close to the Sun and then swing them back into space. A comet's tail is its most recognized feature. When far from the Sun, a comet's nucleus is very cold, and its material is frozen. This icy nucleus changes radically when a comet approaches the Sun. As a comet travels near the Sun, its developing tail it can lose several hundred million tons of dust and vapor can extend for millions of kilometers.

"And this thing is going to hit the Earth?" interrupted General Draper.

"No, all calculations indicate that it'll just miss us," answered Williams.

Draper frowned, the eyebrows on his elongated face drawing together to form a single line. "What! If it's going to miss us, what's the problem?"

"General, the comet will have a tail several million miles long. As I just mentioned, most of the time the tail of a comet is composed of dust and water vapor. We don't understand all the details, but we've confirmed the material in the tail of this comet is radioactive. So highly radioactive in fact, that even from many hundreds of million miles away, we have no problem detecting it. The entire tail of the comet will fall under the effects of Earth's gravitational field. Massive amounts of this radioactive debris will be drawn into Earth's orbit. It's estimated that every living thing on earth will be exposed to a dose of about fifteen hundred roentgens of radiation in the first month. That will be enough to radiation to wipe out ninety-nine percent of all life during the first year of exposure. After the radiation levels peak, in about six months, the radioactive debris will slowly break down and much of it will burn up in the atmosphere. After about fifteen to twenty years, radiation levels will return to normal." As Williams explained he felt as if a giant weight was lifted from his shoulders. The word was out; he was no longer the senior person in control of this information.

"Could you explain in more detail what'll happen because of this radiation?" National Security Advisor Baker asked.

"Of course. As the comet passes, the radioactive material will be drawn into orbit around the Earth. It will, over a period of a few months, spread out and eventually encircle the planet. Every inch of the Earth's surface will be affected. The amount of radiation we're talking about will have an almost immediate effect. We estimate the first deaths will occur within twenty-four to forty-eight hours. After that, the death toll will climb at a devastating rate. Within a few months, almost everyone will be dead."

"People respond differently to exposure to radiation, so some will survive, but the number will be very few, and those who do survive will be extremely susceptible to some cancers, especially leukemia. Sterility and birth defects will also affect many of those who survive but remain exposed.

"Most animal life will be wiped out. Creatures deep in the oceans will probably be okay, but the sea life at shallower depths will die off. Some species of insects will be wiped out, but others will flourish, plants will also be impacted. Some will do fine in a more radioactive environment, while others won't."

For a long period of minutes, nobody said a word, all three men just stared at Williams as they tried to absorb what they'd heard.

Nathanial Atkins was the first to speak. "Is there any way this data could be wrong?"

"No, sir, it's confirmed. A University professor brought it to our attention about three months ago, and we've been checking and rechecking the data ever since," Williams responded quietly.

"When will this happen?" Atkins continued.

"Just under three years. We're estimating arrival on or around August 24, 2026."

"What options do we have?" Admiral Atkins demanded.

"At this time, we're not aware of any viable options. We're certainly looking for any possible solutions, anything which might change the situation. But as yet, we have nothing to offer," Williams answered.

"Are you saying we'll be watching this thing screaming through space for the next three years and there is nothing we can do, except wait for it to get here and kill six billion people?" General Draper snapped.

Williams inhaled sharply. "Gentlemen, that's exactly what I'm saying."

The National Security advisor rose to leave. "Mr. Williams don't go anywhere until you hear from me and obviously, don't discuss this with anyone. I want the name of that university professor." He glanced over at the representatives of the Joint Chief. "I'm going straight to the White House. Keep a lid on this until I've spoken to the President."

Chapter 8 – Day 940

Colonel Finch walked across the flight line to the waiting Army staff car; by the time he got there, he was cold and wet and utterly disgusted with himself. Here he was, being summoned to the Pentagon to provide an update on the work he and his team were doing, and he was going to walk in there resembling a drowned rat.

He dropped into the back seat of the staff car and forced himself to relax. The moisture seeped through his clothing and he cursed again because he hadn't bothered to check the weather report for Washington DC before he left home.

As the driver worked his way through the busy noontime traffic, Matt's mind wandered back to the question which had nagged at him ever since he'd been summoned to the Pentagon. After all the years of work on this project, no one had ever shown anything more than mild curiosity about the work he and the team were doing at the Arizona facility. Now, unexpectedly, he was being ordered to report to the Pentagon to provide an in-depth report. Probably some recently appointed one star wanted to start digging into the project. Someone must have accidentally come across a report of their latest success and wanted in on it now that it was showing real progress, Matt figured.

Or possibly, someone was all worked up over there being a fatality. Those types would completely miss the success the rest of the project experienced, and they tended to make a whole lot of noise. Before you knew it, people believed evil experiments were being conducted by the Army, and innocent people were being killed.

Matt forced himself to calm down, he was getting worked up just thinking about the possibilities, but it would be better to wait and see what was really going on. By the time he'd managed to calm down, they were arriving at the Pentagon. As he got out of the car, he was reminded again of his wet, and less than perfect appearance.

Upon entering, he was met by a US Army Major. "Sir, I've been asked to escort you to your meeting."

"I certainly wasn't expecting an escort, but please, lead on Major. I've only been here twice before, and I don't have any idea where I'm going," replied Fitch.

The Major grinned. "Colonel, I've been assigned here for two years now, and I often get lost in this maze."

They arrived at the conference room eight minutes later, and the Major said indicated the door with a brief dip of his head. "They'll be with you in just a few minutes, sir." He turned on his heels and left Matt alone.

The conference room was large; there was a substantial bar with a mirror at one end. The other end held all the equipment needed for video conferences. The conference table in the center was large and appeared to be made of mahogany. Twelve leather chairs surrounded the table.

Matt set his briefcase on the table and strode to the mirror by the bar, to see if there was anything he could do with his disheveled appearance.

As he was straightening his shirt the door opened and General Lee Draper came in. The General caught sight of Fitch by the bar and said, "Don't you think it's a bit early for a drink, Colonel?"

From the expression on the General's face, it was apparent he was at least half-joking. But the shock of seeing one of the Army's highest-ranking officers walk in through the door had Matt staring at the General incredulously, just the same.

"Relax, Colonel. Get your butt over here and take a seat. I've only got twenty minutes to get you up to speed, and then we have a conference call to make," General Draper said with a slight smile.

Fitch quickly took a seat across from the General, confusion obvious on his face.

"Colonel, I've read your reports, and I find your whole project fascinating. But I need some straight answers now. We'll let you know what we can, as we progress. Right now, I need a clear picture of where this Sleeper Project is, and where it needs to go," the General explained.

"Yes, sir. Have you seen the report I filed two months ago?" asked Fitch.

"Yes, that's why it was decided to get you involved. No games, Colonel. Was this as successful an experiment as your report makes it sound?"

"Absolutely sir. In fact, probably more so. As far as I'm concerned, the fatality was irrelevant to determining the success of the test. And while there were some extremely minor hardware issues, these have been addressed, and those failures helped prove that our fault tolerance was up to speed. Since submitting that report, we've just about finished analyzing the massive amounts of data which was automatically recorded during the tests and there are no other new issues to report. The sleep project is a success, far more so than we had even hoped for," Finch admitted. He couldn't hide the burst of pride in his voice as he spoke.

"Good, that's what I was hoping to hear. What else is needed for you to go live with this?" the General asked.

There was a definite pause before Fitch responded. "Go live? I guess that depends on what you're looking to do, sir. The only application of this technology that we can come up with is for long-term space flight. Or possibly, to sleep people with specific diseases until cures are found."

The General leaned back in his chair. "Let's say, hypothetically, I wanted to take a group of people and put them to sleep, completely unsupervised for up to twenty years. What would that take?"

Matt did a few mental calculations before he answered. "With a few minor modifications, we could do it now, as long as we could sleep them in our current facility."

"How many subjects can you manage in your current facility?"

"We're currently set up for twelve at any one time. If needed, we could add half a dozen more units, but it would take some time," Matt admitted.

"No, that won't work," General Draper said, shaking his head. "If we provided you with a suitable environment and all the manpower and funding you needed, how long would it take to be set up and ready to deal with about one hundred thousand people or more, and put them into this sleep state for twenty years?"

"One hundred thousand!" Matt repeated. The question completely threw him - the logistics alone were inconceivable. "If the facility was large enough, had enough power, and was ready for us to start work on today, we might be ready in about five to ten years." Even as Fitch said this he could see the displeasure on the General's face and he continued hurriedly. "Sir, if I had a better idea regarding what you need, I could give you more accurate answers."

"Okay, Colonel," Draper said after a pause. He slid a small black notebook binder across the table to Matt.

The first thing Matt noticed was the words TOP SECRET in large red letters.

"You're not to discuss this with anyone. I don't pretend to understand the scientific part of this, in fact, the folks at NASA don't understand it fully either, but it seems that in less than three years some blasted comet is going to irradiate the Earth's atmosphere. The radiation levels will be high enough to kill almost everything on the planet."

Matt's mouth dropped open and the color drained from his face.

"We're working this problem from several angles. The data has been confirmed, it's definitely coming here. The chances of us stopping the comet or altering its path are about a million to one. Underground bunkers are a possibility, but the problem is that everyone would need to stay in them for at least ten years – probably more like twenty. Of course, there's no way to get more than a tiny percentage of the people into them; but still, it's better than nothing. Your sleeper program is about the only possibility, but even if we could get the one hundred thousand units ready, we're still talking about saving less than one out of every four thousand people in this country."

"Suffering a mixture of mild dizziness and some nausea, Matt responded quietly. "Sir, please tell me this a hypothetical scenario."

"No, Colonel, this is about as real as it gets."

Matt stood and walked over to the bar. "In response to your earlier question, sir, I no longer think it's too early for a drink. What can I get you?"

"Scotch," the General responded.

Matt filled two glasses with a couple of generous fingers of scotch and hurried back to the table. "Sir, from what I remember a comet is mostly ice. I don't remember radiation being a common concern."

"Apparently, that's true. There's something very unusual about this particular comet though, and we don't have any clear answers."

Matt sipped the whiskey, thinking hard. "Sir, there's no way we can sleep a significant number of people for that period. The power requirements are enormous. We might be able to work up a small nuke reactor to run automatically for a while, but there's no way we can do this on a large scale; it just isn't feasible without a lot more preparation time."

"Alright, Colonel, what can you offer?" Draper asked.

"Sir, I'm still processing this. I'm sorry, but I need a few hours to work through the details and come up with something," Colonel Fitch responded.

"I understand, it took me a good week for this to settle in enough so I could think straight. Unfortunately, that isn't possible right now, we have a conference call to make," the General said, as he reached for the keyboard in front of him and activated the camera at the end of the room. The small red light on the front of the camera blinked on, and the camera swiveled to face them.

Fitch was starting to ask the General about the conference call, when he heard a familiar voice from the speaker on the table. "Good afternoon, General Draper. I assume that's Colonel Fitch with you?"

Matt brought his eyes up to the video conference monitor and found himself staring into the face of President Daniel Anson.

Chapter 9 – Day 939

Derek Kline bit into the spicy shrimp and winced. The pain in his left rear molar was intense, it had been worsening for the last three days, but his excessive fear of dentists had kept him from making an appointment until this morning. Now it wouldn't be until Monday before he could get treatment. That meant another three days of this pain before he'd get any relief. The dentist's secretary had been sympathetic, but not sympathetic enough to find a way to squeeze him in today. In the meantime, the best they could offer was suggesting he take Motrin to help with the pain. So far, their suggestion had helped marginally, but not anywhere near enough.

Derek glanced across the table to his friend Robert Walsh. Robert was hungrily eating, and it made him a little envious to see his lifelong friend eating so easily while he suffered with each bite.

Derek and Rob had met in kindergarten and been close friends ever since. When they were ten years old, Derek's Grandfather had bought him his first telescope, and both boys developed a love of astronomy. They spent many summer nights studying the heavens and charting stars. They would often quiz each other about the constellations and the individual stars which made them up. They'd pooled their pocket money and slowly began to build up a formidable astronomy library.

By this point, the boys were as close as any brothers. Where one was, the other was almost always guaranteed to be found. Derek and Rob even went on their first date together, when in tenth grade, they took the Miller twins to the school dance and later spent half the night trying to get the girls to show an interest in astronomy. The date ended when Tara Miller asked why anyone would care so much about a bunch of dumb stars' and her sister Lisa agreed.

Since they each worked only part-time on the campus of the University of Washington while they studied, they tended to be a little short of cash most of the time, which had led them to the All-You-Can-Eat buffet at the Golden Dragon Chinese restaurant today. It wasn't uncommon for them to eat only one real meal a day and they generally chose to make it a big one at some buffet where they could eat enough to sustain them for the next twenty-four hours. Doing this made it possible to get by on as little as ten dollars a day for food and allowed them to put away more of their meager funds for astronomy journals or texts.

The two aspiring astronomers had been on a high for the last several months, since discovering the strange properties of a comet which was traveling towards the Earth. They'd worked with their professor to confirm their data and checked to confirm there was no other record of this comet's irregularities in any of the typical sources.

They had wanted to publicize their findings, but their professor had insisted on discretion. Apparently, he knew of an astronomy program on the East Coast. They had what they thought was a significant finding involving an asteroid several years before. After going public and creating a minor panic, it turned out that there was a calculation with an unnoticed error in it, one which radically changed the 'big find' into a 'big nothing'. The event had caused a significant amount of embarrassment for the school and their astronomy program.

It was this negative publicity which Professor Mallox was determined to prevent. He had quietly forwarded their findings to NASA and was awaiting a response.

The boys reluctantly went along with the decision, but after almost six months, they were getting tired of waiting. One of the few arguments they'd ever had occurred a week ago, when Rob suggested they stop delaying and publicize their findings on their own.

Derek was adamantly opposed to this idea, and the boys had come close to having a shouting match. In the end, they'd agreed to wait two more weeks for Professor Mallox's direction to get answers.

Today it had taken Derek much longer than usual to eat his fill, and much of the time Rob gently harassed him about his dentist phobia and how slowly he ate, but before they'd left the restaurant, Derek had managed to do a good bit of damage to the buffet's supply of Szechwan shrimp.

The two friends left the restaurant feeling uncomfortably stuffed and walked the ten minutes back to their apartment. Both men were in a little bit of a hurry; Rob had a date that evening with Sara, a journalism student, and Derek wanted another six hundred milligrams dose of Motrin to subdue the pain in his tooth.

The boys jogged up the two flights of stairs to their apartment, and Derek retrieved the keys from his pocket and opened the door.

When Rob stepped into the room, he was immediately aware of a strange odor. It wasn't strong and reminded him of old Mr. Cardinal who lived across the street from him when he was a kid and always wore of a slightly citric-smelling cologne.

"You smell that?" Derek asked.

"Yeah, some kinda perfume or something."

"I think someone's been in here. Did you give Sara a key?"

"No," Rob replied, reaching back and locking the door.

The boys carefully searched the place and confirmed there was no one there. They were just finishing their quick search when Rob caught sight of an unfamiliar white strap sticking out from under his bed.

He grabbed the strap and pulled out a navy-blue gym bag. It was less than half full but somewhat heavy.

He carried the bag back to the living room. "Is this yours?" he asked Derek who was surveying the bag curiously.

"Never seen it. Where did it come from?"

"I just found it under my bed, and I've never seen it before either. It looks new."

"Let's see what's in it," Derek suggested.

Rob opened the bag and dumped its contents unceremoniously onto the couch.

"Holy crap!!" Rob exclaimed. Two handguns and five, six inch by eight-inch packages of white powder, along with large stacks of twenty and fifty dollar bills that had also fallen out.

"Why would someone put this in our room?" Derek said, inspecting their find.

"We have to call the cops," Rob stated in a quivering voice.

"What cop is going to believe we just happened to find this in the apartment we've lived in for the past two and a half years?"

"Then let's get rid of it, go throw it in a lake or a dumpster!" Rob demanded, starting to panic.

Derek tried to stay calm. "Slow down and think. If whoever put it here comes looking for it, I don't want to explain why we just threw it away."

"Then what do we do, just put it back under the bed?" Rob yelled.

"No, let's start by getting it out of here. We'll hide it for a few days and then if we've heard nothing, we'll get rid of it."

"Where do you want to hide it?"

"There's that abandoned warehouse on the other side of campus, the one where that fire broke out last fall. I'm sure we can find a place there that'll be good for a few days," Derek suggested.

Glad to have a plan, Rob willingly agreed and the two of them worked to quickly place everything back in the bag. Moving towards the door, they heard footsteps coming up the wooden staircase. Rob checked his watch thinking it might be Sara, but he grew pale when he realized there were more than one set of footsteps, and it sounded like they wore heavy boots.

The boys started backing away from the door and hurried across to the fire escape in the living room, quickly opening the large window which led to the metal stairs.

Just as they were climbing out, they heard someone pounding on the apartment door, and a voice called out. "Open the door, this is the police! We have a search warrant!"

Ignoring the shouted order, they were halfway down the fire escape when they heard their apartment door being smashed in.

They both jumped the last few feet and were up and running, Derek in the lead and carrying the gym bag. They turned down the alley which dead-ended into their building and the sounds of people following them down the fire escape reached their ears.

With every step, they both searched frantically for a place to hide the bag, but nothing presented itself.

Out of desperation, Derek finally decided to throw the bag through a broken basement window in one of the old buildings they passed. Quickly checking over his shoulder to be sure he hadn't been seen, he raced to catch up to Rob.

They ran another two blocks and heard approaching sirens, coming from at least two different directions. Derek pointed down the next alley and yelled, "You go that way, meet me at the entrance to the park in twenty minutes!"

Derek knew he'd been seen as he ran from the fire escape, so he turned onto a side street and tore off his gray hooded sweatshirt, stopping long enough to shove it down a storm drain. Half a block further up, he saw a discarded baseball cap in the gutter, which he quickly grabbed and pulled the filthy orange cap onto his head.

Slowing to a walk when he reached the next intersection, he stepped out onto the main street and merged with the other pedestrian traffic.

Derek found that walking at a slow pace was extremely difficult; he desperately wanted to run, and it took all his willpower to control the urge. He was also fighting the desire to keep looking behind him. He didn't think he'd been spotted since getting rid of the sweatshirt, but he knew he had to blend in with the others on the street.

He kept walking until he approached a Burger King, and slipped inside. He ordered a Coke and took a seat away from the front doors which gave him a clear view of the entrance.

He sat and waited, glancing at his watch every few minutes. He saw police officers walk past the restaurant twice and on one occasion one of the officers glanced in the window, but her gaze didn't lock onto him.

He was still desperate to figure out what had happened. Things weren't making sense; neither of them ever used drugs, and no one had access to their apartment. Still, someone had placed drugs, cash, and guns in their place. The police had been at the apartment within minutes of them returning home, which suggested they'd been waiting for them. But why would someone put the stuff in their apartment and how did the cops find out? Either the police had followed the person who put the stuff in the apartment, or the person who'd placed the drugs in the apartment told the cops. If that was the case, then he and Rob were intentionally being set up for some reason.

The more Derek thought about it, the more he kept coming back to the critical question - why would someone do this? What reason was there to go to this kind of trouble? None of it made any sense.

Ten minutes later, he rose and left the restaurant carrying his drink with him. He crossed the street and casually headed toward the park. If the timing was right, he'd meet Rob right on schedule. The possibility that Rob might have been caught crossed his mind, but he pushed it away not willing to dwell on that.

Approaching the park, he heard a loud male voice behind him call out. "Police! Stop right there!"

The panic continued to override logical thinking, and he never considered stopping. He approached the entrance to the park and dashed inside, his heart sinking when Rob was nowhere to be seen.

On the path, about thirty feet ahead of him was a small female police officer.

Derek never considered fighting her, but he was fast, and she was small. He assumed getting around her would be easy, so he increased speed and ran straight at her. At the last minute, he would dart around her, and she would never catch him.

He heard her command him to stop and watched her reach toward her gun belt. He was about fifteen feet away when she raised a can of CS/OC pepper spray pointing it at his face.

Suddenly everything changed; he couldn't see, breathing was almost impossible, and his whole neck and face felt as if they were engulfed by fire.

The next thing Derek knew he was on the ground, vomiting, warm Coca-Cola coming up through his nose and Szechwan shrimp coming out of his mouth. The orange ball cap had come off and was under his cheek. He was still fighting for breath and seeing was almost impossible. He was frantically rubbing his eyes, but that only seemed to intensify the pain.

Without warning, a hard object slammed into his back, forcing him flat to the ground. Small hands grabbed his wrists and pulled his arms behind his back. Resisting any further was impossible and he felt the cold steel on his wrists and heard the clicks as the handcuffs tightened.

The officer got off him, and he experience a mild sense of relief when her knee was removed from his spine.

Through the pain, Derek could hear the female officer involved in a conversation with what he assumed was another police officer, but he couldn't make out what they were saying.

After what seemed like an eternity face down on the cold ground, he felt hands on either side of him, roughly lifting him to his feet. His breathing had improved slightly, and he could see a little better, but tears were still rolling down his cheeks and his face and eyes still felt as if they were covered in acid. He heard someone tell him he had the right to remain silent, but the rest of what they said was drowned out by his next bout of vomiting.

He was assisted in the walk to the park exit and held for several minutes until a police cruiser pulled up.

By the time he was pushed into the back seat of the car, the effects of the spray were wearing off enough to see the bloody and abraded face of Rob when he half landed on him. Rob's face looked as if he'd fallen hard against the pavement and there was a terrified look in his eyes.

Pushing himself into a seated position, Derek noticed through the Plexiglas shield separating the front seat from the back, that there was a familiar looking navy blue gym bag with a white shoulder strap sitting on the front passenger seat.

Chapter 10 – Day 939

Early the next morning Colonel Fitch was back at the Pentagon, this time seated in General Draper's private office. It was quite spacious, and there was a large rug in front of the General's desk. The emblem of the United States Army was imprinted in the rug in bright, eye-catching colors. Judging by its pristine appearance, Fitch got the impression that the unspoken rule was to walk around the rug, and not over it.

Numerous photos were displayed on the walls revealing the different units the General had served in during his career.

Matt was still annoyed at being blindsided by an unexpected conference with the President, even though it seemed as if his briefing to the Commander in Chief had gone better than he would have expected.

He'd told the President the same thing he said to the General. He needed time to put some things together before he could promise anything. There was no way they were going to be able to get a plan in place to sleep more than a few thousand people with their time frame. Even then, that could only be done if there was a facility large enough, ready for them to start working on immediately.

While the President hadn't been overly pleased with the news, he hadn't revealed any surprise either.

Following their conference call, Draper dismissed him for the day, instructing him to come up with what he could. He was to report back at 0800 the following morning.

Matt had left the Pentagon and taken a long walk through Arlington National Cemetery, one of his favorite places to visit when in Washington. He'd known a good number of men who were now buried there. It was a quiet place, where he could think and wouldn't be disturbed. The weather had cleared, and the temperature was in the low eighties, so he found the walk was quite relaxing, despite what he'd just learned.

The whole comet story still didn't seem real. It sounded more like a scenario for some type of a training exercise. While Matt knew it was real, for now, he'd approach it as he would any problem, either real or fictitious.

After two hours of walking and thinking, he found himself back at his hotel, although he couldn't recall making a specific decision to return.

That night, Matt went to dinner at a steakhouse across from the hotel. He enjoyed a medium well porterhouse and baked potato with a salad. Following that he went for another walk and came up with a few prospective ideas. After a while, Matt went back to his room and thought over these kernels of ideas some more, making some notes and working over possibilities. Most of these he immediately dismissed.

Finally, he picked up the phone and called James Cowan. After six rings the phone was picked up by James' wife, Kathy, and from the sound of her voice, Matt could tell she'd been asleep. Fitch glanced at his watch and saw that it was almost three in the morning, which meant for the Cowans it must be about midnight. Fitch was shocked; he would never have imagined that it was this late.

"Kathy, this is Matt Fitch. Sorry to wake you, but is James there?" Cowan said.

There were some muffled words, and after about twenty seconds, James spoke into the phone.

"James, sorry to wake you," Fitch began apologetically.

"Is something wrong? Are you still in Washington?" Cowan asked. He too sounded half-asleep.

"Nothing's wrong, and yes I'm still here. Some interesting things are going on here, some big names are really interested in the Sleep Project. I'll be stuck here at least another day. I have an early morning meeting with a Four Star who's got lots of questions. I need to know something; would it be possible to design a capsule that could hold more than one person?"

There was a brief pause while James pondered the question. "I don't see any reason why not; we've always done separate capsules to better monitor individual responses and systems, but there's no reason we can't place more than one person in a capsule."

"How many people could you probably fit in a single capsule?" Matt asked.

"I've never thought about it, but I guess it would be possible to design a capsule that could hold a many as a dozen, maybe more."

"Thanks, that gives me a place to start," Fitch said.

"I'll think about the idea and see if I can come up with anything else. What's this all about, anyway?" Cowan asked.

"I'll give you as much info as I can when I return, but they might be giving us a larger facility and want us to try something on a much larger scale," Fitch answered evasively.

"Sounds exciting, let me know as soon as you're back in town," Cowan said.

Fitch hung up the phone and lay down, although he continued to think about the problem for another hour before falling asleep.

* * *

Now here he was in General Draper's office, on less than four hours sleep, and still, he had no solid answers.

Draper walked into the room and sat a pot of hot coffee on the desk. Fitch chuckled inwardly when he saw the General intentionally circle around the ornate rug in front of the desk. He looked over at Fitch. "You still mad about the unexpected chat with the president, Matt?"

"What makes you think I was mad, sir?" Fitch responded.

"I could see it in your face; if I hadn't been wearing these stars, you would've probably killed me. Right?"

"Right," Fitch agreed.

"Have you come up with any ideas?"

"I think it might be possible to build larger sleep capsules, ones that will hold about a dozen people. That should make it possible to greatly increase the number of sleepers. But every day we delay in getting started, decreases the number of units we'll get functional," Fitch explained.

"Good. The problem is we don't have a facility ready for you to move into yet. The amount of radiation coming off the tail of the comet indicates we're going to need to be at least twenty feet below ground. The Air Force is currently working on a new NORAD installation near the Arizona/Utah state line, to replace the Cheyenne Mountain facility outside Colorado Springs. I talked to the President about getting control of that. It's massive and will be completely self-sufficient. Unfortunately, it isn't currently scheduled to be operational for another two years," Draper said.

"Well sir, I'll investigate my end of it, but without a facility, we have nothing to offer. Currently, I see the sleeper project offering a way of providing a rebuilding team to the people that survive either by standard underground shelters or out of sheer good luck. There's no way we'll be able to do a hundred thousand sleepers. I can't even guess how many we can do, but every day without a functional facility decreases the numbers. I'll need to see the facility before I'll be able to give you an idea of what we might be able to offer," Matt explained.

"That certainly isn't what I was hoping to hear, but I'm not surprised. I'll move things along as fast as I can on this end. In the meantime, start planning everything needed when you have a facility and get everything moving as much as possible," Draper instructed.

"Sir, you said yesterday that other avenues are being pursued. Can I ask what they are?" Matt asked.

The General took a moment before responding. "I suppose there's no reason not to tell you. As you can imagine, we're keeping this as quiet as possible – the complete anarchy and panic we could expect if this were known would be devastating. There are less than ten people who know about it currently. There are some people from the Air Force who are looking at altering the comet's course with nukes. No one thinks they'll be successful, but everything must be tried.

Some others are looking into underground shelters, but I think I'd prefer to take my chances in the open rather than wait in a hole for ten years or more. Undersea shelters are also being considered, the technology isn't there yet, but some are hopeful. I got stuck with the suspended animation idea – no offense. Personally, I think simple underground shelters will be the primary direction of choice, they can save the most people," Draper said.

Matt got to his feet. "Thank you, sir. As I said, I'll get things moving as much as possible. Let me know when there's a place available for us to work."

"I'll move things along here as swiftly as possible. In the meantime, contact me immediately with any new ideas, or if there's anything that's holding you up," Draper said.

With that, Matt found himself dismissed. He returned to his hotel, packed, and by 1300 hours, he was airborne and heading west.

Four hours later Matt pulled into the driveway of the duplex he'd lived in ever since his divorce seven years earlier.

His wife had held out as long as she could, but in the end, she'd admitted she could no longer handle the military life. Matt had been transferred every few years, and that was something which had sounded exciting when they first got married, but after ten years she just couldn't continue doing it. They'd remained friends, and neither of them had failed to see the irony in the fact that ever since the breakup, Matt had been stationed permanently at the Arizona facility.

This wasn't the first time Matt Fitch had been given a seemingly impossible task to perform. Over time, he'd learned that the best way to deal with these types of problems was to do nothing at all, at least for a little while. Stopping and thinking first tended to produce better results than diving blindly into a situation. So that evening, all he did was place a call to James Cowan.

He informed Cowan that he wouldn't be in the next day. He hung up and went down to the basement to dig out his golf clubs.

The next day probably wasn't the best golfing he'd ever done, but it wasn't the worst either. But more importantly, he now felt clear-headed and ready to get to work.

Chapter 11 – Day 936

Professor Rupert Mallox was the head of the Astronomy program at the University of Washington. He'd been teaching astronomy for eighteen years, ten of them at the U of W.

The discovery of the comet's properties by two of his students a few months ago was by far the most significant discovery in his department's, if not the world's, history and he'd forced them to rerun their calculations four times before he'd accept their results.

Rupert had since tried several times to get someone to investigate and confirm the comet's apparent radioactive properties. Over the last few years, there'd been several false alarms regarding asteroids and meteors which could hit the Earth. These concerns had caused significant anxiety to the public before they were determined to be nothing of importance.

After several unsuccessful attempts at getting anyone to take his comet claims seriously, he'd given his brother-in-law a call. Rupert's wife, Deborah hailed from New York and her brother, Martin, was the aide to the senior US senator from Florida.

Martin knew the right people to talk to, and in no time at all, the good folks at NASA had reluctantly agreed to look into the matter for him.

Rupert suspected there would be a reasonable explanation as to why this threat was no more severe than any of the others. Nevertheless, this data seemed to very clearly show an imminent threat, and it needed to be checked out.

Armed with a phone number Martin had given him, Rupert called weekly to see if there was any information regarding the comet study. So far, there'd been no word other than to say that it was being looked into.

Rupert Mallox was starting to think he was being blown off, and it was time to come up with a new strategy. Possibly informing the media that something was found but that its criticality was undetermined and that NASA was looking into it, would get something moving, but he certainly didn't want to start a panic, or make a statement about something that would later be proven wrong; his reputation would be destroyed if he allowed that to happen.

As if there wasn't enough excitement in his life, last week he'd been contacted by the Pentagon. Apparently, there was an opportunity for someone with his background to be involved in a classified project, dealing with suspended animation and space travel. Rupert had declined the offer immediately, despite the project sounding fascinating and knowing it would be a great opportunity. He'd spent four years in the Marine Corps after high school and had seen first-hand, the inefficiency and waste of time and resources that inevitably occurred when the government was involved in a project. He'd sworn he would never deal with that nonsense again.

Three days ago, he'd been contacted again. He was asked to reconsider and at least hear more of the classified details. The man he'd spoken to assured him that if he knew all the details, he'd definitely be glad to be on board and offered information regarding his starting pay, should he take the position. He promised to consider the offer and call them back.

He'd discussed the situation with Deborah, and while the prospect of doubling his current salary would be fantastic, she pointed out that if he was miserable in his work, no amount of money would be worth it.

Rupert returned the call and declined the offer again, but his curiosity had been peaked. Maybe he should call back and talk to them again, hear what they had to say. He sent himself an email reminder at work, planning to call back on Monday morning.

Rupert and Deborah had spent a busy Saturday doing yard work and then headed out for a nice dinner of steak and lobster, followed by a presentation of Macbeth which the University's drama students were producing.

There was heavy traffic leaving the campus, and it took twenty minutes more than usual to get home. By the time they arrived, the rain had increased and thunder rumbled in the distance.

The garage door opened as their 2019 Suburban approached. Rupert skillfully backed the oversize vehicle into the open spot beside his own 2020 Lexus. He opened the door, careful not to bump the other car and headed to Deborah's side of the vehicle.

They went into the house, and Rupert pushed the button by the door to close the garage door, but the door didn't move. Rupert and Deborah exchanged confused glances and Rupert pushed the button a second, then a third time, but nothing happened. Finally, he went back over to the Suburban, opened the door, reached in and pushed the button on the remote. The motor engaged and the garage door closed in its usual fashion. The Mallox's exchanged confused looks as Rupert returned to the house.

Rupert looked up the phone number for the garage door company and wrote it down on a sheet of paper. He would have his wife call the number in the morning and have the system checked for a fault. Having completed this little task, he removed his shoes and dropped into the recliner in the family room.

He decided to read the Seattle Times before heading off to bed. His friends often teased him about his habit of still reading actual newspapers, rather than the electronic version but he liked the feel and smell of the actual paper. He could already hear the water running as Deborah got into the shower. He usually read the paper before dinner, but with all commotion leaving for their night out, he just didn't have time.

On page two of the paper was an article about a local drug raid. Apparently, police and federal agents had raided the apartment of two local college students. Officers had seized several thousand dollars' worth of cocaine and two firearms. At the end of the article were the names of the two students involved, Derek Kline and Robert Walsh.

Rupert was stunned, so shocked by this news he felt mildly nauseated. Both of the boys were in one of his classes. In fact, they were the ones responsible for discovering the radiation coming from the comet. He knew them both well, and he never in a lifetime would have suspected either of them to be wrapped up in something such as drug dealing. They were excellent students, who always put one hundred percent effort into every assignment.

After reading through the article, he folded the paper in his lap and sat in the chair thinking. He had to admit to being both shocked and disappointed by Derek and Robert's behavior, although he still found it hard to believe.

Rupert got up and headed into the kitchen. He threw away the newspaper without looking at the trash can. His aim was good, but on this particular occasion, if he'd looked into the trash, he might have seen the three nine-volt batteries lying at the bottom of the can.

Rupert headed to the bathroom, brushed his teeth, and undressed. He couldn't stop thinking about his students. He was genuinely bothered by this news, he had been quite fond of the two young men, and now he felt betrayed by their actions.

He climbed into bed, thinking he really needed to discuss this with his wife. But not tonight, Deborah was gently snoring, and he'd never wake her just to talk over something he'd seen in the paper, even if he did know the boys involved. Even though he was tired and had a long day, he found he still needed about forty-five minutes before he could settle off to sleep.

Sometime later, exactly how long he couldn't be sure, there was a noise which sounded like a heavy object falling, and it woke Rupert.

He peered around in the semi-darkness and immediately knew something was wrong.

He couldn't see, his breathing was painful, and his eyes were burning. He began to cough. In seconds, his head had cleared enough to allow him to understand what was going on. The whole room was filled with thick smoke.

He jumped out of bed and started shouting Deborah's name, but there was no response. His panic rose; Deborah was a severe asthmatic, and smoke caused terrible attacks.

Turning back to the bed he felt across the mattress for her, frightened to discover she wasn't there. He ran to the doorway, his breathing extremely labored and he coughed continuously in the acrid air.

Rupert tripped over something near the door and he fell, striking his head hard on the door frame. The pain in his head and neck was severe, and he was aware of blood running down his face. Blindly, he felt around for what he'd tripped over. His hands found hair first, and then skin, a nose and lips. Deborah! He continued to feel around until he located her arms and struggled to lift his wife from the floor. He could hear her wheezing as she fought to breathe, and when he got her up onto her feet, he wrapped one of her arms around his shoulders as he half dragged, half carried her from the bedroom.

As quickly as Rupert could manage, he headed for the door leading to the garage, since it was the quickest way out of the house. He opened the door; the smoke seemed even thicker in here. He felt the wall, groping across until he found the button for the garage door. He pushed the button repeatedly before he remembered that it wasn't working.

He made a swift decision. It would probably take longer to get into the Suburban and find the remote. They would have a better chance of surviving if they went back inside and went for the front door. He grabbed Deborah again and dragged back into the house.

His breathing was worsening, and his strength was almost gone. His head was pounding and the sensation was getting more intense by the second.

The crackling sound of fire and the glow of flames was getting closer.

Finally, he could go no further. He released his wife of twenty years, swearing to come back as soon as he had the door open. He started crawling; his motions growing more and more difficult with each passing second.

After what seemed like hours, he reached the door and grabbed the doorknob, reaching up to fumble with the deadbolt until finally, it opened. Unconsciousness was only moments away, he was certain. He twisted the knob and yanked the door. He'd made it!

Rupert was confused when, after only two inches of movement, the motion of the door came to a crashing stop. He shook it several times before he realized the security chain was hooked. It took an extra moment to process this, because in the twelve years they'd lived here they had never used the chain. He tried to pull himself up onto his knees to release it but he was far too weak; he fell back to the floor with a crash. Now he was so exhausted, he couldn't even raise his head. The last thought to cross his mind was that if just one of the three smoke detectors in the house had gone off, they probably would have gotten out.

Chapter 12 – Day 936

James Cowan sat in front of his computer. He was intrigued by the idea Fitch proposed. There was no reason why it couldn't work in theory, but it would take a lot of engineering. He'd worked steadily on the concept the whole day before and was making significant progress. Fortunately, Fitch was due in this morning, and hopefully, there would be answers and he'd give James a better idea as to where this was going.

At 0800 Matt Fitch walked into Cowan's office. Cowan looked up and said, "This is the second time in as many months that you've been on time. I'm starting to get nervous."

"I considered sitting in my car listening to the radio for another twenty minutes, just so I wouldn't have to take this abuse," Fitch said with a grin.

Cowan smiled. "I've been working on your idea, and I think I can make it work."

"Good, I need a live, short duration test as soon as possible," Fitch responded.

"How soon are we talking?" Cowan asked.

"I want it to begin next week."

"Are you serious?" Cowan responded quickly, but he could see from the look on the Colonel's face that he was completely serious.

"It doesn't have to be a big test; three to five subjects and they only have to be out a week. It just needs to be enough to prove we can do this," Fitch explained.

"I don't know if we can pull it off that fast. We need an airtight chamber in which we can manually control the atmospheric pressure. Not to mention rounding up test subjects," Cowan advised.

"We have unlimited resources for this; if you need special equipment, locate it. I'll have it here. If you can't get test subjects, let me know. I'll have some brought in."

Cowan stared at his counterpart with wide eyes. "What's going on? The military may be promoting and funding this project, but I'm still the project lead. I need to know what's going on."

There was a long pause before Fitch spoke. "Let's take a walk." He turned and headed for the door.

Cowan got up quickly and followed his friend. From the tone of his voice and his expression, James could see that Matt was troubled. He decided to just follow along for now and let the Colonel talk when he was ready.

They headed outside and across the parking lot. It was still early, and the air was crisp. As soon as they got outside, Cowan wished he'd grabbed his jacket. He briefly considered going back for it. However, from the look on his friend's face, he decided it would be better to just stick it out.

On the other side of the small road which led to their isolated facility was a grassy clearing with picnic tables and a little pavilion setup. The seats at the picnic table were still wet after a late night rain shower, so both men stood as they talked.

"Unfortunately, there are details of what I'm going to say that are classified and I'm under stringent orders not to discuss them. However, let's say the military is concerned with the possibility of nuclear or biological threats that could wipe out almost all life forms on the planet. They're looking for a plan to have in place in the event of a mass disaster. Underground and undersea shelters are also being developed. They want us to be a factor in any scenario. I, or should I say we, have been tasked with getting this thing moving. I suspect they're going to want us to move ASAP to get a standby facility prepared. The idea is, we could sleep as many people for as long as it takes for the world to be habitable again. We've proven our technology works, and now they want us to set it up for actual use. I want the test complete so that when I hear more, I have something positive to tell them." Fitch felt guilty as he spoke, but he'd been unable to convince Draper or the President that anyone else needed the information. Draper had helped put together this story, and Matt was under strict orders to stick to this plan.

There was a definite look of suspicion on James' face, but he didn't question the story.

"How complete does this test need to be?" Cowan asked.

"I think we need a pressurized environment and we need to place a few subjects out for five days and conduct a successful wake-up. If we need a couple of other people in the test area to monitor events and manually change bags of SF016, I don't care. We've shown we can automate the process. In honesty I don't care if it's all held together with duct tape," Fitch stated.

Cowan smiled. "The main sleep chamber can be pressurized; all we need to do is remove the covers from five of the capsules and shut down the computer systems in those capsules. We can monitor everything from the main computer in the chamber. The SF016 will need to be handled differently, and we'll need staff in there. However, it should be no problem. We won't need to deal with waste management; there will be no output in such a short test. The individual capsules will serve as nothing more than a bed. If you can get the five test subjects and they all check out medically, we can start on Monday."

Fitch knew disbelief must be written on his face. "You already had this figured out?"

"It came to me last night after I talked to you. By now they probably have the cover doors off the five capsules and the individual capsules systems tied into the main computer." Cowan answered with a grin.

Chapter 13 – Day 932

Stanley Waldorf and Tony Jackson walked into the Midnight Lounge and took seats near the back of the dark, smoke-filled bar. The smell of stale beer was heavy in the air.

Stanley had picked the Midnight Lounge for this meeting since he'd never been there in the past and probably wouldn't be seen by anyone who knew him. He only needed ten seconds in the building to decide he'd never be back again.

The out-of-the-way seats they'd chosen helped ensure their conversation would remain unheard and Waldorf positioned himself so he could see anyone approaching.

Whenever anyone came close, he would signal Tony, and their conversation stopped.

These two men had never socialized in the past; in fact, they had no use for one another. Waldorf had tried unsuccessfully, about a year before, to have Jackson fired from NASA for an inappropriate act he and his girlfriend had been caught engaged in on NASA grounds during work hours. Unfortunately, today the two men had things they had to discuss.

The Deputy Director spoke first. "We need to discuss this comet situation."

Jackson nodded. "I know, I can't stop thinking about this and the fact that it's still being kept from the public."

Waldorf continued. "I agree, it's not right to keep this kind of thing a secret. I know Williams was at the Pentagon for a few days last month and I know there are some people here working on a solution. But people need to know this; the government isn't supposed to keep something like this from the people."

"True, but what can we do about it?" Tony Jackson asked.

Waldorf suddenly signaled with a chopping motion of his left hand, and the two immediately stopped their conversation.

"What can I get you, gentlemen?" asked the waitress.

She was medium height, a little on the chunky side and which short, spiked blonde hair. The stud pierced into the center of her tongue gave a slur to her speech and Stanley wondered if she was going to start drooling.

"Nothing," Stanley said contemptuously.

"I'll have a Diet Coke," Tony said.

Clearly disappointed with the minimal order, the waitress left to fill the order.

"I don't know, but something needs to be done," said Stanley.

"What if we were to go to the newspapers? I know a guy at the Washington Times who would love to be the first one to get this information. By the time Williams found out, it would be too late. They couldn't fire us, or the cover-up would look even worse," Tony suggested.

"True, that might be a good idea," Waldorf agreed, "but I want to talk to Williams before we do anything. Maybe he knows more than he's said, but I think it's imperative this information comes out."

After thirty minutes of further discussion, it was agreed that Waldorf would approach his boss in the morning and learn whatever he could.

* * *

At 0830 the following day, Administrator Williams was seated at his desk drinking his morning coffee when Stanley walked in and closed the door.

"You got a minute boss?" asked Waldorf.

Williams looked up, irritation visible on his face. There wasn't much in the world he liked less than being interrupted in his office by an unexpected visitor.

"You've got one minute. I've got stuff I'm working on," answered Williams.

Waldorf slumped into a chair. "Tony Jackson and I have been talking about this comet. We have a big problem with information this critical being kept from the public," he explained.

"You think we should just tell everyone that the world is coming to an end? Can you imagine the chaos? There'd be panicking, riots, people would stop working. The whole infrastructure of the country, no, of the entire world, would collapse! Do you think that's a good idea? This way at least people can enjoy the last few years they have, instead of living in panic and fear!" shouted Williams.

Waldorf had never seen the boss react this way, but he forged on. "People still have a right to know. Tony wants to go to the media, and I agree with him." As he spoke, he saw the color drain from his boss's face and the anger on his face disappeared, replaced by worry.

There was a long pause before Williams spoke again. "I'll make a deal with you. Keep this quiet for one more week. I'll make some calls to the people who are dealing with this thing and tell them we need some answers. I promise I'll keep you informed. Deal?"

He would have argued with his boss some more, but he'd never seen him react to anything like this. He had not even heard of anyone changing colors the way Director Williams had just done. Waldorf decided to drop it for now, but in seven days, he and Jackson would tell the world.

As Waldorf left the office, the Administrator called after him. "Have you told anyone yet?"

"Not yet" he responded grimly and left.

As soon as Waldorf had gone, NASA Administrator Williams pounded both fists on his desk and rose, and starting to pace the room.

This was a big problem; there was no way Draper would be holding a press conference to explain the truths behind the comet anytime soon.

After a few minutes of thinking, he snatched up the telephone, punching in a special number he'd been given. He had been ordered to contact General Draper urgently if anything regarding the comet arose.

He dialed the number, and it was answered by a voicemail system. "This is Mr. Williams here in town. I believe we have a Code Omega. Please call me when you can. Thanks." Williams felt foolish talking about codes, but those were the instructions that had been agreed upon.

Less than five minutes later, his phone was ringing. "Williams here."

"What is it Director?" asked the General with a hint of concern in his voice.

"I have two people on staff here, the first is one of my department directors, Stanley Waldorf and the other is an astrophysicist named Tony Jackson. They were the ones in charge of putting together all the data I first brought to you."

"And?"

Williams squirmed uncomfortably in his chair. "Well, they're really agitated and want to go to the media with the information about the comet. I talked to Waldorf, and there's no changing his mind. I've convinced him to wait one more week, and I told him I'd see if I could get the powers that be to agree to release the information. He went along with waiting the week, but they're both committed to letting the public know. Can they maybe be detained for a while or something? I'm convinced that they'll start talking otherwise."

There was a long pause before Draper spoke. "I'll see what can be done, but it's imperative that we confirm if they've told anyone yet."

"No, General, I'm certain they haven't said a word. I asked the question specifically, and Waldorf claims to have kept quiet up until now, but he and Jackson seem convinced the public has a right to know," said Williams.

"You were right to call me about this; I'll see what I can do." General Draper hung up the phone and cursed, slumping against the back of the chair while he thought. In less than a minute, he was back on the phone.

Chapter 14 – Day 932

Cowan slowly walked across the parking lot to his new dark blue Dodge Durango. He was already fond of this vehicle even though he'd owned it for less than two months. His only regret was in choosing such a dark color – in the hot desert sun, it became so uncomfortable late in the day. Actually, Cowan still couldn't understand why he'd decided on that color. He'd lived in hot southern climates all his life and always chosen light colored vehicles.

He unlocked the SUV with the remote on his key ring and the engine turned over immediately. Fortunately, today was a bit colder than usual, and with just the windows open, he found the vehicle quite comfortable.

As he drove, James at work. It seemed as if the whole scope of the project was suddenly taking a drastic turn. He wasn't bothered specifically by the change, but not having a clear understanding of the goals of this new project made him uncomfortable.

The story Matt gave him had more holes in it than Cowan cared to count, but he suspected there was probably some truth to it. James assumed the Colonel was being ordered to keep a lot of the details confidential.

Regardless of the real reasons for the changes, what they were investigating now was stuff they'd only briefly considered in the past. Now they were going to get to try some of them out. If things went well, some of the long-standing plans for implementing a real sleep event would need to be completely revisited.

Still contemplating the path they were following, Cowan suddenly realized he was only a couple minutes from his house. He thought back on the drive home and was disconcerted to realize there were large parts of the trip that he had no recollection of. While this had certainly happened before, it still troubled him each time it happened. He always imagined that had he gotten involved in a minor accident, he might not have even noticed and just kept driving.

He slowly turned onto his street and almost had to stop for Tuffy the black lab, who was wandering down the middle of the road. Tuffy had lived in the neighborhood as long as Cowan could remember. He was old now and slow, and mostly, if not entirely deaf.

One of Cowan's favorite photos of his son was of him playing with Tuffy when he was a tiny pup. As Cowan thought about it, he realized the picture must be close to fourteen years old now, which meant this canine was at least ancient in dog years, if not older. Cowan smiled at the thought and decided he didn't mind waiting a minute for Tuffy to make it past his driveway. As he got out of the car, he paused for a moment and took another look at the neighborhood mascot as he continued his slow journey.

He entered the house calling out, "Kath, I'm home."

"Out on the porch," came the faint reply.

Cowan went upstairs to the bedroom, quickly slipping off his shoes and socks and changing into shorts and a polo shirt, then went back downstairs to the kitchen. Finding no clean glasses, he opened the dishwasher and took out one which was still hot. He almost dropped it before he got it to the sink and ran cool water over it for several seconds. James then dried it before adding ice, and a healthy serving of iced tea from the clear plastic pitcher in the refrigerator, pausing to add two generous teaspoons of sugar and heading out to the porch.

Kathy looked up at him and rolled her eyes. She could never understand why anyone would sweeten their tea that way, but she'd grown up in Manhattan. Sweetened tea was something she'd never tried until she and James met in college and she'd been definite regarding her aversion to the drink.

She was standing by the grill, and James inhaled the delicious scent of chicken breasts, smothered in barbecue sauce. A pot boiled on the side burner of the grill and rice bobbed in the water. He noticed that she'd prepared the table, and dinner was just minutes away.

"Hi, it was cooler out, so I thought we'd try eating out here," Kathy said.

"Great idea, that smells great. What did you do today?"

"I went to work for a couple hours. Since I'm leaving in the morning and I'll be gone for several days, I wanted to make sure things were in order in my classroom. I can't believe classes will start up again in less than three weeks."

"I know, it seems like school just got out. I bet you're already excited about getting a room full of sixteen-year-old punks who have no interest in American History."

Kathy grimaced. "James, I can't believe your attitude sometimes! Most of the kids are good kids. I'll confess that many of them don't see the value of learning about Columbus or the Emancipation Proclamation, but at that age, I didn't either."

"That may be true, but what am I supposed to think? When I ask you what interesting things happened at work, you tell me about Sandy being pregnant, or Mike who was expelled for fighting, or Marsha, who you caught cheating on a test. I don't hear many stories about Dave who aced the test because he spent all weekend studying just to succeed in your class because he realized its value to his future."

Kathy smiled as she answered. "Well, I can see that you might walk away with the impression that they're a bunch of losers, but that's only a small percentage of them. Most are good kids."

Cowan held a large glass plate out for Kathy, who removed the chicken from the grill and shut off the propane gas.

They finished prepping the food then sat at the table. Both closed their eyes and took a moment to give thanks for their food before they started eating.

Kathy looked over at her husband. "Is something bothering you? You seem preoccupied?"

Cowan was surprised by the question. He didn't feel preoccupied, but he had to admit that he was thinking a lot about what Matt Fitch had told him. Apparently, Kathy knew him very well if she could notice he was a little off.

"Matt got back from his trip today. It seems the Pentagon wants us to move beyond the concept phase. They want to create a facility where significant numbers of people could be put to sleep for long periods of time. The idea is that in the event of a nuclear or biological war, or some other global disaster these people could sleep until it was safe to come out again."

"Interesting idea, but how many people could you actually sleep at a time?" Kathy asked.

"That's the part which makes no sense. I can't see us being able to sleep more than a few hundred, maybe a thousand at the most. Even that would probably take years of preparation. Besides, where would we do this? We certainly don't have a facility available which could withstand the kind of global disaster they're talking about. Even if we did, we'd need constant power and a staff to maintain everything. We haven't even completed all the automation. A scenario like they're proposing would take ten years to get going, and Matt Fitch is making it sound like it needs to be in place tomorrow."

Kathy smiled at her husband, knowing he'd already spent a lot of time thinking about this. "Sounds to me like the kind of challenge that you so desperately enjoy."

James smiled back weakly. "You know, it could be. But with them holding back so much information, it's just a huge frustration."

Chapter 15 – Day 931

Cowan walked back into the infirmary where Captain Travers and a physician were completing the medical evaluations on the five volunteers Fitch had rounded up.

"Amy, how long until you're ready to begin?" Cowan asked.

"We're finishing up now, and we'll move into the chamber from here," she answered.

"Good. Do you guys have any questions?" Cowan questioned, looking at the test subjects.

They all glanced nervously at one another before one of them spoke up. "All we know is we were ordered to report here for some tests and that we'd be sleeping for five days."

"So you didn't volunteer for this?" Cowan asked.

"Sir, we were just ordered to report here at 0700," another of the test subjects answered.

"In the Army, that is volunteering," Travers offered.

Cowan understood, but he was none too pleased. "We've been working on what we refer to as the sleep program. It could be considered a cross between suspended animation, and a drug-induced coma. While sleeping in our systems, the normal body processes slow to almost a stop. Our last group was out for five years, and they aged about two days each year. We've made some significant changes in our processes and need to see how they work. The Pentagon has placed a rush on this, and they want it done immediately. That's why we didn't have time for our regular selection process. There will be an IV in your arm and a mask on your face. You'll breathe a special gas, and the drug in the IV will put you out quickly. There will be equipment hooked to you that will monitor your heart rate and blood pressure, as well as temperature and breathing. You won't dream or be aware of the passing of time. You'll awaken feeling slightly confused and nauseated, but this will pass quickly. Any questions?"

"Has anyone ever died during one of these tests?" a tall female volunteer asked.

Travers answered before Cowan could respond. "You'll have medical personnel in there with you at all times, and if there is any problem, we can easily end the test."

Cowan wondered if the soldier, young and nervous, had noticed that his last question had been avoided.

Once the exams were completed, the test subjects moved into the chamber. Their shirts were removed before they were placed in the open capsules. The short duration of the test avoided the need for the waste removal systems to be used.

"Is the Colonel planning to be here for this?" Travers asked.

"He had to fly back to Washington last night; He expects to be back tomorrow," Cowan responded.

"Any idea what's with these trips of his?" the Captain asked in a low voice.

"Seems like Washington has heard about what we're doing, and they're really interested, even considering expanding the project," Cowan said. He watched as a technician attached blood pressure cuffs to the arms of each test subject, and the IVs were started.

After the electrodes for the cardiac monitors were attached, a positive pressure face mask was applied and Travers and Cowan left the chamber, leaving a physician and two technicians behind.

The heavy steel door sealed the chamber, and the room was pressurized to make conditions in the chamber the same as they would have been inside individual capsules. The test subjects were asleep within ten seconds from the first traces of SF016 entering their systems.

* * *

Cowan was at his desk studying a technical diagram on the computer screen when Fitch entered the room. "How is the test going, James?" asked Fitch.

"So far they've been asleep for forty-seven hours without incident. The technicians are working in shifts, and the Doc is just hanging out. They're bored, but I guess that's good. Also, I have some great news; we have completed the tests of the new biological scanners. They'll maintain a constant watch for biological contamination during the sleep process. This should prevent the need for the further precautionary use of biohazard suits when entering the sleep chambers. Explained Cowan excitedly.

"Great news," Fitch said continued. "James, they want us to do it," Fitch said.

This got Cowan's attention. He quickly spun his chair around and stood. He started to speak but caught himself. He stared at Fitch and noticed his uniform and his lower jaw dropped.

"Oh, my!" was all he said as he stared at shoulder boards of the man's dress uniform. These looked like the same shoulder boards that usually had the shiny silver eagles of an Army Colonel. Today they each had a single gold star, perfectly centered.

"Yea, that was my reaction too. They're really serious about this project, and they want me to have all the clout I need to get it done. I guess they figured a mere Colonel would've trouble getting enough stuff in gear to get it done."

"Congratulations Matt. This is wonderful," Cowan said as he shook his friend's hand.

"Thanks. I'm excited too. Are you in the middle of anything that can't wait?" asked General Fitch.

"No, I was working on designing the automatic systems for a larger sleep chamber," Cowan answered.

"Let's go talk," Fitch suggested.

Captain Travers walked into the room. "Welcome back, Colonel," she said walking over to the desk to pick up a three-ring binder.

"You're mistaken, Amy. The Colonel didn't come back," Cowan said with a smile.

Captain Travers looked across at the two men in confusion, before her eyes fixed on the gold stars on General Fitch's uniform. "Congratulations, sir! You must have really impressed them with what we're doing."

"Something like that," Fitch said. "How is the test going?"

"So far everything is fine. We're having trouble maintaining the pressure in the chamber; it was never designed for this kind of thing. But it looks like we'll be able to make it work for three more days."

"Good. James and I are going to leave the building for a while. I want you to meet with both of us in my office at 1300 hours," Fitch instructed.

"Yes sir, General, I'll be there," Travers answered.

After the men left the building, Cowan became aware of how quiet the General was. When Cowan had inquired about his trip to Washington, Matt hadn't even responded, apparently lost in thought. Cowan decided to give the man the time he needed. Clearly, something was bothering him.

They walked silently for several minutes until they were quite a distance past the picnic site. When Fitch stopped, he looked around, revealing surprise regarding how far they'd walked and then started back to the picnic area.

Today the tables were dry, and Fitch sat down on top of one of one of them before he spoke. "They want it done."

Cowan silently waited for Matt to continue.

"They want a fully-functional sleep facility, one where a large group of people could be placed in the event of a disaster. A facility ready and stocked so that as soon as a threat was detected, as many people as possible could take the long nap and wake up when it was clear," Matt explained.

"Matt, we could never create a facility that will hold a large number of people," Cowan protested.

"This isn't intended as a survival shelter. It's intended to sleep a specially trained group of people, whose function will be to help the survivors rebuild. The general populous will be going to underground shelters, large, modified mines, and specially built bunkers, possibly even undersea sanctuaries to wait things out.

"The planning of these shelters is in the hands of a different group. The estimate is still less than one percent of the population will be able to make it to a shelter. Our part is to sleep the ones needed for rebuilding; physicians, engineers, farmers, teachers and many others, as well as a formidable military force to deal with what they find when they awaken. Our facility won't just house the sleepers but all needed equipment, including vehicles, aircraft, computers, weapons, farm equipment, and even a small but advanced hospital. There is even talk of a special sleep chamber for livestock, but I don't think that will actually happen," Matt explained.

"Do they have a location for us yet?" Cowan asked.

"Yes, but it's still under construction."

"When will it be completed?"

"Unknown. It's currently in the hands of the Air Force. It will be turned over to us as soon as I get there to take control," Fitch said.

"You're saying, the Air Force has a massive underground facility partly constructed, and they're going to just hand it over to us so that we can make a 'What if' facility? That makes no sense. There has to be a lot you aren't telling me." Cowan argued.

"I know, but James they'll lock me away if I reveal any more details. They might even arrange for you to disappear too. It's that secret," Matt warned.

"This is making me very uncomfortable," Cowan exclaimed.

"I know. I'll try to keep you as informed as I can. I can't tell you many other details, but I promise not to lie about it either. Can you live with that for now?" Matt asked.

Cowan sat in silence for a few minutes, thinking it over before answering. "I can live with it. For now"

Fitch nodded.

"Who else at this facility knows the full details?" Cowan asked.

"You're the only one who knows anything right now. From what I understand, I'm only one of fourteen people who know the classified information. This afternoon we're going to brief Travers and I'll keep the two of you in the loop as much as possible. The three of us will be the team which makes this whole thing come together. I wish I could tell you more James, I really do. Personally, I could use someone to talk to this about, but my orders couldn't be clearer." He got to his feet, brushing the back of his pants. "We need to get back."

As they walked Matt added, "I'll be flying to the new facility in Arizona tomorrow. I'll officially be taking charge of the site in the afternoon. As soon as this current experiment is completed, I want you and Travers out there. We have a ton of work to do and not much time."

"Why the sudden rush to get this done?" Cowan asked.

"I was told to get it up and running ASAP," answered the General.

Cowan could tell this was one of those situations where his friend had chosen his words carefully. He wasn't lying, but there was definitely more to it than Matt was revealing.

"I want to start discussing the details with both of you, but I'll be tied up this afternoon after we talk to Travers, and then I'm leaving in the morning," Matt said with a frown.

"Why don't you and Amy stop over to my place this evening? We'll grill some steaks and go over everything. Kathy is visiting her parents in Kansas this week, and DJ is back at college so there won't be anyone else there," Cowan suggested.

Matt pursed his lips. "Okay, that works for me. We'll ask Amy."

"Great," Cowan said. "Let's say 1830."

Chapter 16 – Day 929

It was early in the evening, and Tony Jackson was coming to the end of his evening jog through the park. It was busy tonight, with numerous joggers utilizing the paths. The evening was pleasant, sunny and warm, and so far the predicted showers had held off.

His girlfriend Lori had gotten him to take up jogging a year and a half before, just after she'd convinced him to quit smoking, and he was pleased with what the exercise had done for him. He was never short of breath anymore and had energy to spare. Usually, they jogged together almost every night, which had been good for their relationship. Ending up back at his apartment for a joint shower was always a plus, too.

This evening, he was jogging alone. Lori had flown out of town that morning, she was attending a seminar for work and wasn't scheduled to return for four days.

He was more than halfway through the park, just coming up over the top of a small hill when he saw a tall brunette jogging toward him. She appeared to be in her mid-twenties, with the most unbelievable body he'd ever seen. She was firm and muscular, not like a bodybuilder, but there was very little body fat on her. She wore a one-piece, black spandex running suit with a red stripe running down each side. There was a dark green fanny pack resting over her right hip. As she passed him, she gave him a good looking over, followed by a sly smile.

Tony couldn't believe it; he was almost thirty-six years old and it had been at least a decade since any woman had checked him out like that.

He'd only traveled about another thirty yards when he became aware of someone coming up behind him. He moved across to the right side of the path, thinking to let them pass. He'd tried to get past some of the less considerate runners on some of the narrow paths in the park and knew how that kind of thing could be frustrating.

The person behind him moved up next to him and he glanced over, surprised to see it was the brunette again. She smiled again, and his pulse quickened. She had the cutest smile, with the whitest teeth he'd ever seen.

She matched his speed, and they ran together for about a hundred yards. Then she looked over at him again, winked, and put on a burst of speed. He increased his own pace and caught up, and this time he winked at her. He was rewarded again by that brilliant smile, and after a couple of minutes, she increased speed again. This time he had to really work hard to catch her. They were just approaching the east entrance to the park where he usually stopped because his apartment was just a short walk from here, the right distance to cool down after a good run. Tonight though, he decided to keep going. He was going to run for as long as she did or until his heart exploded, whichever came first.

The gorgeous woman stopped, leaning over, hands on her knees and fighting for her breath. Tony was also struggling; leaning against the iron rail fence next to the gate to the east entrance. Just as his breath was returning, he felt something touch his butt. He twisted his head around and there she was, with the most mischievous look on her face.

"That was a great run, but I bet you're good at things other than running?" she said in the most seductive voice he'd ever heard.

"You bet I am," Tony agreed without the slightest hesitation.

"Do you live close by?" the brunette asked.

"Sure do, just a couple blocks up the street," Tony agreed.

"Then let's get moving, big guy," she responded.

Without examining the invitation too carefully, Tony guided her gently by the arm, and they left the park quickly.

Neither spoke on the way to his apartment. Tony was thinking about how his friends at NASA would never believe this story. He also enjoyed his good fortune that this was the week Lori was out of town. This couldn't have been better if he'd planned it himself. Several times, he looked over at the brunette on the way to his apartment, and each time she looked back at him with an excited, eager expression on her face.

When they approached his apartment door, he fumbled with the keys before letting them in. "How about a shower?" he suggested eagerly.

"Only if you'll be in there too," she said seductively.

"Wouldn't have it any other way," Tony said, scarcely able to believe his luck.

He walked into the bathroom, already pulling off his sweat-soaked tee shirt. It took a second before he noticed his new friend had stopped in the bathroom doorway, her hand inside the fanny pack. He knew something was wrong the minute he looked at her face; focused and dangerous, any remnant of the fun and sexy woman he'd met in the park had disappeared.

The weapon cleared the pack, and in a swift and obviously well-practiced move swung toward his head. Tony tried to move his arms to protect himself, but they were still tangled up in the armholes of the shirt and by the time his brain had registered what was in her hand, it was too late to even scream.

The silenced .22 automatic popped twice in rapid succession and two neat holes appeared on Tony's forehead. The small caliber bullets didn't have the energy to exit the back of his head, but they bounced around inside his cranium, tearing up brain matter as they went. His body landed half in the bathtub, with his feet hanging out. He twitched several times before all movement stopped.

The assassin returned the weapon to her fanny pack and picked up the spent shell casings, placing these in the fanny pack as well. She felt her victim's neck and discovered a faint weak carotid pulse.

Straightening up, she went to the refrigerator and found an almost full, half-gallon container of orange juice. She removed the lid, drinking thirstily and then went back and rechecked Tony's pulse, slowly shaking her head. She retrieved the weapon from the fanny pack and added a third hole to Tony's head.

This shot she angled explicitly, so the bullet would travel into his brain stem. Again, she checked his pulse, satisfied that this time there was none. She noticed a sizeable crimson pool forming on the floor of the bathtub, where the side of Tony's head was partially blocking the drain.

Placing the pistol back in the pack she removed a small rag; she snatched up the third shell casing and then took a moment to wipe off the handle of the refrigerator, the only surface in the apartment that she'd touched. The cloth went back in the pack and carrying the remaining orange juice, she calmly left the apartment.

Chapter 17 – Day 929

The water pressure increased in Cowan's ears as he descended. He remained submerged, swimming as hard as he could. When he broke through the surface, he took a deep breath of the warm desert air. An evening swim was his favorite way to relax when things were on his mind. The in-ground pool was quite a bit larger than most. When Kathy had suggested getting it, their son was participating on a swim team at school, and it made sense to get something that he could swim laps in.

As he was toweling off, he heard a car outside the front of the house about twenty minutes earlier than the time they'd designated. He waited until he heard the car door close before calling out a greeting.

Amy Travers appeared on the deck, stopping beside the large gas grill. She wore a pink blouse and tight-fitting blue jeans along with sandals. This wasn't Amy's first visit to the Cowan's home, she'd been here several times since joining the Sleep Program and she and Kathy had become good friends.

"Are you swimming tonight?" Cowan called out.

"No thanks, I've got too much on my mind right now," Amy answered.

"That's when I enjoy a swim the most; it helps clear my head," Cowan said, climbing up onto the deck. He disappeared into the house and returned after a few minutes, dressed in a polo shirt and shorts, his feet bare. "After today's meeting with Matt, what could you possibly have on your mind?"

"None of it makes sense. There's a lot of stuff he's not telling us," Amy Travers admitted.

"Yeah, I think he wants to, but he can't," Cowan said.

"I keep getting these crazy scenarios in my head," Amy responded. "Whatever it is, it's big.".

Now Cowan understood. His friend who was never on time for anything in her life had been early tonight for a reason. She'd wanted to beat Matt Fitch here, so they'd have time to discuss the situation they'd both been dragged into.

Cowan motioned her over to a couple of patio chairs, and they sat down.

"Matt made it clear that while he couldn't talk about it, anything he did say would be the truth. From what he's told us, it seems certain they want this in place immediately and for us to be able to sleep as many people as possible. The only explanation I can find is that there's an impending threat and they want an option," Cowan surmised.

"How long can this possibly be kept quiet? There are more and more people becoming involved. Nothing stays a secret long."

\They heard another vehicle in the drive and a few minutes later the General walked out, carrying a drink he'd made for himself as he came through the house. He'd been here often enough to understand how things worked at the Cowans. "I can only imagine what you two have been discussing," he said with a sly grin.

Amy's face heated. This was one of the few times she'd seen her commanding officer without a uniform.

Cowan ignored the comment. "I'll get the steaks on the grill, and after we eat, we can get started."

They enjoyed a delicious meal of steak and salad, their conversation deliberately neutral, before they all went into the house, gathering in the living room.

"I know you two are struggling with this. For now, let's just proceed as if what I told you are all the details. Theorizing about this won't get us anywhere. I have a blueprint of the new facility, and there are some things we'll be working with other agencies on as this develops. We'll be the core team initially, but there will be others joining us as things get moving. Not only do we need to organize the implementation of the sleep systems, but we'll also be involved in designing training plans for the future sleepers. We'll be assisting in determining what equipment needs to be stored for use after the wake-up. We'll also assist in developing protocols for the team to follow, once the awakening occurs. There will be plenty of other areas we'll be involved in, but that should give us plenty to think about."

Fitch unrolled a set of blueprints he'd brought along with him. "Until early this week these were classified at the highest levels. Now they're ours."

The diagrams revealed a massive underground complex. There were areas designated as offices, command and communications centers, a gigantic power station, and vast areas which weren't yet labeled. Miles of tunnels were designated, snaking through the facility. Some areas appeared to be several stories high. There was even an underground water supply, fed directly from the Colorado River. There were also immense open areas on the lower levels that were easily the size of five football fields.

"The Air Force's current facility at Cheyenne Mountain was intended to survive long enough for them to make sure all our missiles were away. They could even survive a near miss. Some have speculated they might even survive a direct attack if the weapon had a minimal payload, but that's always been doubtful. This newer facility was planned to withstand anything and allow personnel to hole up for as long as necessary. We're expanding on that and making some changes. We'll continue to enlarge this place, to allow for more and more sleep capsules," the General explained.

"This place is amazing," Cowan said.

"How much of this is completed?" Amy asked.

"It's mostly completed now," Fitch explained. "Several major modifications will need to be made. It's mostly tunneled, that's why we'll need to make the design changes soon. I'll get started tomorrow, and I need you both there by the end of the week. Let the rest of the team do the follow up at the end of the current experiment. As soon as they're awake, call me, and I'll have a chopper here to collect you."

"If these people are going to sleep for ten years or more, what're we doing for a power source? We'll need massive amounts of power," Cowan pointed out.

"We can thank the Navy for solving that problem. They have a new small reactor which will be able to run that long easily. It's still too large for their carriers, but the next generation will be smaller. This one is so large because of all the automation. It takes care of itself; the Colorado River will be used for its cooling. We'll have nuclear engineers as sleepers, and I bet you can come up with an automatic wake-up sequence in the event of any problem."

"Sounds good," Cowan answered. "When will the reactor be operational?"

"They brought it online two weeks ago."

"Already! This thing is moving along quickly," stated Cowan.

"Just wait. This is only the tip of the iceberg. There is lots more coming, General Fitch said.

Chapter 18 – Day 928

Stanley Waldorf was feeling a bit uneasy, unable to stop thinking about the last meeting he'd had with the Administrator. The boss had never behaved that way before. He'd been expecting to get summoned back to the Administrator's office, but five days had passed and he'd heard nothing.

Williams had been friendly today when they passed in the hall. There was no agitation; it was almost as if their previous conversation never occurred. Stanley knew Williams well, and there was something in the man's eyes which made it clear all was not forgotten.

To top that off, Tony Jackson didn't show up for work today and no one had seen or heard from him.

Stanley pulled his 2018 Lincoln Town Car into the traffic and headed for the highway. It was time to head home, and he was going to try and stop thinking about work.

Approaching his home, his Android smartphone rang. "Waldorf here." Stanley thought this was how important people answered phones, and he was a deputy director at NASA. That made him important.

His wife, Barb, was on the phone. "Stan, could you stop and get me a pound of hamburger on your way home? I'm making lasagna for dinner, and I just noticed I don't have the meat."

Stan was extremely annoyed by the request. He was sure Barb had spent the whole day on the phone, or in front of the TV watching her ridiculous soap operas and dumb court shows. If she'd gotten off her lazy butt, she could have taken care of this herself. She stayed home all day, but she expected him to do her work too, it was getting out of hand. He decided it was just about time to tell her so, but right now all he wanted was for his dinner to be cooked. "Yeah, I'll get it," he said curtly and disconnected the call.

He pulled into the parking lot at the grocery store and got out of the car. Walking away, he noticed a black van with tinted windows pulling into the spot next to his Lincoln.

Stanley went directly to the meat counter and grabbed a package of burger. He was heading for the checkout lane when he noticed Stacey Miller standing at the dairy counter. Stacy was good friends with his wife, the one she spent hours on the phone with. He'd never liked Stacy, she seemed much too independent and he knew she always got what she wanted with her husband and that he did nothing without first consulting her.

His own wife had tried that once, and there'd been a significant battle before he finally got that nonsense under control.

He saw Stacey glance over at him, the expression on her face one of disgust. Stanley just glared back. How was it that Stacey could harbor that much disrespect for him? What had Barb told her, which made her look at him like that? Tonight, he was going to find out what that wife of his was saying about him.

There was a new register just opening as he arrived, and Stan quickly squeezed his way in so he didn't have to wait. He suspected this was probably the first thing which had gone his way all day.

Approaching his car, he noticed the owners of the black minivan trying to open their passenger door. The man was fumbling with the keys, and the woman was holding a bag of groceries. Stanley briefly considered the fact that their van had arrived just after him and he'd only grabbed the burger and made the quick escape through the newly opened checkout lane, yet these two were already out with a full-size bag or groceries.

His quick escape started to seem a hollow victory, especially when he got a better look at the woman standing beside the mini-van. She seemed to be in her mid-twenties, with beautiful brown hair and a fantastic body. *Where did I go wrong?* Stanley thought.

The couple noticed him, and the man spoke with a friendly smile. "Go on, we'll be a moment,"

Stanley muttered a brief thanks and started to squeeze past them, reaching into his pocket for the keys.

When he reached for the car door, he felt a sharp stabbing pain in the right side of his neck. He whirled to the right and saw the brunette holding a syringe with a needle attached. He started to speak, but the keys were ripped from his grip by the man to his left, and the sliding door on the van behind him was wrenched open. He tried to yell, but his tongue seemed swollen and numb. He was dizzy, and his breathing had become labored.

A powerful set of hands grabbed him from inside the van and dragged him in. Stanley was aware of the door closing, and the familiar sound of his Town Car's engine starting. A female voice from the front of the van said something he could not understand before he became aware of the vehicles movement.

By now, Stanley could barely breathe, and he was aware of a heavy sensation in his chest. He tried to look around, but couldn't get his head to move. Something was very wrong, but right now he couldn't be sure what the problem was. In fact, he realized he wasn't even sure at the moment what his own name was.

The van traveled eastward, eventually stopping at the marina where an impressive speedboat was tied to the dock. The still-breathing form of Stanley Waldorf was stuffed into a large plastic container and removed from the van by the brunette and her partner.

Stanley's Lincoln Town Car didn't show up at the marina, in fact, at that moment it was backing into a self-storage locker, twelve miles away. The person renting the locker told the locker's owner that they were taking a position as a missionary in the Congo and would be gone for three years. Even though this was a bit unusual, three years rent in cash easily persuaded the owner to accept the arrangement with no further questions. The door to the storage locker was closed, and the padlock locked shut.

* * *

A dolly was used to load the large plastic box marked SCUBA equipment onto the boat. The box was placed in the back of the boat, and the mooring lines were untied. The boat slowly moved away from the dock and headed east out into deeper water, continuing to gain speed.

After fifteen minutes, when the shore was no longer visible, the boat slowed to a stop.

Stanley was removed from the box, dragged to the back of the boat and laid flat on his back. The man collected a set of ankle shackles, and these were woven through the three holes on a concrete cinder block and clamped to each of Stanley's ankles.

While this was being done, the brunette fastened handcuffs which had been fed through a second cinder block to Stanley's wrists.

Together the two of them rolled Stanley and the blocks off the back of the boat. Just as he fell into the water, the brunette saw Stanley's eyes snap open for the last time.

The two assassins stayed kneeling by the back of the boat until the last of the air bubbles had surfaced. The brunette slowly got to her feet and removed a dark green fanny pack from around her waist. Ensuring it was zipped tight, she threw it into the water. The weight of the .22 automatic and the silencer was enough to quickly sink the fanny pack, taking with them the rag, the three spent shell casings, a 3cc syringe and the key which belonged to the padlock of a self-storage unit.

Chapter 19 – Day 926

The helicopter flew north, following the Colorado River. Cowan and Travers sat in the back, enjoying the view. The aircraft made a sharp turn to the right and continued for almost another mile before it made a gentle descent at the base of a massive mountain, coming to rest on a dirt landing pad. All visibility was briefly lost when the rotor blade kicked up a massive dust cloud.

An army Lieutenant driving a Humvee met them. "Sir, Ma'am, I'm Lieutenant Parker. General Fitch asked that I meet you and give you a ride," the short Hispanic officer said.

The Lieutenant took their bags and loaded them in the Humvee. After Cowan and Travers climbed aboard, Parker glanced back at them and asked. "Is this your first time here?"

Cowan and Travers both answered, confirming it was their first visit.

"Well I don't know how much you know about the place, but I'll tell you what I can on the way up," Parker offered.

As they approached the mountain, they saw an opening at the base of the mountain.

"That helipad you came in on is temporary. The permanent pad will be on the other side of the mountain, it's under construction now."

They were rapidly approaching the tunnel entrance. It was recessed into the base of the mountain, a good fifty feet in diameter and was covered by a massive, blast resistant door, four feet thick. The door was currently open, and a huge dump truck was backed far down the tunnel. The far end of the tunnel was at least a half-mile away and that door was open as well. Even from this distance, it was clear the other end was a much wider opening.

Driving through the tunnel entrance, the Lieutenant gave them a running commentary. "This was supposed to be the new command and control center for NORAD, so many of the design plans are similar to their current facility. The reason this is designed with an opening at each end is so that in the event of a nearby impact from a nuke, the pressure wave would literally pass through the mountain instead of slamming into it. If needed, the blast doors can shut in less than half a minute, and they weigh about fifty tons each. That's twice the size of the doors at the original facility."

The Humvee stopped, and they climbed out. Cowan suspected a jetliner could sit in the tunnel he found himself in, with room to spare. In front of them was a huge hole in the floor, a platform visible about two hundred feet down.

"That's an elevator, similar to what you'd see on aircraft carriers. All types of vehicles will be going up and down on that thing all day long." As the Lieutenant spoke, there was a loud humming noise and a slight vibration moved the ground beneath their feet. It took a full minute for the elevator to reach the top and riding the elevator up were two of the most enormous dump trucks Cowan had ever seen, each piled high with dirt and rocks. The trucks exited the tunnel through the larger of the two entrances and as soon as they were clear of the exit, two more were moving into the tunnel. They traveled side by side, stopping on the elevator pad. The elevator was descending before the trucks had completely stopped.

Cowan saw there were multiple recessed doors on either side of the tunnel. The Lieutenant directed them to the first door on the right. He pressed his palm and fingers firmly against a square of Plexiglas which was flush with the wall at chest level. Immediately the door slid to the left into a recessed hole in the wall, and a mechanical sounding voice spoke. "Good morning Lieutenant Parker."

Parker rolled his eyes. "When they first got this system online, I thought the computer voice was really cool, but if you're going through these doors twenty or more times a day, it gets a bit annoying," he stated.

They stepped through the door and started down a corridor. Cowan noted that the walls and ceilings were all steel. The floors were covered with carpeting, but he assumed it was steel under there, too. The passage reminded him of the ones you saw on a ship.

Lieutenant Parker was bringing up the rear and saw Cowan glancing around. "Sir, all the rooms, and the corridors are individually fashioned steel structures. Each of these structures rests on a bed of very large springs, and each of those springs weighs close to a half ton. In the event of a nuke strike, or even an earthquake, the springs will drastically reduce the movement and therefore decrease the damage in here."

At the end of the corridor, they approached another large door. There was another plexiglass plate on the wall and Cowan pressed his right hand against the plate. Immediately the computer voice said, "You are not authorized to enter this area."

"Let me, Sir, You aren't set up yet," said Parker, as he moved to the front of the line.

"Good morning Lieutenant Parker," said the voice as the door slid open.

They stepped into a spacious elevator and as soon as the door shut, they began a rapid descent. The doors opened again, and they stepped out into the center of another wide corridor. There was a door to the left, at the end of the passage, marked 'COMMAND CENTER.' To the right, there were several doors on either side. There was another elevator at the far end; above its door was a sign that read 'ENGINEERING'. The small party turned to the left passing another door marked 'MESS HALL', which didn't have a Plexiglas palm reader. Across the hall from the Mess Hall was a door marked 'HEALTH CENTER'.

Parker's hand worked the scanner, and the double doors to the Command Center opened, revealing a lot of activity. Technicians were standing on yellow ladders, running orange fiber optic cable from conduits in the wall to computer terminals. New systems were being installed, and the far wall was being painted. There was a large central console with four chairs facing it, off to the right. Most of the electronic work seemed to be centered around this console.

They located General Fitch in a recessed office off to the far left. As soon as he saw them, he was on his feet and moving toward them at a rapid pace. "James, Amy, glad you're here! Things are a little crazy."

"Sir, this facility is amazing!" Travers exclaimed.

"It sure is. I'm still a bit overwhelmed myself; fortunately, it isn't too hard to find your way around."

"Will this place meet our needs?" Cowan asked.

"Definitely, with the changes I've ordered, I think it'll be close to perfect."

"We saw a little on the way in here, but I'd sure like a complete tour when there's time," Cowan said.

"Let's go. The sooner we get the tour completed, the sooner I can get you both working," Fitch agreed. "I assume there were no problems with the last experiment?"

"None sir," Amy agreed. "They all woke up without incident. The staff is packing up and awaiting instructions."

"Good. We have a lot to do, and in all honesty, I don't even know where to start." Fitch pointed towards the console they'd noticed before. This is the central control area; from here we've got access to over a dozen communication satellites. We can communicate with any military or civilian group we need to contact. There are some new satellites, which are going to be launched in case of a disaster. When the sleepers awaken, they'll be able to use them for communication with the shelters, and monitoring what's happening all around the planet. There are seventy-five external and just as many internal cameras. The external cameras are spaced out so we can see every inch of ground up to five miles out from the facility. There are also terminal imaging and sound detection systems all around the perimeter. All of that's monitored from here."

"We can also open and close the main doors at the tunnel entrance. Originally, the idea was to make it so we could collapse the main tunnel from here with remote explosives, now though, I think we'll scrap that idea. We can assume control over all the automatic functions from here, including elevators, fire suppression, and water flow. If necessary, we'll even be able to manage the main power and computer systems from right here. I plan to make it so we can monitor and manage the sleep capsules from here too. If you've got any suggestions, I'd welcome them."

Cowan nodded, his eyes scanning the system. "Sounds good. I'm sure we'll come up with some ideas as we get a better feel for the place."

Travers nodded her agreement.

The trio left the control room and started down the corridor. The first door on the left revealed the Health Center. The doors parted without any security checks, and they entered into a hall. On the left was a large open area, measuring about one hundred square feet. "This was intended to be a small fitness center. Ideally, I'd love to keep it and even expand it but I'm waiting to hear whether that will be possible. The medical facilities were designed to hold a small clinic, but obviously, we need to expand those plans to a fully-featured hospital, and medical labs. We'll also have to have the ability to synthesize required drugs and medications. I've spoken to the engineers, and they're working on plans to make this area twenty-five times larger than it is now."

They came across an Air Force Captain who was briefing an Army Major in a small office off to one side. Fitch drew Cowan and Travers across to the doorway and knocked against the wall. "Excuse me, gentlemen."

The two officers got to their feet swiftly when they realized it was General Fitch standing at the door.

"Major Stephen Cross, Captain Warbler, I want you to meet James Cowan and Captain Amy Travers. They're my team, here to get things moving for our mission." Introductions were made before General Fitch added, "Major Cross will be the Senior Medical Officer and his support staff is already in route to the facility. Captain Warbler will be taking up another position outside."

They left the men to continue their discussion and advanced further into the Health Center before Fitch spoke again. "Captain Warbler was the senior medical officer before we took over. We offered him the opportunity to stay on, but he declined. Cross is a good man, with experience in almost every kind of environment you can imagine. There will be eight physicians working under him, and they have an extensive area of expertise, everything from pediatrics to neurosurgery."

"They were approaching a large room marked 'TRIAGE'; inside there was a tall male Air Force nurse treating a worker who'd suffered an injury to his arm. The injured man sat on a hospital bed while the nurse rinsed dirt out of a jagged laceration on his upper arm.

They were headed back down the hall when Cowan asked, "How did the transfer of command go?"

Fitch pursed his lips and. "Actually, it was extremely smooth. Someone paved the way so that when I got here, there were no issues. In fact, the facilities commander was Colonel Will Franks, but the Air Force arranged to have a Major General here to make sure things went well. I suspect he was sent directly from the Pentagon and laid the law down before we had even landed. Everyone was quite accommodating and he treated me as if I was the one with two stars. The biggest problems we're having with the transition are coming from me trying to get up to speed without revealing too much information, and the modifications we need to make. There are still a bunch of Air Force personnel here, making sure we have things under control. I made it clear to my superiors that I'm in no hurry to replace them. If they know what they're doing, I think it's best to let them stay."

Approaching the next door on the right they entered the mess hall. This room was partly finished, and some crude furnishings were scattered around. There was the aroma of pizza in the air. There was a small buffet line open and several and a few small tables were occupied.

"At least the important stuff is ready," Travers commented.

"True. But I'm sure this will all have to be ripped out," Cowan responded.

"Exactly," Fitch agreed. "This was designed to serve about three hundred people, but we need to be able to handle several thousand. The engineers have confirmed the expansion is possible. The problem is, when these people wake up, we don't know what they'll face. They'll need a sizeable amount of food, perhaps enough for one or two years. That means a massive amount of food storage space, including warehouse-size freezers. I don't think eating MREs for two years will cut it," Fitch explained, referring to the military's pre-packaged Meal Ready to Eat packets which could be eaten anywhere, anytime and would last on the shelf for years.

"They hopefully will have plans for the Health Center and the Mess Hall ready soon. I plan to triple the number of workers we have on the site. There are already housing quarters under construction outside for the workers, and after the wake-up, they'll house some of the former sleepers," the General explained.

They left the Mess Hall and headed further away from the command center. "Hopefully they'll have plans for the Health Center and the Mess Hall ready soon. I plan to triple the number of workers on site. There are already housing quarters under construction outside for the workers, and after the wake-up, they'll house some of the former sleepers," the General explained.

They passed the elevator which had brought them down to this level and came across more doors on either side of the passage. "These rooms are mostly built, but again, they'll need to be expanded. I suspect this is where we'll house the sleep capsules. The architects checking to see how far they can be expanded. I suspect initially there will be a core team of about one hundred and fifty to two hundred sleepers who will be awakened, to investigate the situation outside. When the time comes to start rebuilding, the rest will be woken. We'll also need to have specific individuals who are keyed to awaken if specific circumstances occur, such as a medical emergency, a fire, or a reactor issue. The systems will constantly monitor outside environmental factors, and if specific parameters are met, key personnel will then be awoken to make a final decision," Fitch explained.

At the end of the hall was another large elevator. The sign above it Fitch touched the plate in the wall and a detached voice spoke. "Good morning, General Fitch." The elevator doors slid open.

Fitch started talking as the elevator descended. "This level houses all the behind-the-scenes stuff including the reactor room, waste disposal facilities, water purification, and computer center. There'll be a need for a manufacturing center; they'll need to build anything they don't have, along with having the capability to create things which won't survive for long periods of time, such as batteries. They'll also be installing the print shop down here."

"Sir, why will they need a print shop?" Travers asked.

"When everyone wakes up, they'll need to contact the survivors. The ones in shelters will be contacted by radio and given instructions regarding where to go. The few who manage to survive outside of the shelters will be located by satellite or aircraft able to track their heat signatures, and leaflets will be dropped to them from aircraft the sleepers will have access to. There's no way of knowing how many people will survive, so we want to make sure they have the ability to produce a million or more leaflets if necessary," Fitch explained.

After what seemed like an eternity, the elevator stopped, and the doors opened. They stepped out and walked straight down another long hall. There was considerably more noise in this area and Fitch led them to the computer center. After the doors parted for the General, they stepped inside and noticed the temperature was much cooler than it had been in the hall. The room was one hundred feet long and at least fifty feet wide and contained row after row of computers in tall racks. Most of the equipment, Cowan found he couldn't identify.

"We plan to have web-based applications which tie into the databases here. We want to have as much information as possible available for the sleepers. Whatever they need to know, we want that information readily accessible. Everything from the chemical composition of Viagra to how to build a Zamboni. It'll all be in there and readily available when the time comes. These systems will also monitor everything during the sleep and will be responsible for sounding alarms and initiating the wake-up sequence. These systems will have as much redundancy built into them as possible. We want each system to be able to experience multiple component failures before the system has to go down" Fitch explained.

An Air Force Major and Army Major approached them. "General, are these your team leaders?" one of the men asked.

"Yes, they are. Can you get them taken care of?"

"Of course, Sir. Can you two come over here? We have all your information. We just have to assign your clearance. Sorry you had to come down here for this, there will be a security station up top, just off the main tunnel, that can do this in the future, but it's still under construction," explained the Air Force Major.

Cowan responded. "No problem, we're getting a quick tour anyway."

'I just need you two to place each of your hands against this when I say."

He held up a small square box. In the center was a Plexiglas plate similar to the one that was seen by the doors. There was a cable running out to the back of the box, and it plugged into the USB port in a laptop computer.

"Captain Travers, when the machine says your name press one hand then the other on the reader."

The major typed on the laptop's keyboard, and the computer voice spoke from the computer. "Captain Travers." Amy placed one hand on the plate and then the other. As soon as she removed her hand, the computer spoke again. "Captain Travers, Complete."

After several seconds voice was back "Mr. Cowan." Cowan completed the procedure in the same fashion and with the same results.

"General, did you want them to have full security access?"

"Yes, Major, access to everything," stated Fitch.

Leaving the computer center and headed for the reactor room. Approaching the entrance, they saw an Air Force Lieutenant Colonel standing in front of the door. He spoke up when they approached. "Sir, we're doing some calibration testing of the radiation detection sensors. If you require it, we can stop, but we'd have to start over, and we've been at this for four hours already."

Fitch shook his head. "No, we can come back later. This is my team, James Cowan and Captain Amy Travers. Can you give them a brief overview of the power systems?"

"Of course, sir." the Lt. Colonel turned his attention to James and Amy. "This is a new design in nuclear reactors. It's all automated and can run without refueling for five years if it's under full load, much longer if less than a full load is required. It's similar to the reactors on Navy ships, except their designs are much older. This one is state of the art," he explained.

"Have you been given information about the expansions we're doing, and the energy requirements for our equipment?" Cowan asked.

"Yes sir, General Fitch went over some of that with me when we got here. I don't know what you folks are doing, but he gave me some estimates on power utilization."

"Will the new power requirements be a problem?" Cowan questioned.

"No, sir. We're currently providing power for this whole facility and all the outside construction projects in this compound. We're running at right around three to five percent capacity. I estimate by the time your equipment is all up and running, we'll be just below seven percent of capacity."

"Excellent. When would be a good time for us to return for a tour?" Cowan asked.

"Late this afternoon, or anytime tomorrow would be fine."

After visiting the heating, cooling and ventilation systems, as well as the water purification and waste removal systems, they took a different elevator system up; and as it was ascending, Travers spoke up. "Everything we saw looks great, but some of it will need an overhaul. None of it was designed to be completely unsupervised for twenty years. There are few backup systems in case of a failure, but all of that will need to be upgraded."

"I agree with Amy," Cowan said.

"I agree too. Amy, let's add that project to your plate," Fitch announced.

"Should've kept your mouth shut, Amy," Cowan said with a laugh.

"I wouldn't laugh if I were you; I already have a list of things for you to help me with," Fitch said, his eyes twinkling when he looked at Cowan.

The elevator opened onto a short hall. They passed through a thick steel door, currently open but it could be shut to seal the hall off, and reached another closed door. This opened, again without an electronic palm scanner and they stepped out into the central tunnel where they'd first entered the mountain. Cowan noted they were considerably farther down the tunnel than the entrance where Lieutenant Parker had first led them through.

"So far, everything you've shown us is down from here; is there anything up?" Travers asked.

"The elevator you first came down in will also travel upwards. There are two unfinished conference rooms and a big space which I plan to make into an off-duty lounge. There will be some personnel quarters there too. I'm not certain how many, it all depends on how much they can tunnel out. There are also several passages to the top; they carry cables for antenna arrays, radar, and environmental scanners. There's also a small crawl space which leads to the top for maintenance of those systems."

Fitch led them out through the wide mouth of the tunnel to where easily a hundred men and women worked on constructing a building which resembled a large hotel. "I ordered this work to begin the day I got here, and they're moving at a decent speed. We'll be tripling the number of workers on the underground complex at least, and we need somewhere for them to stay. As soon as this building is complete, they'll be starting an identical one beside it."

Travers noticed that work was being done on the permanent helipads and the large lights that would make for safe night landings. Because she had previously flown helicopters for the Army, this immediately caught her attention.

Returning to the tunnel, they walked about a third of the way down its length before stopping. Giant recessed double doors stood on either side. Fitch went to the ones on the left and they entered a long hall. At two locations along the hall, there were huge open doors that when shut, would completely seal off the hall. The last doors at the end opened into a massive cavern, easily the size of four football fields and perhaps fifty feet high.

"This will be one of two primary sleep chambers. Across the tunnel is an identical room, and there will be a second level in both, so we'll have twice the floor space you see here. One of the first things you two will be doing is get the rest of the team down here. These need to be converted into atmosphere-controlled chambers. The second level will be going in next week, then it's up to our team to do the rest. Make sure they know that any resources they need are already approved. Since these chambers are already physically large enough, this is where we start."

They left and walked back into the central tunnel. "I'd take you down to the main storage area, but there's too much activity going on right now. Essentially, it's just a giant empty chamber. It'll be divided into different areas, to store different categories of equipment. The computers will keep track of each item and in where it's stored. It'll contain everything we think they'll need in the future; building material, vehicles, computers, weapons and medical equipment." Fitch explained.

"There's an awful lot of planning going on here Matt. Who else is going to be involved in this? As we move forward, the ability to maintain secrecy will quickly become impossible," Cowan noted.

"I know. I have a meeting in DC about all this next week," Fitch stated.

Chapter 20 – Day 827

Several months later, General Draper, General Fitch, Admiral Atkins and National Security Advisor Baker met at the Pentagon in Washington DC.

"Gentlemen," Draper began. "Let's start with a quick overview of what's occurred to date and see what steps need to be taken. Up until this point, we've utilized every means at our disposal to keep the details of the comet's radioactivity a secret. The comet itself is becoming widely known about because of the spectacular light show it'll create when it passes close by. In fact, in the last week, I've seen or heard mention of it several times in the media.

"As you've all said on more than one occasion, we need to start bringing more people into the game. It seems impossible to avoid expanding the number of people with full knowledge of this event at this point.

"I've been dealing with the Air Force, and General Peebles is the only officer over there who knows exactly what's going to happen. He's working on a plan to use nuclear weapons to modify the course of the comet. If we could get the weapons out far enough into space, there might be a chance, but it's not probable. His people are working out new theories but the possibility of success is minimal.

"Teams are already scouring the country looking for places to develop shelters. As sites are located, we're determining the requirements. There's minimal concern regarding surface contamination, any radioactive debris will burn up in the atmosphere; the problem is that while the stuff is in orbit, it'll be hitting everything with its radiation. Consequently, there's no concern regarding clean up after the fact. NASA is still sticking to their current timeline, the comet is still on the same course and gaining speed at the anticipated rate. Remember, the closer it gets to the sun the faster it'll move.

"Our next issue is the selection process for residents of the shelters and the sleeper capsules. I'm willing to hear arguments on this matter, but I fully agree with the preliminary requirements proposed. The sleepers need to predominately be young single people who have the specific skill sets we need. I still believe a high percentage of military or prior military should be included in the group because they know how to follow orders and understand discipline. Any comments?"

"We probably want to maintain close to an even balance for male and female." Secretary Baker suggested. The others all agreed.

"Sir, how are you planning to contact and recruit roughly a hundred thousand shelter inhabitants, and ten thousand sleepers, without the word getting out to the rest of the population? There will no doubt be people who turn down the prospect of being involved, and then they become a huge risk for revealing the situation to the greater population. It's a perspective problem which can't just be ignored," Fitch questioned.

"If we pre-select them, we can always just kidnap them off the streets as the date draws closer," Admiral Atkins responded.

"True," Draper said. "But I think we'll need to have these people cooperative."

Baker spoke up. "I already have a couple working on putting together a list of people who are experts in their fields. When the time is right we will contact them. "We'll mention that we're working on a plan involving shelters to be used in the case of a chemical, biological or nuclear event, and ask if they'd be interested in participating. It will be clear if they agree, that they'll be rounded up when and if something happens and that they should be ready to leave at a moment's notice. They'll understand that they'll be in the shelter for an unknown period, one that could be extensive. If they agree, then we'll arrange a more intense interview and provide them with the necessary instructions. Of course, we'll make it clear that this plan is precautionary and hopefully will never actually need to be utilized. We'll use a similar approach with the sleepers, but they'll be required to commit and when the training starts, they won't be able to back out."

"Are there any other questions or suggestions?" Draper questioned.

When no-one responded, he continued. "The President has made it clear to National Security Advisor Baker and myself that the sleeper team is not to be a military force, run by the military. There will need to be a military component, but its overall command and control are to be non-military. The reason I've suggested single people is it will be easier to segregate them for an extended period, for training purposes, before sleeping them. And I think it's important to point out that of course, there will be no children in the sleep capsules. The sleepers are a group selected for their rebuilding skills and will not include anyone unlikely to be able to perform that role. The selections for the shelters will be coordinated differently. Family units will be encouraged and we'll have to carefully select the people who will be allowed to go to the shelters.

"Psychological screening must be included considering they might have to stay underground for twenty years. Medical and security people will also be needed for each shelter. Also, we need to look at factors such as personal potential. High school dropouts and drug addicts wouldn't be selected; we need to utilize only those people who can successfully contribute to the group. We need to remember that less than ten percent, of one percent of the population, will get a shelter. We'll try to increase that number, but it's currently our best-case estimate.

"We all know that there are some would be very upset with the selection process, so it will need to be kept absolutely classified. For the same reason, we're trying to keep this quiet from the rest of the government. I'm sure we can all envision every congressman out there causing enough of a stink that we would lose almost five hundred sleep capsules to them. Let alone the other officials who would try to weasel their way in. It's paramount that everyone chosen meets the criteria we've set, with no exception. All the sleepers will have to undergo a significant amount of training. General Draper and I have been discussing this, and they all need to be cross-trained in many areas. Everyone must be competent with standard weapons and tactics, as well as basic medical procedures. As we've said before, we've no idea what these sleepers might encounter, but they'll have no backup and must be able to handle any threat themselves. If someone is a mechanical engineer, he still has to be trained in something important that he can be doing when there is no engineering work to be done."

"Unfortunately, that means we aren't going to be sleeping. We'll be provided with a shelter, I can make that happen but that's all. Now let's hear from you, we need to get all your opinions so we do this right.

Admiral Bob Atkins was the first to speak. "We're working on the construction of undersea shelters, but I don't think we'll have room for more than a few thousand people. There is a good possibility that they won't be able to stay down long enough to wait this thing out. The selection process will be the same as we use for the underground shelters. Also, there are many technological roadblocks we'll need to overcome to make this work."

Fitch spoke next. "We've got numerous changes to make to the facility, and a ton of work to do to get the place ready for sleepers, but the work already completed is fantastic, and the facility is much further along than I'd hoped. As long as we continue to get access to the resources we need, we'll be ready."

"It sounds like things in regard to the sleepers are on track; we need to increase the pace in looking for sites and building the new shelters. "We've been looking at several possible candidates to lead the mission. I want us to reconvene after lunch to look at the candidates and see if we can come to an agreement on the selection. If in the meantime any of you can suggest any other names for consideration, let me know."

The meeting broke up shortly afterwards, and Fitch left the room. As he strode down the hall he heard his name being called and turned to see General Lee Draper following him. He stopped and waited for the four-star General to catch up. "Yes, sir?"

"Do you mind if I join you? There are some things I want to discuss," Draper announced.

"Of course not, sir.

Draper led Fitch out of the Pentagon and had his driver take them to a nice Italian restaurant which was about ten minutes away.

They entered the dimly-lit restaurant, and a waitress led them to a large booth in the back.

Once seated, Draper spoke up. "I wanted to make sure that if any obstacle comes up, regardless of how small, you let me know. We need your facility operational ASAP. The big event isn't scheduled for another two and a half years, but I want you to keep expanding the site. Every additional sleeper we can cram in there is another life saved. Let me know what we can do."

Fitch clasped his hands together on the table. "Sir, I'll keep things moving as fast as I can, obviously. Give me a few weeks and I'll have a better idea as to what we can offer."

"Sounds good. Have any of your people figured out what's going on?"

"My immediate team are smart enough to know something is up. There's just no way with a construction of this size that couldn't know that this isn't just a standby facility. They don't know the nature of the threat, however, or the date, but every day they're a little closer to figuring it out," Fitch explained.

"I guess it's time. Bring Cowan and Travers up to speed. No one else though, and I want them signing a non-disclosure agreement. Make sure they know the consequences if they reveal anything – it will involve imprisonment."

"Understood, sir," Fitch responded. A sense of relief swept over him, keeping this to himself had been incredibly difficult and for all the work Travers and Cowan were doing, they deserved to know the truth.

Returning to the conference room after a pleasant meal of tortellini, washed down with a glass of Chianti, the two men took their seats at the table.

NSA Baker addressed the group first. "Gentlemen, we've collected a list of several candidates we want to review as a group. The person we select will be approached and given the opportunity to take command of the Sleepers."

After a discussion lasting a little more than four hours, the group was unanimous in their decision to approach Doctor R. J. Anderson with the offer of the role of Sleeper Command.

R.J. had formerly served in the US Army, after graduating at the top of the class at West Point. R.J.'s military career was excellent; achieving high marks in everything from leadership to marksmanship. R.J. had been on the fast track, and promotions were coming thick and fast. After ten years though, R.J. surprised everyone by resigning from the army and returning to college to finish a doctorate degree in international studies. For the past eight years, RJ had been working with the United Nations and personally led disaster relief efforts on four different continents. A military background and proven leadership skills, along with the disaster relief experience, made RJ the perfect candidate.

Chapter 21 – Day 825

Doctor Anderson was visiting Harvard University as a guest lecturer, speaking about disaster management in third world countries to a group of about two hundred graduate students. As the lecture ended, there was the traditional opportunity to ask questions. RJ was hoping there would be few, if any questions; there was a three PM flight back to New York, and if things went well, RJ intended to be on that flight.

The students left the old lecture hall a few minutes later, and RJ quickly started packing up notes and books. Glancing up RJ noticed two men approaching from the back of the hall. Perhaps there would be some questions after all, but with a second look, it became apparent that these men weren't students. Both stood too tall and self-assured, and they wore expensive suits. You almost never saw students wearing suits.

"Can I help you with something?" RJ asked.

"Doctor Anderson, I'm Agent Adams, and this is Agent Shea; we're with the FBI." Both men flashed their identification. "We've been instructed to escort you to a critical meeting taking place in Washington DC."

RJ frowned, placing a few sheets of paper into the briefcase. "What's the nature of the meeting?"

"I'm sorry Doctor, but we haven't been informed. We were just told to get you there, ASAP. There's a plane waiting for you at Logan Airport."

"I'm sorry, but I can't just drop everything. My schedule is too busy to just run off without more information."

Agent Shea smiled. "I understand." From the inside of his jacket, he withdrew a plain white envelope and handed it to RJ.

RJ studied the envelope for just a moment before tearing it open and read the contents three times before shoving the letter back in the envelope. "Okay. Take me to Washington."

On the drive to the airport, RJ considered the sudden change in events and took out the letter again. Staring at the Presidential seal at the top, then President Daniel Anson's signature at the bottom, RJ glanced back at the salutation.

The first thing the President needed to understand was that absolutely no one – not even the President of the United States – got to call her Rebecca.

* * *

Rebecca Anderson grew up in a small middle-class town, with two loving parents. Rebecca had been named after her grandmother on her mother's side. When Rebecca was fourteen, her father was killed in an automobile accident, an accident which also left her mother mentally impaired and unable to care for her teenage daughter.

Rebecca had moved in with her maternal grandmother, who was the only other relative in the area. About a year later, her grandmother's boyfriend had moved into the home. Rebecca never liked Scott Winfield, who made a habit of making inappropriate comments to her. He was frequently intoxicated, and during those times he was even worse. Shortly after moving in, Scott started sexually abusing her. At first, Rebecca did nothing, but she eventually built up the courage to tell her grandmother about the abuse. Her grandmother had refused to listen; insisting there was no way Scott would do something like that. In fact, she'd seemed angrier with Rebecca, for saying anything in the first place.

Weeks later, Rebecca's grandmother arrived home from work early and walked in on Scott holding Rebecca down, while he was trying to get his hand inside her clothes. Rebecca caught sight of her grandmother backing out of the room and later acting as if nothing had happened. Rebecca talked to her again, this time in tears, begging her grandmother for help. Her Grandmother had slapped her across the face and demanded this subject never be brought up again.

From that day forward, everyone had known her simply as RJ. She would not allow anyone to call her by the name which she shared with the grandmother who betrayed her.

Three months later, the body of Scott Winfield was found floating in a local river with his throat slashed. The body was discovered in an area where Scott often fished. No footprints were found near the scene, not even Scott's, and it seemed clear that someone had made a special effort to erase them.

His fishing pole, beer cooler, and a lawn chair still sat by the river. His wallet was still in his pants pocket, and there were seventeen dollars still in it.

No one ever found the knife used to slit Scott's throat. The Sheriff suspected Scott had fallen asleep or passed out from drinking all that beer, since there were twenty empty cans by the chair, and his attacker had quietly snuck up behind him.

The authorities questioned everyone, including RJ, but no suspect was ever located.

Twenty years later, RJ sometimes awakened from a nightmare and could again feel the sensation of Scott's hot blood pumping out all over her arms.

* * *

The FBI agents were as good as their word; they delivered her to the waiting jet and told her someone would be there to meet her when she arrived in Washington.

The flight was uneventful. The flight crew had provided some sandwiches, chips, and Pepsi. Later she'd reclined her seat and tried to sleep but found the never-ending questions running through her mind made it impossible.

Finally, she brought her seat back up and picked up a copy of USA Today, which had been provided with her food. On page three she came across an article entitled "President's Disaster Shelter Plan passes in the House."

Yesterday, after much debate Congress, with a two-thirds majority approved funding for President Anson's plan to implement disaster shelters around the country. With the ever-increasing threat of chemical, biological or nuclear terrorism aimed at the US, the president received approval to begin construction of shelters which will provide a safe environment for people in the event of such an attack. Sources report that the president lobbied harder for these shelters than he has for any other spending requests he'd made. Critics call this plan wasteful and compare it to the never used nuclear bomb shelters that sprang up at the height of the Cold War.

RJ put the paper down, shaking her head, and wondered if she really wanted to get involved with these people.

Upon landing, the plane was met by Agent Kathy Muller, who escorted her to the waiting car. "I assume you can't tell me what this is about either?" RJ asked.

"Sorry Doctor Anderson, I was just asked to meet you here and make sure you got to the White House ASAP."

Arriving at the White House, RJ stepped out of the car and was met by a smartly-dressed woman, wearing a gray skirt and a white shirt. She didn't identify herself but led RJ in through the main doors and up a flight of stairs, indicating a conference room on the left, where two men stood.

"Here you are, Doctor Anderson," the woman said.

RJ stepped inside, surveying the two men. The first was a tall white male, wearing an Army uniform. She could see from his shoulder that he was a four-star General, and when he turned to look at her; she recognized him as General Draper. Eight years before, when she'd still been serving in the Army, he'd been her divisional commander. While she'd never met him personally, she certainly knew of him and his reputation.

The other man was a bit older; an African American male of medium height. She'd seen him before and knew he was National Security Advisor Jeremiah Baker.

Mr. Baker looked at her and held out his hand, "Welcome. I'm Jeremiah Baker, National Security Advisor and this is General Lee Draper, Dr. Anderson. Or do you prefer RJ?"

She took his offered hand. "RJ is just fine, sir." She turned to look at Draper. "General Draper, I've heard much about you."

"Likewise. We have some matters we need to discuss with you. Would you like to take a seat?"

RJ sat down on one of the padded chairs at the conference table. "I was under the impression I was meeting with the President."

"Depending on how things go here, you probably will be," explained Baker, who sat down in a seat opposite her.

"We have an unusual situation, a matter of national security; in fact, this matter is so highly classified that we won't be able to give you specifics until you agree to participate. Generally speaking, we're preparing a team to assist in disaster relief and rebuilding following a massive natural disaster. A disaster we believe is imminent. This team will be involved in training and preparation beforehand, and when it's safe following the incident they'll start rebuilding," Draper explained.

"Sounds exactly like my kinda thing, sir."

"If you're going to join this, you'll be involved full time immediately and must remain committed to this project until the end."

"Who's running this? DOD?" RJ asked.

Draper shook his head. "This isn't a military endeavor; although the Department of Defense is currently in charge. When this becomes a disaster recovery operation, the command will be civilian, but there will be a military arm in place to be utilized as required," Draper explained.

"Why is the military so involved at this point in time?" RJ questioned.

"Like we said, this is so highly classified, we aren't releasing any of this information. The military oversaw this project before we ever knew there was going to be a need for rebuilding. Since the army was already running things, the President agreed they should oversee preparations," said Baker.

"If I agree, who will I be working for?"

Baker and Draper exchanged awkward glances before Draper responded. "To be honest, that hasn't been finalized. For now, you'd be working with us, but you'd report directly to the President."

"How many people are on the rebuilding team?"

"Eventually, we hope to have over ten thousand," replied Baker.

RJ stared at him. "Ten Thousand! What exactly is it that this team will be doing?"

"They'll be working with the survivors to rebuild."

"Where is this disaster going to happen, and what kind of disaster are we talking about that we could need a team of that size?"

After a moment of silence, Draper responded. "Unfortunately, we're unable to give you that kind of information until you sign on."

RJ only just refrained from rolling her eyes. "How do you expect me to commit to this, without all the facts?"

"I understand the difficulty, RJ. However, I'm afraid this is the best we can offer you," Baker said.

"How many other team members have already signed up?"

"Actually, you're the first," Draper admitted.

"Why am I the first?" Even before she received a response, she already had a sinking feeling in her stomach.

"RJ, we want you to command the team to rebuild after this massive natural disaster."

RJ had dozens of questions jumping around in her mind, but all she could do was sit back and stare at them.

President Anson strode into the room. "RJ, good to meet you," he said, holding out his hand.

RJ couldn't help but smile. Apparently, the President had already been informed about her name preference.

"Good to meet you, Mister President."

"How much have they told you about this project?" asked the President.

Before she could answer, Draper spoke up. "Sir, she knows the basic information we agreed on, including the role we want her to play."

"So, what do you think? Are you interested in the offer?" Anson asked.

"What little I've heard has been overwhelming, sir. I really don't know what to think right now," RJ admitted.

Anson nodded. "I completely understand. We all had that reaction initially. I must inform you, this needs to move forward and quickly. I've been told you're the best person for this job, so I'm hoping you'll accept it."

"Yes, sir. How much time commitment is involved?" she asked.

"If you're involved in just planning, just over two years," answered Draper. "You'll have to sign an agreement stating that you understand this information is classified and you'll be imprisoned if you disclose any of it."

"If I agree to lead the team, how long?"

RJ caught three men looking at one another, apparently universally uncertain how to react to the question. "I assume this is one of those questions which are better answered once I have all the details?"

"Yes," Baker agreed. "I think it is."

"Can I see this agreement I'll have to sign?" She had to admit, if nothing else, her curiosity was piqued.

Draper slid it across the table to her.

RJ quickly skimmed the agreement and then pretended to read it through twice more. It gave her a chance to think uninterrupted. She'd been on many disaster relief missions. She'd never heard of one in which over ten thousand people were utilized. What kind of disaster would you train for two years beforehand? Better yet, what type of disaster could you predict over two years *ahead* of time?

RJ suddenly recalled the article she'd read on the airplane on the way to Washington. Things started falling into place and she looked up.

President Anson, NSA Baker, and General Draper stared at her anxiously. All of the sudden they saw the color drain from RJ's face. She stared at each of them in turn and reached for the pen.

"Looks like she figured it out," Baker commented.

Chapter 22 – Day 820

Lieutenant Parker pulled up beside the helicopter landing pad and stepped out of the Humvee. It was a cool morning, and it felt good to be outside.

He heard the sound of the approaching helicopter and got back in the vehicle, shutting the windows. He wanted to keep the dirt the chopper would kick up out of his vehicle.

RJ Anderson stepped out of the UH-60 Black Hawk and hurried across to where the Humvee was waiting.

"Ma'am, I'm Lieutenant Parker. I was sent to bring you to the facility." Parker took her overnight bag, placed it in the vehicle, and climbed into the driver's side.

RJ couldn't help but notice all the activity going on as they headed away from the temporary chopper pad and traveled towards the base of the mountain. "Things look busy," RJ pointed out.

"Yes Ma'am, ever since General Fitch took over. Within three weeks of his getting here, they'd tripled the number of people working here. This continues night and day."

"It seems to be a long drive from the chopper pad to the facility," RJ noted.

"True, but the pad is temporary; eventually there'll be several permanent ones near the west tunnel entrance but unfortunately, they won't be available until most of the construction is completed."

"What kind of security do you have here? I haven't seen any guards."

Parker responded, “There’s a perimeter fence one mile out. Your aircraft didn’t start descending until you’d cleared it. There are two gates, manned round the clock. Guard and dog patrols inside the perimeter. The rumor I heard is that the orders are to shoot anyone who breaches the perimeter. There are also more guards at the tunnel entrance.”

Parker drew to a stop in the central tunnel and they took the elevator down to the Command Center. General Fitch was sitting at a desk in the back office, working on a computer.

“Sir, Doctor Anderson is here,” Parker announced.

Fitch stood up and held out his hand. “Glad you’re here, RJ.”

“Thank you, Sir.”

He shook his head. “Feel free to call me Matt; you aren’t military anymore.”

“Okay, Matt. Are things always this hectic around here?”

“Yeah, this is about normal. I’ve been here three months, and if anything, things are getting crazier.”

As they spoke, RJ was surveying the setup. The command center measured about twenty-five feet square, and there were computer monitors everywhere. Four seats were congregated around a large central console and each station appeared to be identical.

One of the stations seemed to be configured for communications and monitoring external environmental factors. The second monitored internal systems, including the reactor. The third was for controlling the sleep chambers. She couldn’t determine the purpose of the fourth station.

“Okay RJ, are you ready for the grand tour?”

“Sure, let’s get started.”

Stepping into the hall, RJ was immediately aware of the thick blanket of dust in the air.

“When this complex was first built, there was going to be a total of about eight hundred people working here. We’re now planning for ten thousand. Over the past three months, we’ve been enlarging everything. The Health Center is now twenty times larger than it was just three months ago. The mess hall is fifteen times larger, and we’ve added a second level specifically for food storage. There are several warehouse-size freezers, all with multiple redundant systems. There should be enough food stored for your team for about two years."

RJ was impressed with the amount of work that had been accomplished in such a short amount of time.

After running her through the reactor room, Fitch showed her the manufacturing facility which had recently been added. "You'll be given every conceivable piece of equipment, but things will be needed later that weren't considered, and obviously, parts will fail. Your team should be able to fabricate almost anything you need in here."

"It seems like you've considered everything," RJ commented with a smile.

"We've tried to, but I suspect you'll be awake less than a week before you think of the first thing we've overlooked."

They took the elevator up to the central tunnel and walked down the corridor that led to Main Sleep Chamber One. They stepped through the large open door and RJ noticed that not only was the room much larger than she'd expected, but the walls had all been created from stainless steel. There were several workers, on scissor lifts, working on plumbing and ductwork at the ceiling. To one side she saw a set of stairs leading to a second level.

Cowan and Travers were standing in the middle of the room studying a set of blueprints. When the General approached, Cowan looked up, "Morning Matt."

"James, Amy, I want you to meet RJ Anderson."

Cowan nodded and smiled. Amy offered a friendly wave.

"As soon as we have this facility completely operational, RJ will assume command," Fitch explained.

"Has anyone explained the sleep process to you yet?" Cowan asked.

"Over the past week, I've spent quite a bit of time reading all the reports that have been filed. I have a basic idea about how it all works."

"Good. Let me show you around then," Cowan offered.

The two of them walked off, leaving Travers and General Fitch to go over some changes to the set of blueprints Travers and Cowan had been studying.

"There will be row after row of special beds in this room, twenty-five hundred here and the same number upstairs. There's an identical room across on the other side of the central tunnel but currently, it's about two weeks behind in construction. There are two more chambers below here, on the main floor. They're much smaller and designed to hold the team who will wake up first. Those men on the ladders above us are finishing up the piping which will supply breathing gas, SF016, and the wake-up medications. The tanks containing the SF016 are up in the highest point of the mountain. Gravity draws it down as needed, and there's a computer that monitors for leaks. The system will immediately awaken the on-call technician if a leak develops. We haven't been able to agree on exactly how much SF016 will be needed for ten thousand plus sleepers for a period of twenty years, because everyone metabolizes it at a slightly different rate. Consequently, we've taken our best guess and tripled it. All the other systems in here will give out long before you run out of SF016.

All the waste removal plumbing will be in the space under this floor," he continued. "You can see that there's a backup source for everything. If there is a problem with the SF016 lines, a secondary source has been built in. That kind of redundancy is the same for everything," Cowan explained.

"If all body processes are stopped, why is waste removal a concern?" RJ asked.

"In truth, the body processes aren't stopped, just dramatically slowed down. With the continual infusion of SF016, which contains a combination of water and nutrients amongst many other things, there is still the need for waste removal. The urine output for a sleeper is on the average the same in one year as it would be in a day if they weren't sleeping."

RJ found she was impressed. There were pipes and conduits running all over the ceiling, but they were exceptionally well organized and were even color-coded.

"I read in one of your reports that approximately ten percent of the sleepers used in the tests have needed to be sedated. Is that because of a side effect of the SF016?" RJ asked.

James smiled. "No, in almost all the earlier tests the sleepers have been in individual capsules. There isn't much room in them, and most people experienced claustrophobia, and because of that, some of them have had a tougher time than others and needed to be sedated. For your team, there will be very few individual capsules. Most will be contained in large open chambers like this. You can think of this room as one huge, individual capsule which has five thousand sleepers in it. The only people who will need individual or small group capsules will be those people who might be required to wake up individually and make repairs, deal with emergencies, or confirm that it is, in fact, time to wake the others."

"That makes sense; I've got another question if you've got time."

"Actually, I have a little over two years," Cowan agreed with a smile.

RJ chuckled at his dark sense of humor and continued. "There's something else I don't understand. I've read about studies which have proven that long-term immobility actually speeds up the aging of bones and muscles."

James nodded. "That's quite true; there have been several studies over the past few decades. There was one in 1966. It showed that three weeks of immobility aged the bones and muscles by as much as twenty years. That's one of the reasons why we've been working for so long on what's now known as SF016. Putting someone to sleep was the easy part; stopping the aging process and keeping muscles from starting to atrophy was the challenge. SF016 is not a single drug, but a mix of thirteen different compounds which work together with the breathing gas to create the full sleep effect."

"It all sounds very impressive, but I won't pretend to completely understand it," RJ admitted.

"I understand. The important part is that it's working well, and we're progressing faster here than any of us had even hoped," James explained.

"How long until this chamber is complete?"

"Another nine months at least. We've got lots of testing to do. Also, the systems for monitoring the sleepers aren't installed yet. The chamber across the hall will be about a month behind this one by that point. Then we'll work on the smaller chambers upstairs. Also, we were just told there needs to be a sleeper chamber for livestock down in the pit. They just started tunneling that one out. Half of my technical staff has returned to our facility in Arizona to conduct testing of the sleep process on animals. If we aren't careful, this place could turn into the next Noah's Ark."

RJ was confused and asked, "What's the pit?"

"Come on, I'll show you."

They walked out to the main tunnel and turned to the left. A short distance down the tunnel they came to a massive opening in the floor. Cowan walked across to a palm reader and placed his hand firmly on its surface. "Good morning, Mr. Cowan. The elevator is ascending" a mechanical voice announced.

It was almost a full minute before the large circular platform rose into a position flush with the roadway in the tunnel.

"Step on the platform," Cowan ordered, and RJ stepped on. Cowan placed his palm on the reader again. "Good morning, Mr. Cowan. The elevator is descending."

Cowan stepped onto the platform as it began a slow descent into the pit. "There will also be a normal elevator; it's supposed to be operational in a few weeks," he explained.

The descent was quite slow, but when they finally reached the bottom, RJ was amazed at the size of the area. It was probably around twenty times the size of a football field. The ceilings had to be close to fifty feet above the floor. Most of the area she could see was finished. Steel walls and floors were in place, and the lights were mostly hung.

Behind them, a group of men were carving a new tunnel off the back of the room.

"This area will be partitioned off, once it's determined where everything will be kept down here," Cowan explained.

"So, this is all storage."

"Correct. The list of everything that will be put into storage for you keeps growing. This room will be very full."

"Looks good, is that where the animal chambers will be going?" RJ asked, pointing to the tunnel under construction.

"Yes, it'll be about the size of one of the large chambers upstairs, but a single level." They stepped aboard the platform, and it began to rise.

RJ returned to the command center and found Fitch.

"How long will you be with us RJ?" the General asked.

"Tomorrow evening I head back to Washington. I'll be working with General Draper on team selection and training. I'll be spending most of my time on that. I'll stop out here every few weeks to see how things are going and to provide any insight that I've gotten."

Chapter 23 – Day 730

Senator Wilfred Cogshell sat in his first-class seat on the Boeing 747, en route from Amsterdam to New York. So far, the flight had been delayed, the takeoff rough, and the food only adequate. To make matters worse, the guy in the seat next to him was snoring loudly and reeked of stale cigarette smoke.

Senator Cogswell had spent the last two weeks meeting with representatives from five different European governments, and he was using the time to look over the many pages of notes he'd taken during the past two weeks.

He came across a notation which he'd made while speaking to the Russian Foreign Minister. The Foreign Minister had officially requested the United States government investigate a matter for them. The administrator of the Russian Space Program had heard several reports that the comet approaching Earth had some traces of radiation present. They suspected there wouldn't be any significant problem resulting from it but asked that the US government confirm their suspicions.

He entered a note in his iPad to remind him to place a call to the Administrator of NASA in the morning. Cogshell had met the Administrator several years before, when he'd showed up at NASA and requested a personal tour. Cogshell couldn't remember the Administrator's name off the top of his head, but he recalled that he'd been a fat, arrogant man, who made it seem he'd been put out to provide the tour.

In the morning, he would be sure to place a call to him.

* * *

Administrator Williams sat alone in his office. Other than the monthly reports he submitted to General Draper, he'd had no other contact with the man in over three months. The last time Williams had contacted Draper, it had been to report the concern regarding his Deputy Director and another employee going public with the comet story. Less than a week later, one of them was dead and the other missing. Even after all this time, there was still no trace of Deputy Director Stanley Waldorf, and Williams was certain he was dead. He was also convinced the phone call he'd placed to General Draper was the cause of both deaths. Williams had to admit that as bothered as he was about what happened, he hadn't been surprised by how the matter was handled.

Now there was another possible problem. Some US Senator wanted NASA to investigate a comet which was approaching Earth. Even worse, the request came directly from the Russian government. As much as Thomas Williams didn't want to call Draper, at least he knew the call wouldn't get anyone killed. While having a Senator whacked would be a small challenge, he wouldn't put it past Draper. However, taking out the entire Russian government might be a little too messy even for the arrogant General.

Reluctantly, Williams picked up the phone and dialed the special number. A voicemail system answered the call and Williams left his message. "This is Mr. Williams across town; I think we have another Code Omega. Please call me when you have time. Thanks."

As in the past, the call was returned in just a few minutes.

"Williams here."

"Mr. Williams, I understand we have another problem?"

"Yes, General. I was contacted by Senator Wilfred Cogshell from New Jersey. He's just back from a trip to Russia. While there, he was asked to investigate something for the Russians. Apparently, the Russians have been talking about our friend in space and noticed its peculiar qualities. Their initial projections apparently don't yet predict the danger. They just want confirmation that we, too, see no impending danger. I already have an official response prepared for the Russians on the matter. It says we're tracking the comet and all our projections show that it'll miss the Earth. I've mentioned that some mild radiation has been detected but we don't see it as being a threat."

"Have you sent it yet?" Draper asked.

"No, I wanted to check with you first."

"Good. I agree with your statement to them, but don't send it yet. I need to discuss this with the President first. I'll call you back,"

Williams started to respond, but realized that Draper had already disconnected.

Two hours later, Williams was told to make the call. He left a message for the Senator, confirming the findings he'd relayed to Draper.

In the next eight months, Great Britain, Argentina, Australia, France and Canada also made inquiries regarding the comet's radiation levels.

A month after that, the story made it to the public; first in a few newspapers and later on prime-time news. It took only a few weeks for everyone to begin talking about how this long-awaited comet seemed to have a little radiation associated with it.

Nobody figured out the reality of the situation.

Chapter 24 – Day 302

RJ stepped from the classroom and into the hot desert sun. The time was 1330 hours, and already she was exhausted. She'd awoken at 0500 with the others who were spending the next four weeks at Training Site Alpha. By 0530 she and two hundred and fifty others were one mile into a five-mile run. At 0700 they were having breakfast, and by 0800 they were in the classrooms. Every sleeper had their skill set personally evaluated by RJ and her team. Primary skills were built upon, and new skills were learned. Specifically, what capabilities were added to the sleepers' resumes were determined by a combination of the specific interests of the individual, and the needs of the team.

All sleepers would learn basic medical skills, as well as basic engineering, construction and combat skills. This would be over and above their primary skill, such as teaching, farming or another skill which would be needed in the new world they would awaken into.

The previous night, RJ had eaten dinner with a thirty-two-year-old Hispanic female named Mia. The young woman held a degree in molecular biology and would be responsible for the fabrication of medications and immunizations. Today though, she was in class learning about plastic explosives and other demolitions.

Prior to her arrival at Alpha, she'd spent three months training as a surgical assistant in a military hospital in Europe, a skill added to her post-awakening resume.

Mia had joked with RJ about how much her life had changed since the two of them met and RJ smiled at the memory of the conversation; she wondered how Mia would enjoy rappelling out of the helicopter later this evening.

RJ got into the Humvee and headed for her office. In fact, the office wasn't anything more than a small portable trailer. She had similar areas setup at all four training sites, and moving between them, she simply transplanted her computers and documents and in a very short amount of time was back in business.

Entering the trailer, she was immediately hit with a blast of cold air. She had one of the only air-conditioned locations in the compound. She glanced at her watch; she was scheduled to meet up with another group at the rifle range in twenty minutes. Unfortunately, she had another issue to deal with first.

She settled in front of her computer and adjusted the small camera on top. In moments, a window popped up on the screen stating she had an incoming call. She accepted the call and found herself staring into the face of her deputy commander, Brad Warren.

Brad Warren was, like her, former military and he'd spent most of his career in the Army Corps of Engineers. Brad was involved in many international projects; building and rebuilding were topics he could easily relate to. He'd retired with the rank of Major three years ago, and now at the age of forty-four, owned a small engineering firm. Since being recruited into this project, his brother was now running the business.

Brad Warren was one of the more unusual people on the project in that his wife Jill, an experienced helicopter pilot and an instructor was also a future sleeper. Jill was at Alpha this week too, conducting training for the students who were practicing rappelling from the helicopters. She'd spent the previous four weeks as a student at Alpha, working on her combat training and she had crossed trained several months before at training site Delta in communications. Most of her time, however, was spent working with other sleepers who wanted to make flying helicopters their second or third skill.

RJ smiled at Brad, “How are things at Bravo?”

“I’m glad my medical training is almost over, I can’t take much more of this. I’ve been in class for ten weeks, and the six weeks before that I was teaching an engineering class. I need a break. I’d pay for a few days on the obstacle course or the firing range,” Brad announced.

“I know what you mean; I feel the same way at times. I’m flying out to the mountain for a few days, to see how things are going. Before I left, I wanted to discuss the situation you emailed me regarding.”

“This guy, Dale Carter, is a real pain in the you know what, RJ. I understand why you selected him, but he’s infuriating the other two nukes. He struts around, blabbing on and on about how much he knows and how little everyone else knows. The other nuclear engineers are ready to kill him. They’re both ten years older and have twenty times his experience. This kid might have been top of his class, but he’s a pup with an attitude problem. We need these three to work together to keep that reactor working and to eventually start training their replacements. I think one of the others punched him out the other night. He showed up in medical class with a bloody lip, but he won’t say what happened, and I quit asking. He was quiet for a day or so, but that didn’t last. I think we’d be better to kick him out.”

“I’m not ready to kick him out yet. Even if we did, what then? He certainly can’t just be allowed to leave, not with everything he knows.

“I’ll make sure he and I cross paths soon and have a little chat. In the meantime, I’ll have him dragged in for a repeat psych exam. I know it isn’t something we normally repeat, but I’ll set it up to make it clear to him we think he’s has a problem. I’ll make sure the results of the exam show he needs to spend some time with a counselor and. If he thinks we might cut him loose, he might get his act together. He understands that being removed from the program means he dies in less than a year from radiation sickness,” RJ explained.

“I’m willing to give it a try, but this kid is so arrogant I don’t think he believes we’d even consider getting rid of him” Brad agreed.

"Let's see what happens, and I'll make sure to talk to him too. Do you have any questions for me to get answers for while I'm at the mountain?"

"I'm just curious about a timetable for moving in."

"I'm supposed to work on that with General Fitch while I'm there," RJ responded.

"Good. One other thing, one of the sleep experts needs to be going with us, in case there are any issues during the long sleep. Has that been worked out and when will they start training? We'll need to get them started soon."

"That will be covered this trip too. I'll let you know what we decide."

RJ disconnected the call, got up from her chair and took a small bottle of cold water from the refrigerator. She hesitated in the cool air conditioning for as long as possible, then pushed the door open and stepped into the desert sand. Climbing into the Humvee, she could already feel the sweat starting to trickle down her neck and back. She shifted into gear and started out for the firing range wanting to complete the last of her shooting drills for the week before leaving for the mountain.

* * *

Three hours later, she'd completed her training, packed her gear and gotten her files and laptop together. She'd showered and was waiting for the helicopter which would take her on the two-hour trip to the mountain.

She sat in the cool office and looked out over the helipad. She heard an approaching aircraft and three minutes later a UH-60 Black Hawk was sitting on the pad. RJ waited until the rotors stopped turning then headed out to the pad. Ten minutes later, they were airborne again and heading north.

When the Black Hawk landed, the first thing RJ noticed was that they'd landed on the opposite end of the mountain. The permanent helipads were now in place, and they were able to land on the concrete surface instead of in the sand.

She stepped from the helicopter and began the one-hundred-yard walk to the tunnel entrance. Behind her were the three completed buildings which the workers now considered home. Nearing the gate, she was met by an armed sentry. She placed her hand on the scanner at his station and was immediately granted access. She boarded a waiting Humvee and rode the half-mile long journey into the mountain.

She swiftly became aware of two things. First, the noises of the heavy machinery used for digging and tunneling were gone. On her last visit, six months ago, they'd still been digging and cutting rock out, and no matter where in the facility you went, there was the constant sound of heavy earth-moving equipment.

The second thing RJ noticed was an odd pungent smell in the air, which reminded her of burnt rubber or plastic. She was sure the smell hadn't been present the last time she was at the mountain.

She proceeded down the brightly lit corridor and past the mammoth elevator which led to the pit. She placed her hand on the scanner on the wall by the recessed door. "Good afternoon, Miss Anderson." She was greeted again when she called the elevator and it descended to the main floor of the complex. When the doors opened, the burnt smell was much stronger, and she could hear the ventilation fans running at full power. She entered the control room and went to the office she shared with Matt Fitch, but the office was abandoned. Several technicians were in the control room, going about various tasks.

She sat down at the desk and accessed the computer, requesting it to locate General Fitch. She rapidly received a response, confirming that the General was in the engineering area.

RJ briefly considered heading to engineering but decided against it; instead, she had the computer bring up all the status reports which had been submitted since her last visit.

Reading the reports, RJ was pleased with the progress. The enlargement of all the planned areas was complete. The hospital was finished, the mess hall was almost complete, and the second level freezers and food storage areas had been completed for a week. In fact, the freezers were online, and all backup systems were checking out just fine.

The sleep chambers for the command staff on this level were mostly complete, as were the livestock chambers. The primary sleep chambers had been completed a month ago, and there were currently five test subjects in each of the five thousand bed chambers. They'd been placed in the deep sleep two weeks ago and were scheduled to remain asleep for another two weeks. So far, there had been no problems.

The living quarters for many of the two-hundred-member initial wake up team were due to be finalized in the next few weeks.

RJ made a mental note to get up to that level and take a look around. Her quarters were going to be up there, and she was anxious to see the progress.

Deciding she was hungry, she had the computer locate General Fitch again, confirming he was still in the engineering area. She sent a signal to the intercom closest to him. After the wall unit beeped, a voice answered. "This is Cowan."

"James, this is RJ. Could you please let the General know I've arrived and I'll be in the mess hall when he has time?"

"Sure RJ. He's here and says he'll be there in about ten minutes."

"Great, thanks."

RJ logged out and headed for the mess hall. When she arrived, she treated herself to a cheeseburger, fries and a large salad. She found a large booth along the wall and sat down to eat and was almost done when Fitch and Cowan entered the room. Both men grabbed a drink before sitting down with her in the booth.

"Amy will be catching up with us too; she'll be along in a couple minutes," Fitch explained.

"Good. I was reading over the status reports. It seems as if everything is moving along right on schedule. By the way, what is that smell? Smells like something burning," RJ commented.

"There was a fire in the laundry area. They'd just finished installing the last of the equipment in there, and it was being tested. No one was in the laundry room and suddenly, the computers were signaling a fire alarm. It took a few minutes to get people down there to get it out. It seems one of the large dryers shorted out. There isn't much left of it. There's a team down there working on clearing up the mess. It looks as if a couple of the units on either side of the defective one are ruined too, but the rest are okay," Fitch explained.

"Glad this happened now, instead of after the sleep," stated RJ.

"Agreed," Travers said, joining them at the table.

"We have some timetable issues to discuss. We need to decide which one of you two is joining us for the big sleep, so we can get the required training started," RJ said, glancing from Cowan to Travers.

"I think Amy should go with you, she's almost as knowledgeable as I'm about the sleep process and I can finish up here while she starts the training," Cowan announced.

Travers turned to stare at Cowan, surprise evident on her face.

"Amy, if there are issues during the sleep, can you deal with them?" RJ asked.

Travers thought for a minute or two. "I suspect I could handle almost any problem, I've been working closely with James for some time now."

General Fitch spoke up. "James is clearly the most experienced person when it comes to the sleep process, and while I'm very pleased with Captain Travers abilities, it only makes sense for the most qualified person to go. This whole project revolves around the long sleep and anything we can do to guarantee its success is paramount."

"I'm afraid I have to agree," Travers said reluctantly.

Three sets of eyes turned on Cowan. After a few seconds, he slowly shook his head. "No, I can't. I won't go. I won't leave my wife to die, while I hide out here." The idea of leaving Kathy to die while he sought safety wasn't something he would even consider. When they'd married twenty-four years earlier, he'd promised her that he would be with her unto death. He'd never lied to her, and she'd never let him down. He couldn't let her die alone.

"James, this project needs your expertise. We need you there in case there are any problems," RJ responded gently.

"Sorry RJ. I won't leave my wife." The tone in Cowan's voice was determined and it was clear this was not something he'd budge on.

"Hey James, isn't your wife a teacher?" General Fitch suddenly asked.

"Yeah, she teaches high school history. Why?"

Fitch turned to RJ. "Do we have a need for another teacher on the project?"

"Well, we originally wanted to sleep twelve teachers but cut back to ten to make room for another nurse and a molecular biologist. But we kept a few beds in reserve for this type of situation," RJ said reluctantly. RJ liked Cowan and understood his concern.

"What do you think, James?" the General asked.

"I'll have to discuss it with her, She knows something is going on, not the details. But she is too smart to have not connected many of the dots. I don't know if she'll be willing to leave our son behind."

"How old is he?" RJ asked.

"DJ is twenty-two, he's a senior in college."

"I can't do that one for you. Sorry."

Cowan nodded, sadness in his eyes. "I know."

"James, I could guarantee that he gets a spot in an underground shelter if she agrees. There is lots of flexibility with who we put in the shelters," Fitch added.

"I'll head home tonight and discuss it with her. I think she might agree."

"Good. The next thing we need to cover is the move in date," RJ said. "Is there a plan in place?"

"Yes. Next month we start bringing in supplies– vehicles, food, tools, construction equipment, building supplies, etcetera. Most of the delivery schedules are already in place. In six months, the livestock arrives. We'll have a three to one ratio of females to males in all species and the females will be impregnated before their arrival, which will almost double the number of each species we take with us."

"One month before the comet's arrival, the primary sleepers will arrive and immediately be put to sleep. Two weeks later, the two-hundred-man advance team will start to arrive and be put to sleep, except for your immediate command staff. They'll enter the mountain a week later and immediately be sealed in. Then you and any others of your choice will remain awake and in communication with the rest of us. You'll witness the comet's arrival, and we'll maintain communication for as long as possible. You'll enter the sleep capsules when you decide it's optimal. This was all decided some time ago, but can be modified as necessary," explained the General.

RJ thought about it for a minute. Inwardly, she was horrified at the realization she would soon be sitting in the command center, watching the world die all around her. Despite that knowledge, the plan sounded good, and the timeline was close to what she'd envisioned.

"That sounds good me. I'm curious to see some of the living quarters and the completed sleep chambers."

Cowan spoke up. "If you don't mind, I need to make arrangements to head home for a couple of days. Kathy and I need to have a long discussion about what we're going to do."

"In that case, I'll show you what we've accomplished while you've been gone," Travers offered.

"Sounds good to me." The two of them got up to leave.

Once the doors closed behind the two women, Matt looked over at his friend. "Do you think Kathy will really sign on?"

"If she realizes it's the one chance to guarantee our boy gets in a shelter, I think she'll do anything."

"Good, let me know how things go."

Cowan got up to leave, and as he went Fitch made a mental note to contact General Draper. Cowan's son would have a place in a shelter, whether James and Kathy chose to sleep or not.

* * *

Cowan climbed aboard the UH-60 Black Hawk and was quickly airborne. Checking his watch, he realized it would be about seven PM when he arrived home. He sat back and enjoyed the fast flight across the desert, and as he traveled, he mentally rehearsed the fantastic story he was going to tell Kathy. She'd been curious about his work, and up until now, he'd been somewhat vague. Tonight, the unbelievable story would come out, and in truth, he had no idea how she would take the news.

Chapter 25 – Day 302

During the drive to work that morning, Air Force Colonel Roger Barrett thought again about the highly unusual events which had taken place over the last few weeks.

As the commanding officer of the remote, desert missile testing facility, he and his team were responsible for scheduling and conducting the tests of many different types of military hardware.

For the past few weeks, he and his team had been working with the Army on preparing for the testing of some new classified missiles. He hadn't been able to learn much, other than they were highly classified and exceptionally large. It didn't seem to make much sense. His facility was typically used to test smaller weapons, missiles that would only travel a few hundred miles at most.

In the case of larger missiles, these tests were usually conducted on the coast. That way if there was a problem and the rocket had to be destroyed, the debris would fall harmlessly in the ocean.

This week's launches would break that rule. Today was the beginning of a week-long string of missile launches from his facility and it was by far a most unusual project, for more than just a few reasons.

The missiles in question were a design that he hadn't seen before, and the one time he'd questioned the payload, it had been made crystal clear that the specifications he'd been provided were all he required.

Nor had he been made aware of the details regarding where these rockets would be coming down. Based on their size, it was apparent that they'd be traveling a long distance. Typically, he would be involved in the briefings which covered all these details.

Adding to the mystery, was the fact that an Army four-star was running the project.

Colonel Barrett arrived at the gates of the Air Forces facilities' only entrance and presented his ID to an Army Corporal who studied it and looked back at Barrett repeatedly before granting him entrance. It was a far cry from the usual routine when Barrett's normal security personnel knew him and after a cursory glance at his face, would allow him to pass.

Driving into the facility, located deep in the Mohave Desert, he was stunned by the increase in security. Heavily armed US Army personnel seemed to have been posted all over the base and his regular Air Force Security was all but unseen, and those few he did see were more heavily armed than usual.

Barrett pulled into in his reserved parking spot, somewhat surprised it was still available given that the Army had taken over everything else on his base. He walked the short distance to the mobile command trailer, again showing his ID, this time to a young soldier armed with an M4 assault rifle.

It was just after nine and the mobile command trailer was already heating up rapidly under the desert sun. Barrett stood in the control room, and the more he thought about the strange situation, the more uneasy he felt.

The launch countdown was progressing, and there were at least a dozen people packed into the control room. Half were his staff and the other half Army.

Some of his team were making a final visual inspection of the rockets, and they were being escorted the whole time by stony-faced soldiers.

When the report came back as all clear, he picked up the special phone which had been installed for this project. It was answered immediately. "General Draper," boomed the voice at the other end.

"Sir, this is Air Force Colonel Barrett, all preparations are complete, and we're requesting final launch clearance."

"You are authorized to launch on schedule. Contact me if there are any problems," Draper said.

"Yes sir," Barrett responded.

Three minutes later, the first of the two rockets lifted into the sky, riding on an ever-fading plume of fire. Thirty seconds after that, the second rocket lifted off.

While Barrett and his team conducted their post-launch procedures, he snuck a glance at the digital display an Army officer was studying closely, and he was shocked to see the course and trajectory of the rockets. They weren't going to be coming down at some remote site; in fact, they weren't on a trajectory that would place them in orbit either. The reality was, they were heading out into space.

Now Barrett was confused. The only things ever launched deep into space were automated robotic spacecraft, used for studying objects in space. If that were the case, why were they launching twenty rockets over a ten-day stretch and why all the secrecy?

These people were treating these things like nuclear weapons rather than space probes and that thought gave Barrett an idea which he quickly dismissed. After all, launching nuclear weapons into space was a more ridiculous idea than any of the other scenarios he'd come up with.

Colonel Barrett shook his head. None of this made any sense.

Chapter 26 – Day 302

Bill Etcher was driving fast, almost recklessly. He was furious and found that he almost wanted to be stopped by a cop. This idea was tempered when Bill remembered he didn't have a license and he'd go back to jail if he got stopped. He slowed the old pickup just a little as he entered town, spotted the tavern on the corner and made a quick decision. With brakes squealing in protest, he brought the truck to a stop.

This tavern was one of his favorites, he would frequently stop here for an hour or more before heading home from work. He'd been planning to go directly home tonight, but after what had happened, he knew he couldn't face his wife, Marsha without indulging in a few drinks. There were times when she was the most uncaring person in the world and his anger increased as he thought about how she was going to react to his news and what she would say. She'd automatically assume that his getting fired at work today was his fault. She would whine and complain, probably even dare to suggest his drinking was to blame. He knew the speech; he'd certainly heard it plenty of times.

Actually, he was glad he'd been fired; he'd needed a reason to search for a better job. After all, he was thirty-five years old, and he could do better than working for ten dollars an hour making tacos.

Six hours a day four days a week of making tacos was more than he could stomach, especially when he had to report to that punk kid.

'The punk', as Bill frequently called him behind his back, couldn't have been more than twenty-two years old.

Anyone in his position would have a few drinks before work. What right did the punk have, telling him he couldn't drink before he arrived at work to make stupid tacos! What he did before work was his business!

Yeah, the more he thought about it, the more Bill Etcher was glad he got fired. His only regret was that he didn't punch the punk's teeth in before he left!

He got out of the truck adjusted his overalls and guided his overweight body to the entrance. He pushed open the old wooden door of the tavern, stomping up to the bar.

"Bill, you're looking more bothered than usual. What's the matter?" asked the large woman with the bleached blonde hair who worked behind the bar.

Bill leaned against the bar. "I got fired."

"Here let me get you a beer, I'm sure you can use one," the woman said.

"Thanks"

A brown bottle with the cap removed was set down in front of Bill, who drank it down in three quick swallows.

"Get me a couple more, babe."

The blonde set two more beers down in front of Bill – and ten minutes later, two more.

An hour and a half after entering the bar, Bill finally decided it was time to head home.

He climbed back into the old Ford pickup and headed for home. He was feeling much better and knew stopping at the tavern had been the right choice.

He pulled into the driveway next to the trailer they'd lived in for the past two years and stopped with his rear wheels on top of the small bush his wife had planted the previous fall. Bill did not remember the name for the stupid bush only that it was supposed to have red flowers; so far it had had none.

He stumbled up to the door and tried to push the key in the lock. After repeated attempts, he gave up and pounded on the flimsy white door.

Marsha was a scrawny woman with long stringy hair. She never smiled, long ago realizing the mess her life was. She came to the door and opened it, and Bill shoved his way in. "The locks broke; my stupid key wouldn't work," Bill grumbled as he dropped into a faded blue recliner with cigarette burns.

Marsha quietly pulled the ignition key from the truck out of the trailer door lock, then switched keys and demonstrated that the lock was working perfectly well. "Looks like it works fine to me," she said, as she threw the keys to him.

Bill tried to catch them but missed. Reaching for the keys which dropped to the floor, he almost fell out of the chair.

"You're pathetic," Marsha said, heading for the kitchen.

"You shut up! I had a hard day, and I don't need to put up with this when I come home. Bring me a beer."

"Hard day? Is the stress of taco making too much for you, or did you get fired again?"

"Shut up woman! You don't know what you're talking about." Bill's anger surged, as he realized everything was falling apart just as he'd feared.

Marsha stomped back into the room and stared him in the eyes. "I don't know what I'm talking about? Well, I do know you're a loser and a drunk, who can't even hold down a job making tacos."

This derisive statement was more than Bill could take. On the second try, he managed to get to his feet and screamed, "You'll never talk to me like that again!"

With one hand, he shoved her backward. She stumbled back and fell onto a small table which held a potted plant and both the plant and table were crushed under her weight. Bill didn't wait to see if she got up, or hear the familiar threat to call the cops. He yanked the front door open, ripping the top hinge from the wall as he did and stormed out of the trailer.

After starting the engine he stomped the gas, and the truck shot forward and crashed through the two garbage cans before continuing into the backyard. Amazingly, Bill managed to get the truck stopped, put it in reverse and stomped the accelerator. The tires spun before the truck rocketed backward, leaving deep trenches carved in the dirt and only just missed hitting the trailer. The neighbor's mailbox wasn't as fortunate and got flattened as the vehicle made it out of the driveway and onto the dirt road. Bill slammed on the brakes, got the truck back into drive, and headed down the road as fast as he could.

By the time he got to the end of the dirt road, there were already two calls made to the local police department.

The dirt road intersected with a single lane paved road and Bill managed to keep the truck on the road when he made the turn. The radio was blasting, and Bill couldn't even hear the noise of the engine over the loud country music.

The only time Bill almost went off the road was when he swerved to hit a cat on the side of the road. He felt a little better when he felt the bump under the wheel as he successfully flattened the old half-lame cat that was always seen by the road in this area.

Bill was traveling at close to eighty miles an hour when he neared the town limits. He was approaching the two-lane highway which bypassed the downtown area when he noticed the blue and white flashing lights coming up behind him. He knew there was no way he could stop. Having no license meant jail for sure. He tried pushing the accelerator pedal further to the floor, but it was already against the carpet. He glanced around and realized he was already approaching the highway and there was no way he could slow down enough to stop at the stop sign. In his fuzzy mind, he thought this could be an opportunity to get away from the cops.

Just as he reached the crossing, a vehicle passed directly in front of him. Just before impact, Bill saw the other driver turn and look directly at him, saw the look of horror on the man's face.

Bill's pickup impacted with the driver's door of the Dodge SUV at eighty-eight miles per hour.

Immediately upon impact, Bill's unrestrained body slammed against the steering wheel with enough force to crush all the ribs in his chest and destroy almost every organ in his thoracic and abdominal cavity. Bill Etcher was dead from internal hemorrhaging before the pursuing police cruiser had come to a complete stop.

In the other car, the driver's door, floor, side and roof of the SUV had been pushed in over two feet. As the steel intruded into the driver's compartment, the restrained operator of the Dodge had his left arm, shoulder, ribs, pelvis, and femur crushed. Two of the fractured ribs were forced inward and punctured the driver's left lung. At the same time, the left side of the driver's head struck the car's doorframe with an enormous force. Blood vessels in the driver's head ruptured and started bleeding into the brain. The impact also fractured the driver's neck instantly.

When the first police officer reached the Dodge, the driver had no pulse. The officer considered starting CPR but swiftly realized there was no way to get the driver out of the crushed SUV, because of the immense amount of damage the vehicle had suffered.

Thirty-five minutes later, the fire department got the car cut apart enough to free the trapped body. Just before the man was placed into a body bag, the officer retrieved his wallet and driver's license. He walked back to his cruiser and got his clipboard, and from the license, he copied down the victim's name, *James Cowan.*

Chapter 27 – Day 299

The steam rose steadily from the hot water in the shower and the naked woman stood underneath it, motionless for a long time. Every surface of the small bathroom was covered with moisture, created by the thick humidity.

Eventually, the influx of steam tapered off, and finally, the woman began moving, slowly at first but her pace increased as the hot water ran out and the shower grew colder and colder. Eventually, when the water was too cold to be comfortable, she slapped the valves closed, and the water stopped.

Amy Travers stepped out into the steam-filled room and began toweling herself off with little enthusiasm. Wrapping the towel around her body, she slowly wandered out of the bathroom and down the narrow hall to her bedroom.

She settled quietly on the side of the bed, staring into the closet for several minutes. Finally, she shook her head violently from side to side a couple times, wiped away the tears from her eyes, grabbed a dress uniform, and put it on. She quickly dried her light brown hair and pulled it back into a ponytail, then left the bedroom.

On the way out, she stopped in the kitchen, grabbed a bottle of Tylenol from the cupboard above the sink, and swallowed two capsules down without water. Approaching the door, she grabbed the regulation black purse which hung on the coat rack and left the apartment.

Amy descended the stairs and stepped out into the sunshine. There had been some rain the night before, but already the ground had dried, and dust was blowing across the complex in the light breeze.

She crossed the parking lot, approaching her seven-year-old Honda. She'd considered replacing the car, but with all that was transpiring on the project, purchasing a new car seemed pointless.

She'd been talking to some of the future sleepers who had recently purchased expensive new vehicles. According to what they'd told her, their thinking was that they could at least play with their new toys for a few months. By the time anyone started to notice they were behind on the payments, they would be sleeping, and the lien holders would be worrying more about survival than collecting payments.

While it sounded like good thinking to Amy, she couldn't bring herself to worry about a car in the middle of this crisis. If her car died and needed to be replaced, she admitted to herself that she would probably go all out, but until then she had much more to worry about.

Getting into the car, she was immediately aware of the humid, musty smell and a quick glance around confirmed she'd left the passenger side window down during the night. The front passenger seat had soaked up the rainwater, and was slowly drying out, but leaving the musty smell all through the interior.

Usually, she would have placed her purse on the seat beside her, but today she threw it in the back seat in disgust. She left the parking lot, going a little faster than she should and headed for the highway.

As she drove, she thought about the weekend three months ago which she'd spent in Reno with Kathy Cowan and how many funny and flattering stories they'd shared about James. She had been touched by how deeply in love Kathy was with her husband, and how close Amy herself had felt to him.

Ever since the tragic accident three days ago, she'd been analyzing her own feelings. She didn't love Cowan, but she suspected that if he hadn't been married and she had allowed it, she easily could have fallen in love with the man.

She pulled in to the parking lot at the funeral home and was pleased and pleasantly surprised to see how many cars were there already. As busy as James had always been, she didn't picture him as having more than a few close friends. Apparently, she was wrong.

She walked to the entrance, and a tall, balding man wearing a gray suit opened the heavy wooden door for her.

She removed her hat and entered the chapel area, a rather large room filled with chairs. Two aisles led to the front where a dark wooden casket rested on a pedestal; it was almost completely covered with flower arrangements and a podium sat in front of it. Amy couldn't help but notice how from this distance, the casket looked like a sleep capsule and somehow, that seemed fitting.

Centered on the casket, facing the mourners, was an eleven by fourteen-inch framed photo of James, which Amy recognized from the den wall in the Cowan's home. The podium was centered at the front of the room and partially obstructed the view of the casket.

Standing near the front of the room was Kathy Cowan; she was talking with a thin, tall young man. From the man's features, Amy was confident this must be DJ Cowan.

Ever since Amy had grown close to the Cowans', DJ had been away at college in the winter, and busy working or participating in internships during the summer. Amy had always wanted to meet him and was saddened that the long-awaited meeting would occur at his father's funeral.

Amy considered going up and talking to her friend but noticed that everyone was taking his or her seats so, she decided to wait and see her at the end of the service.

Amy found a seat in the back and was getting ready to sit when she saw RJ unobtrusively waving to her from a few rows nearer the front. She moved up and took the seat Matt Fitch and RJ had been holding for her, touched by their consideration.

"How you doing?" asked Fitch in a low voice.

"Not good," Amy whispered.

Before the General could say anything more, a man in a dark suit stood and addressed the mourners. Amy assumed this must be the Cowans' pastor.

"Ladies and gentlemen, we are gathered here to say our final goodbyes to our dear friend, James Cowan. I've known James and Kathy for about twenty years and I've no doubt that James is with our Lord and Savior at this minute, thinking about all of us and the pain we're all suffering."

The pastor spoke for several more minutes, but Amy wasn't focused on what was said, instead retreating into her own thoughts. Amy suddenly became aware that the service was ending, and people were getting to their feet, making their way outside. Fitch stayed behind as Kathy had asked him to serve as a pallbearer and Amy slipped up to the front, speaking briefly to Kathy, and exchanging hugs. "How are you holding up?" Amy asked.

"It's been rough. Fortunately, DJ has been here. We're going to make it through this."

"Let me know what I can do, Kathy. If there's anything you need, I want to be there for both you and DJ."

Kathy managed a faint smile. "I know Amy, you're a great friend. I'd wanted you to meet DJ today, but James' mom wasn't holding up well, and DJ took her home just a few minutes ago."

After a few more minutes of quiet conversation, they hugged again, before Amy left the chapel so the pallbearers could carry the coffin out to the hearse.

As Amy watched the wooden box containing her friend's body being carried from the funeral home she couldn't help but think of James and his wonderful family.

She felt another bout of tears coming, and wasn't certain if the tears were for James, or for herself.

Chapter 28 – Day 90

The helicopter flew low; perhaps a hundred feet above the desert. Occasionally it would climb because of an immovable object on the ground, but just as quickly settled back down into the lower altitude.

RJ rode in the co-pilot's seat, impressed at the skill Amy Travers had developed in the three months she'd been flying again.

Amy had initially joined the Army to fly and had flown helicopters for several years. Unfortunately, the policy of keeping women out of combat had significantly limited her options, and eventually, she'd decided she'd had enough frustration and began to contemplate whether she would take on a new career path or leave the military altogether.

She had a degree in biology from her pre-military life and met then Lt. Colonel Matt Fitch at a social gathering. They'd gotten to know each other and Matt offered to have her transferred to his team. Amy loved the military life and was willing to give up flying in exchange for this new offer.

Since it was essential Amy have some usable skills for after the long sleep, and given the future sleepers wouldn't be bound by current military policies, it had seemed a perfect opportunity to return to flying. Along with basic medical and weapons training, and brushing up her flying skills, Amy had also been managing the sleep team, a role forced on her after James Cowan's untimely death.

At first, the combined stress of training while taking over command of the sleep project was immense. Added to the loss of a good friend and mentor, and Amy was overwhelmed. She managed her grief by diving into her multiple roles, leaving herself no free time and no time to grieve. She was so exhausted after the first month, the flight instructor grounded her and General Fitch had finally stepped in.

Amy had been given a week of leave, and she spent some time speaking with a grief counselor. Fitch continued to assist and support her after she came back to work but by then, she was maintaining a healthier pace, and delegating more and more work to other members of the sleep project. And enjoying a return to piloting which she'd never seen coming.

Amy pulled the helicopter into a steep climb and flew in over the mountain before she rapidly descended directly onto the landing pad at the mouth of the tunnel.

"I think you're enjoying this too much," RJ suggested with a grin.

"I think you're right. I'd almost forgotten how good it feels to fly."

They waited together in the helicopter as the engine powered down. Amy scanned the area around them and saw two fully laden eighteen-wheel semis lined up at the mouth of the tunnel. Beyond them, colossal cranes were lowering the last of the underground fuel storage tanks into the ground.

Getting out of the helicopter they started for the tunnel entrance and were met by a soldier in a Humvee who drove them the half-mile long journey into the tunnel. Approaching the elevator which led to the pit, Amy saw two brand new, identical red and white ambulances lined up behind one another. A woman was attaching magnetic signs to the sides that listed precisely where in the pit they would going to be stored. There was also a large barcode on the label stuck to the side so that the vehicle could be scanned and tracked in the computers.

"Let's go see how things are progressing," Amy suggested.

"That sounds good."

They stepped into the massive elevator at the same time the woman with the signs was stepping off. They stood by the side of the rearmost ambulance and rode the elevator down.

When they got off the elevator, they saw two more tractor-trailers backed into the room. Forklifts were emptying the cargo from the trucks and as they walked past she could see that the enormous chamber was about twenty-five percent filled.

A forklift passed them, carrying three pallets of IV fluids. The second was removing toilet paper from the other truck. Walking past where the forklifts were delivering the cargo in organized areas they could see row upon row of vehicles, including several new cement mixers, bulldozers, and front-end loaders standing in a row.

In the row behind them were four different types of fire trucks and near the northeast corner were several dozen green tractors and other pieces of essential farm equipment.

Amy noticed the vehicles were mostly up on blocks and had their tires removed. They continued walking and saw a new dump truck on blocks; a team was removing the tires and using paint brushes to cover the tires with a foul-smelling substance.

RJ must have seen the confusion on Amy's face. "The rubber in the tires will dry out and crack, long before we wake up, so they remove them and cover them in that gel, which prevents them from drying out. They'll do the same thing with all the belts and hoses, too."

"I guess that makes sense" Amy agreed.

There was an abrupt beeping noise, and they turned to see the two ambulances backing into their designated positions. They started back towards the elevator and made it just in time to ride up with the two empty semis.

"I'm going to check on the two sleep chambers down below," Amy suggested.

"Okay. If you need me, I'll be in the command center," RJ responded.

Amy turned to the right to check on the two smaller sleep chambers on either side of the corridor. She went to the passage on the right that led to the large open room first and was surprised to see the large pressure door was closed, and the digital indicators showed the chamber was pressurized.

She peered through the thick glass window and saw the one hundred and fifty pedestal-like beds, and then noticed six of those beds had sleepers on them, IV lines inserted and masks on their faces. The wires for cardiac monitoring were visible snaking beneath their shirts. This room would sleep most of the team members who would be involved in the initial assessment following the awakening and Amy was pleased to see live testing was ahead of schedule. The guilt she'd suffered over delegating the preparation of these chambers to her less experienced staff faded a little.

Amy left the chamber and headed to the one across the hall. This chamber was physically as large but would only hold fifty sleepers, since the specialists in this chamber could be called upon to awaken during the sleep to deal with problems that developed. Consequently, it had been designed with two pressurized doors and a ten-foot space between them which could be used as an airlock. It was necessary to design the environment in this manner so that people could come and go without causing a problem for the rest of the sleepers.

Amy strode through the two sets of pressure doors and saw the chamber was filled with individual sleep capsules, which better enabled the individual sleepers to awaken and perform needed functions and then later return to sleep.

Captain Travers was glad to see all the capsules were in place. One group of technicians was hooking up the tubing to the capsules, while a second team was attaching the modified hinged covers. Work in this chamber appeared to be right on schedule.

Amy moved to a table at the side of the room and started reading over the progress reports and lists of tasks which still needed to be completed. As she reviewed the work, her appreciation for the rest of her team increased. Not only had they finished the two primary chambers and the main chamber on this floor, but the animal chamber was also scheduled for completion in a month and this chamber in two months. That would bring their work to a conclusion almost two months ahead of schedule.

She contemplated going to see General Fitch, but first, she decided to go back to the pit and check out the animal chamber.

* * *

RJ entered the command center and headed to the office. General Fitch wasn't there, and she soon learned from a technician at a communications terminal that he had retired to his quarters feeling ill.

RJ was looking over status reports when Travers came in from her inspections.

"How are things coming, Amy?"

Amy nodded. "Excellent, everything is well ahead of schedule. The animal chamber will be fully operational in a month. I went and checked it out, and things are looking good. Our sleep chamber is the last one to be finished, but it looks like it'll be done soon. How's everything else progressing?"

"Good. The underground fuel storage tanks are the last major piece of construction. Final deliveries are all scheduled. Most of the food will be here over a month ahead of time," RJ explained.

"Sounds great, what about the animals?"

"They start arriving in five weeks. As soon as they're all here, we'll put them to sleep."

Amy giggled, "Sorry, but talking about putting all the animals to sleep, just sounds wrong."

Chapter 29 – Day 5

Megan Tanner hurried from the gray Chevy pickup in the driveway to the front door of her one hundred and twelve-year-old farmhouse. She'd been delayed working at the bank, and now she was extremely tight on time.

She should have known she was asking for trouble when she'd allowed the Richardsons to schedule an appointment so late in the day. She'd assumed they would just fill out the loan application, and be on their way. If that had been the case, she would have been out of the bank and on her way home on time.

Unfortunately, Mr. Richardson had more questions and concerns about the loan than Megan ever would have imagined. He wanted to go over every possible blemish on his credit and find out from Megan exactly how each could affect the chances of them securing the loan.

Megan repeatedly told him not to be concerned at this point and just to wait for the application to be processed, and then they would deal with the specific issues if there was any need.

However, try as she may, by the time the Richardsons finally left she was almost twenty minutes late leaving work. Her admittedly inappropriate driving had helped makeup about four minutes on the way home, but she was still way behind schedule.

She needed to get dinner ready and on the table by the time her husband, Jake came in from the barn. He was supervising as his workers got the herd into the barn and got the new milking system going.

There had been some problems with the new system the night before and some of the cows were late getting milked. Because of this problem, he'd decided to personally watch over the process for the next few days.

Dinner was already going to be a fast-paced event tonight since it was Tuesday. Their daughter Lauren had a softball game each Tuesday evening at 6:00 pm, which always meant things were extremely hurried at suppertime.

Bursting through the front door, she was greeted by the noticeable smell of tomato sauce cooking.

Mildly short of breath, she hurried through the family room, where her son Ray was sitting in front of the Xbox, playing a video game. All Megan caught sight of on the screen as she walked through the room, was a burst of simulated machine gun fire tearing into the chest of a large animated creature, with a massive head and many eyes. Ray didn't even notice her as she walked past.

She entered the kitchen and found Lauren placing the uncooked pasta into a pot of boiling water.

"Hi, Mom. I figured since it looked you were going to be late, I'd get supper started so I wouldn't miss the start of the game. I hope that's okay."

"I'm sorry I'm late honey. Thanks for getting this started, it's a big help. If you can watch it for me for just another minute, I'll take over and you can get dressed for the game."

"Sure Mom."

Megan went to the bedroom and quickly changed into a pair of jeans and a flannel shirt before returning to relieve Lauren in the kitchen.

As Megan was finishing the cooking, Jake Tanner stepped through the back door and removed his mud-covered work boots. "That smells great hon," he commented.

"Good, but Lauren did most of it before I even got home."

"Really? When did she start cooking?" Jake asked.

"Not sure, she's never shown any interest in anything that couldn't be heated in the microwave, but this came out quite well," Megan admitted.

Within a few minutes, they were all seated at the table working on eating dinner.

Megan had to remind Ray to hurry several times, but they all rapidly finished eating, and they completed their preparations to head to the game.

After a rushed dinner, Lauren stood by the front door anxiously waiting for the others when she noticed a van traveling rapidly up their long driveway.

"Mom, Dad, there's a van flying up the drive," she called out.

"Jake, are you expecting anyone?" Megan asked.

Jake pursed his lips. "Nope, not that I recall."

Megan got to the front window just in time to see two uniformed soldiers climbing from an unmarked fifteen-passenger van. They were both armed, with a pistol holstered on their waist.

"Jake, get over here now!" Megan shrieked.

Jake arrived just as the soldiers were reaching the front door. The bell rang once, and before any of the Tanners could get to the door, the soldiers were letting themselves in.

"Mr. and Mrs. Tanner, I've been ordered to inform you that we have a Code Anvil," the tall man in the lead said.

Young Ray Tanner had no idea what a Code Anvil was, but when both his parents faces instantly turned pale, he suspected this was somehow related to a conversation his parents had conducted with him and his sister almost two years before.

"Is this a test?" Jake said after a long moment of hesitation.

"No, sir. I've been told to inform you this isn't a drill. It's the real thing."

"What's the problem?"

"Ma'am I don't know. In fact, I don't even know what a Code Anvil is. I just know my orders are to transport you and your family to the designated location and to remind you that you have only ten minutes and then we'll take you out of here, ready or not." The soldier's tone wasn't threatening, just matter of fact.

Megan was the first one to react. "Kids, follow me, now!" she demanded and ran to the office which had been set up in a back room.

They followed obediently and saw their mother removing a folder from the filing cabinet which mostly held farm-related paperwork.

Lauren saw the word 'Anvil' in large black letters on the folder.

When their mother opened the folder, the teenage Tanner siblings could see their mother's hands shaking as she started sorting through its contents.

The folder had about twenty different items in it, and Megan quickly pulled out four laminated eight and a half by eleven sheets of paper and handed one to her husband who had come into the room behind the kids. Jake offered his wife a grim smile and immediately sprinted from the room with the form.

"Kids, don't argue, just follow directions. I'll explain what I can when I have time. I don't know if you remember these forms, but about two years ago we went over them and discussed what to do with them. We should've looked at them again, but we didn't get around to it. Each of you needs to go to your room, and under your beds are those two special suitcases I told you never to remove. Take them out and fill them from the list. Don't ask questions. Let me know as soon as you're done. Hurry."

Sensing the tension in their mother's voice, Lauren and Ray headed to their bedrooms. They saw their father inside their parent's bedroom, rapidly filling two suitcases that were identical to the two under each of their beds. While doing this, he was also talking on the telephone. They missed most of the conversation but did hear him say, "I know, and I don't have any details yet, but a family emergency has come up. You'll oversee the farm while I'm away…"

His voice faded out as they reached their own rooms and rapidly started working through the checklists they'd last seen two years before and now barely remembered.

Lauren was in the bathroom grabbing her toothbrush and other personal items when she heard her mother say, "This was never actually supposed to happen." Lauren wasn't sure if her mom was talking to herself, or to her dad, or to one of the soldiers.

The last thing Lauren saw her father do before they left was to carry a full, fifty-pound bag of dog food onto the porch, slice it open with a pocket knife and dump the whole thing next to Sammy's dog bed. As he stepped off the porch, he propped the door open so the dog would be able to come and go as he pleased. It made no sense to her since it would usually take the little Boxer a month and a half to eat that much food.

Once the suitcases were filled, the soldiers loaded them into the van and in a very brief time, they were on the way. The van left the Tanner's home and started for the highway. "Mom, what's going on?" Ray asked.

In the dim light, he could see his mother crying.

His dad was the one who responded. "Kids, about two years ago, the government built a series of underground shelters to be used in case there was ever an attack against our country. We never discovered how we ended up being selected, but we were asked if we would be interested in being guaranteed a space in one of these shelters if there was ever a need. They insisted there would probably never be a reason for us to go to one, but just in case, there was a plan in place to get us there."

"Where is this shelter?" Lauren demanded.

"We don't know. I assume we'll be finding out soon," Jake responded.

"And we don't know what the emergency is that's causing us to have to go to the shelter? Ray inquired.

"That's right."

"Daddy, I'm scared," Lauren admitted.

"Me too, honey."

"Excuse me, folks," the soldier in the passenger seat spoke up. "We have another family to pick up on our way. When we get there, we need you to all remain in the van."

In less than fifteen minutes the van was back on the highway, with the Tanners and a new couple, Steve and Wendy Barnett also on board. The Barnetts seemed to be in a state of shock and had brought minimal luggage. Neither spoke during the trip.

Their journey ended at an old hanger on an Air National Guard base.

They were herded into the hanger, where there were pizzas and beverages available. Each of them was given a yellow armband and instructed to keep it on at all times.

Cots were spread out in the rear of the hanger, and some people were already sleeping on them. Most of the others were walking around and talking. Everyone other than the military personnel wore an armband, and Lauren noticed there were at least four different colors visible.

As they looked for a place to set their stuff, a sudden blasting noise erupted from the PA system. "Blue group, your aircraft is still on schedule for arrival at 1930 hours. Red group, your aircraft has been delayed until 2045 hours and for those of you in the yellow group who are just arriving, be prepared to leave with all your belongings at 2100 hours. Remember, your aircraft will be met by buses, which will take you to final destinations. Please remember that the personnel on duty here have no additional information to provide. Thank you."

The message was repeated with minor adjustments about once every twenty minutes.

During their stay, vans continued to arrive and drop off frightened and confused passengers. Megan saw the same two soldiers who had dropped off her family, return at least once more with other people. While they waited there were several times when a large military transport plane arrived, and several hundred people from their hanger boarded.

Megan wandered around listening to what others were saying, hoping to learn something about their current situation. Unfortunately, it soon became clear that no one knew any more than she did. However, every one of them had a different guess regarding the source of the emergency.

Many people were crying. Everyone was frightened and confused. Repeatedly, she heard people comment about how they'd never actually thought this would happen.

Three hours later, their aircraft arrived, and when they left the hanger, they left behind several hundred people, all members of brown or green groups, who had started showing up after she and her family first arrived.

Chapter 30 – Day 4

General Fitch glanced nervously around the command center. He'd been living here in the mountain for over two years and he wasn't sure if the apprehension he felt was because he'd be leaving what he considered to be home, or because his death was so soon at hand. Because he was sixty, it was impractical for him to tie up valuable space in one of the many shelters throughout the country. The General would be close to eighty years old before it would be safe to leave the facility. Knowing that and having been part of the team which had developed the criteria for people selected for shelter, he hadn't even inquired about getting a space. His most significant regret was that he would never know whether all this hard work had paid off.

Brad Warren stood beside him in the command center. This was only Brad's second time at the mountain; most of the last year and a half had been spent coordinating training for the ten thousand sleepers. They were awaiting the arrival of Travers and RJ who were due sometime in the next hour.

"Were you able to get all your gear stored?" Fitch asked.

"Yeah. It's cramped, but I've seen worse. The hard part was trying to determine what to keep and what to say goodbye to. Actually, I've got it better than most; since Jill and I are bunked together, we have the space for two and that makes it much better. The single quarters are much smaller."

"True, and there are only quarters for seventy-five people. As soon as the sleepers wake up, the equipment comes out of the chambers, and the partitions go up. Most everyone will get an oversized cubicle to live in," Fitch reminded him.

"True. Just thinking about it makes me like my quarters all the more. By the way, are you all packed?"

"Yes, I had to get the commander's quarters cleared out for RJ. I assume she'll move in when she gets here tonight. I have a chopper picking me up later tonight."

"You really have done a fantastic job here Matt." Brad praised.

"Thanks, I had a bunch of excellent people working for me."

While they were talking, Nick, one of the communications techs spoke up. "General, UH-60 inbound from the southeast requesting permission to enter our perimeter and land."

"That should be them," Brad commented.

"Good, grant them permission and have them report up here as soon as they can," Fitch told the technician.

"Yes, sir."

"Is everyone else here?" Brad asked.

"Still waiting on a few stragglers, one of whom is that young nuclear engineer you've been having all the problems with."

"Carter? I should've known. RJ had a chat with him, and he was doing okay for about a week, but then he reverted to his usual arrogant and obnoxious self."

"It sounds like he'll be a real handful; better you than me," the General said with a smile.

Brad rolled his eyes. "Thanks. I'm more than ready to leave him behind. Unfortunately, RJ wants him, but I'm sure that's because she hasn't had to deal with him. I've had more than enough. He's one of the most difficult and unlikeable people I've ever met."

At that time, RJ and Travers walked into the room and Fitch turned his attention to them. "Good evening ladies."

"Good evening. Is everyone here yet?" RJ asked.

"Still waiting on a few, including my problem child," Brad said with another roll of his eyes.

"You may have been right about him," RJ stated. "It's too late now, but I won't hold anything up because of him. If we have to go without him, then so be it." She looked across at Fitch. "How are you feeling, Matt?"

"I can't believe it's almost time. I just wish I could know the final outcome."

"If Carter doesn't show up, we'll take you with us," Travers suggested with a smile.

"Thanks, Amy," Fitch smiled back. Looking at RJ, he added, "Before you relieve me of duty, I want to give you a last look around. There isn't much time to change anything, but I'll answer any last-minute questions you have."

"Sounds good to me," RJ commented, and the four of them left the command center.

They walked to the pressurized door of the first chamber on that floor and looked in. One hundred and fifty sleepers were lying on the pedestal beds. The ends of the tubes and wires were only just visible. Each sleeper was covered by a sheet and RJ shuddered, thinking they all looked dead.

"They've been out for a week now, so far, no incidents. We've been monitoring them from upstairs. There have been no issues with the other chambers, either," Fitch advised.

They moved across the hall and saw the other chamber; this one filled with two dozen different capsules. Some could hold a single person, and others could hold up to ten. Since the lids were closed, it was impossible from this angle to tell that half the capsules were occupied, if it wasn't for the indicator lights on the sides of the capsules. In this chamber alone, there were over two hundred miles of tubing, and almost a hundred thousand different sensors.

The clean sterility of the human sleep chambers was a sharp contrast to what they saw in the animal chamber, located down a short tunnel from the pit. The animals might have been sleeping, but that did nothing to reduce the smell associated with several thousand farm animals crammed in a small space. There was something unsettling about the animals, Fitch thought. Their tubes were clearly visible, connecting to almost every orifice. It was far more disturbing than the dignified way the same thing had been accomplished with the human sleepers.

The four started back up to the main level, and Travers was amazed by what she saw in the pit. The area that just three months ago had been all but wide open was now completely packed with equipment and supplies. The fire apparatus they'd examined wasn't even visible behind the mass of new equipment that had arrived.

There were dozens of Humvees and off-road motorcycles in the foreground. She counted almost as many UH-60 Black Hawk helicopters, and even a few AH-64D Apache gunships.

There were huge cargo planes which she suspected might be C-141's and even a pair of fighter jets. Beyond that, there was a sea of earth moving and construction equipment. Whatever was waiting for them after the sleep, they would be ready.

The group made their way back up to the main level and gathered in the mess hall, where the remaining members of the sleeper project had gathered for a brief celebration. The team enjoyed their last few hours together, sharing stories and many laughs. The whole group grew dead quiet when Amy Travers made a toast to the late James Cowan.

As the food started running out, a double beep sound emitted from the intercom on the wall. RJ walked over to the wall and pushed the button. "RJ."

"General Fitch's helicopter is inbound, should be on the ground in five," a female voice from the command center announced.

"Thanks."

RJ turned and saw Matt getting up from his chair and she walked across to him.

"Well RJ, this place is all yours now," he said.

"Thanks, General." She hugged him briefly before stepping back to allow others to say their goodbyes. The remaining members of the sleep project team were gathering their stuff and heading for the helipad.

"Sir, do you mind if I walk out with you?" Amy questioned.

"Of course not, Amy."

One of the security personnel appeared at the door, taking the General's bags and starting for the elevator.

For the first half of the walk, neither Travers nor Fitch said a word. Finally, Matt Fitch gently placed his arm around her shoulders in a fatherly way. "You scared?"

"No. At least, no more than anyone else is. I keep thinking about Cowan though."

"Me, too. He was a good friend to both of us," Fitch commented.

"Yeah, he was. I was wondering… about his family." Travers paused considering how to word the question she so desperately wanted the answer to.

Before she could ask, Matt finished for her. "Kathy and their son arrived at a shelter this morning. They'll have a good chance."

"Do they know the truth?"

Fitch paused for a second or two. "I went to their house after the funeral. We had a long talk."

Amy knew precisely what he was alluding to, and it helped to know that James' family knew how important what he'd been doing had been.

"I told her about the arrangement we'd made with James the day he died. I told her she could still have a place as a sleeper. She declined, as I knew she would. She'd never leave her son, even if he had a place in a shelter," the General added.

"Good. I'm pleased." She responded.

They walked in silence for a little longer. Approaching the central tunnel, Amy and Matt got into the waiting Humvee and rode it for the quarter mile to the mountain's exit.

They stepped out of the vehicle and paused briefly. "Where are you going to be when it gets here?" Amy asked.

"I'll probably be at the Pentagon with General Draper or possibly the White House Situation Room. We'll be in radio contact with you, for as long as possible."

"Be careful, Matt."

"You too."

They hugged for several moments, before Fitch turned and walked to the helicopter.

Amy leaned against the Humvee until the helicopter was out of sight before she started back.

After she'd parked the Humvee, she set out for the elevator which would take her to the main level. She wanted to check on the status of all the sleep chambers from the remote terminals in the command center, then she would get her quarters in order. As she walked past the pit, someone else was walking toward her from the opposite tunnel entrance. As they both approached the corridor to the elevators, he smiled. Amy could tell the guy was checking her out. A situation she was absolutely not in the mood for.

"Hey babe, can you show me to the command center?" he said.

Travers decided to just ignore him, but he followed her and got into the elevator with her.

"My name is Carter, Dale Carter. What's yours?"

Amy heaved out a sigh. "Dale Carter. I've heard a lot about you."

"Good stuff, I bet.

The elevator doors opened. "Actually, not one word of it was good," Amy responded and walked away.

Chapter 31 – Day 3

Gary Bison stood in the entrance tunnel, watching as the third bus of the evening approached.

Gary had been selected a year ago to be the leader of Shelter Eighty-Seven. Even after all the training and preparation, he still wasn't entirely sure exactly how many shelters there were, but he did know the shelter here in the gypsum mines in Grand Rapids Michigan was considered a Level Three shelter, a large shelter which could hold between one thousand and twelve hundred people for the twenty-year duration.

Level One shelters could accommodate over two thousand five hundred people, and to the best of Gary's knowledge, there were only three or four of them in the country.

As the bus unloaded, Gary watched the passengers disembarking. There was almost no one over thirty years old in the group. There were several families, but none of them had more than two children, and none of those children were under four years old. Each person could bring two suitcases, and in the case of Shelter Eighty-Seven, each individual was provided with a ten by ten living area. In the case of a family, the allocated living space had been doubled.

There were three different cafeterias for the eleven hundred and fifty shelter inhabitants, as along with a well-equipped medical clinic that could deal with most medical and surgical issues. There was a swimming pool and a movie theater, as well as computer facilities and a bowling alley. The fitness center was quite large and there was a large conference center which doubled as a chapel. Two dozen classrooms had been set up which could be used for everything from education to private meetings.

There was an enormous amount of underground storage space which contained everything needed now, and what would be required when this group finally left this underground warren twenty years from now.

The facility was powered by a small nuclear reactor, almost identical in design to the one at the mountain, the only significant difference being that all the automated processes hadn't been put in place since there would be a crew of trained personnel managing the reactor at all times. The reactor was water-cooled, and the water was pumped from the Grand River, two miles away.

Gary was amazed at how this had all been accomplished without anyone at the state or local level becoming aware of what they were doing here. He'd once asked how all this could happen without inspections and proper procedures being followed and was told that a little money in the right places could move mountains.

While he accepted this as truth, Gary never forgot the one inspector who'd come by shortly after he'd asked that question. The man showed up eight or nine months ago and started making inquiries and demanding to see permits. Gary had put him off for as long as possible, explaining that this was a federal disaster shelter, but the young inspector didn't care. All the while Gary was communicating with a person who he knew only as Mr. Roberts. Mr. Roberts' phone number was provided to Gary to use as a resource if any problems arose during preparations.

One morning the inspector was at the gate again demanding access to the facility and was not going to be delayed another day. As the argument began heating up Gary's cell phone rang.

Without answering it, or even looking at it, he handed it to the inspector and told him that the call was for him.

The man had a confused expression as he opened the phone and said a hesitant "Hello?"

The man was listening and getting more and more agitated by the moment. Several times, he tried to interject a comment but was cut off. Each time by a voice that Gary could hear but not quite understand.

After a few moments, the redness left the inspectors face and was replaced by a deathly pale color. He continued to listen for another minute or two and then closed the phone without saying a word. He handed the phone back to Gary and slowly turned and walked to his car.

He was just getting to his car when he turned and looked at Gary with a look of fear in his eyes and said, "Who are..."

He stopped his question and after a long moment got in his car and slowly left.

No one else had come by since, and as curious as Gary was to find out, he never asked anyone who had been on the phone or what was said.

* * *

Gary stopped his reminiscing when the group from the bus approached.

"Mr. Bison. Good to see you again, sir," said a tall black man, who was leading the group. He was carrying a briefcase and was dressed in blue jeans and a white polo shirt, with the logo of a large computer hardware manufacturer on the upper left pocket.

"Senator Collins, welcome back," said Gary, shaking the man's hand.

With an embarrassed laugh, Collins responded. "I don't think I'm going to ever get the hang of being referred to as a senator. Why couldn't they have decided to refer to us as councilmen, or something?"

"I know what you mean; they apparently considered calling all of us site leaders Presidents. Many of us spoke up against that idea, really quick. The thing is, they wanted something with more of an air of authority to it, and senator is what they finally settled on. When you consider the life and death control we'll have over these people, it makes sense for our titles to sound authoritative."

Senator Collins nodded in reluctant agreement, then added, "I almost forgot, I want to introduce you to my wife Jillian, and my daughter Cassandra." As he spoke, he motioned to the two females who'd stopped about five feet behind him and were patiently waiting for the introduction.

Jillian appeared to be about thirty years old and was petite. Gary Bison didn't think she could be any more than five foot four. If Gary's memory was accurate, she was a nurse. Cassandra was about eight years old and was already taking after her father in height. She had long straight black hair that was neatly pulled back into a ponytail.

"I'm glad to meet you both. I've read your files, and it's nice to be able to put a face with the names," Bison said, shaking their hands.

"My dad says you're the boss, is that true?" Cassandra asked.

Gary smiled. "I guess it's true, for the next few years at least, I'll be the boss, after that we might have another boss. But there will be ten other people, including your dad, who will be helping me to do a good job."

Cassandra looked beyond Gary to the entrance of the shelter. She saw the long sloping tunnel which led deep underground. "Is that where we'll be living?"

"Yes, that's where we're all going to live for a while."

"It looks big down there. My mom says that when I can come out of there, I'll be her age."

"That's true; we'll be down there for a long time. But you'll be going to school, and you'll have friends and even finish college."

Before Cassandra could ask any more questions, Jillian spoke up. "It was nice meeting you, Mr. Bison. We'll let you get back to your work, and we'll go and explore our new home."

Gary stayed and greeted a few of the other arriving residents, including Megan and Jake Tanner and their family, and then followed the group back inside. He rode an electric cart down into the shelter where he came across a large open storage area. It was secured with a chain link fence, to keep people from getting into the shelter's provisions.

There was a radiation detector mounted on the wall, and he gave it a cursory glance as he strode by. It was indicating nothing more than normal background radiation currently.

The passage continued down to the main level where all the residential apartments had been set up.

The control center was also on this level, a big room from where all internal cameras and heat and smoke sensors could be monitored, as well as external radiation detectors. There was a console for monitoring the reactor and computer room, and another for communications. From there, they would maintain contact with the other shelters and eventually be contacted by the sleepers upon their awakening.

In the back of the command center was a large conference room, where the Senate and site leader would hold their regular meetings. The next level down held the cafeterias and recreational facilities and in the far back of the shelter, there was even a six-cell jail.

They had a trained, and armed security force, which would provide internal security and the site leader would act as a judge with the Senate as the jury in any problems that came up which warranted judicial proceedings. Incarceration was possible in most situations, but in the more serious of circumstances banishment from the facility could be considered. Gary hoped that banishment from the facility, being sent out into the deadly radiation, would act as a deterrent for most everyone.

He headed to the apartment he and his wife Carley shared with their two sons. When he arrived, he saw that the boys were already in bed and Carley was sitting in the recliner, reading from her bible.

After greeting his wife and pressing a kiss to her forehead, Gary lay down on the bed and thought about what the next few days would bring. The last ten buses would be arriving over the next two days. Then the following day their long imprisonment in this underground shelter would officially begin.

Chapter 32 – Day3

Brad Warren woke feeling tired and unrested. He noticed Jill was already up and gone. Throughout the night, he'd been awake as much as he'd been asleep. He washed up and dressed in the gray jumpsuit which would be the official uniform of the command staff.

Leaving his quarters, he walked down to the main level; RJ was already in the mess hall eating breakfast, she wore an identical jumpsuit. He collected his tray and sat down across from her. RJ looked as tired as he felt.

"Morning. You look tired," he said.

She smiled. "Check in a mirror, you look pretty rough yourself."

"It would explain why I feel this way," he agreed.

"Did you hear Carter arrived last night?"

"No, I hadn't heard. How was his attitude with you?"

RJ smirked when she answered. "When I saw him, Amy had just kicked his ego around a bit, so he was okay. I sent him right to engineering, to get settled in."

"Good, I'll check on him later. Is everyone else here?" Brad asked.

"Yeah, Carter was the last one to arrive."

"That figures. Are we still scheduled to shut the doors today?"

"There's a last-minute delivery expected. Apparently, we're waiting on a bunch of seeds and grains for planting crops. They're almost here, and then we should be able to seal the tunnel doors around noon.

We estimate it'll take forty-eight hours to completely conceal the two entrances."

"Good. Sounds like we're on target," Brad stated.

"Amy is working on getting most of the remaining personnel into their capsules. We need to start our final tests of all the systems."

"Okay. If you don't mind, I'm going to make a quick stop at engineering. I want to make sure there are no problems with our *friend*."

"Let me know how it goes," RJ requested.

Brad turned to the right when they left the Mess Hall and hurried towards the elevator at the end which would take him to engineering. On the way, he stopped at the sleep chamber that housed the capsule he'd be entering in a few days' time.

Amy was already in the chamber, assisting the last member of a ten-person capsule into place. The man was undressed and covered by a sheet which served no real purpose other than to preserve the modesty of the sleepers. He could see the other nine sleepers, but from this angle, he couldn't tell the male to female ratio. Twenty years, naked, that close to other people who you'd only known for a few months at best wasn't a pleasant thought. He knew that if he were in that situation, he'd want a sheet too.

He watched as the IV was started on the sleeper who'd just been added to the capsule. All the man's EKG electrodes were already in place. Another technician reached into the capsule, placing a long catheter tube somewhere Brad didn't want to think about. He decided that he'd seen enough.

As he walked away, he thought back to the catheter tubes and IVs. Would the final sleeper have to hook all that stuff up themselves? He knew that was something he'd never be able to do.

The elevator arrived, and he rode it down to engineering. When the doors opened, he immediately heard yelling. Two of the engineering assistants were hovering near the reactor and seemed to be watching the confrontation.

"Are you a moron? What kind of stupid idea was that? If you were half as smart as you thought you were, you'd know that doing that could easily overwork the cooling pumps!"

When Carter responded his voice had a nervous edge to it. "Easy man, there's nothing to worry about, as long as you closely monitor the pumps, and you'll attain a performance boost of about four percent."

A third voice jumped into the conversation. "Four percent? If you were lucky, you might get three, but that's meaningless. This reactor is already seventy-three percent more powerful than we're going to need. Why would anyone risk taxing the cooling system to gain four percent that isn't even needed? You're an idiot!"

"Gentlemen! What's going on here?" Brad demanded, irritation evident in his voice.

"Carter's messing with the automatic cooling systems. These things are carefully calibrated for safety and efficiency by the manufacturers and meet the requirements of our team. But this IDIOT thinks he can make things better, by ignoring their recommendations and making his own custom changes!" the engineer named Fitzpatrick explained in a frustrated voice.

"Carter, this is the last time I'll discuss this with you. RJ agrees with me that enough is enough. One more incident with you causing problems and we'll kick you out. If the doors are already shut, we'll sleep you and throw you out when it's over. You're far more trouble than you're worth. You need to remember that what you're doing is for the good of a team of ten thousand people. It isn't about you. If you can't think past yourself, then get out now!" Brad turned and stomped out of the engineering area.

RJ was in the control center when Brad returned. "How did it go?"

"They were screaming at each other when I got there. I told Carter that if there's one more incident, he's out. If things go as usual, he'll behave for a day or two. I don't understand how he made it through selection. There had to be better candidates."

RJ remained silent for a few minutes. "His credentials were great. I probably should have booted him, but I thought he would straighten out. Ok, let's sleep him tonight. He's scheduled to be the second on call, right behind Fitzpatrick, for any issues related to the reactor that occurs during the sleep. If he's awakened, he'll need to put himself back out, when the problem is solved. Check with the others; make sure that they're comfortable with him handling issues. If they want, we'll move Waterman to second on call and put Carter last. Also, make sure that he knows the criteria for when to summon help and what he can do on his own.

"Once that's done, turn him over to Amy, she'll show him how to re-attach himself to the sleep systems if needed. Also, tell her to sleep him as soon as she's comfortable with that."

"Sounds good," Brad agreed.

Just as Brad left the room, a beeping emitted from the communications console. "Gate One reports that the last truck we're expecting just entered the compound," A young woman named Abby, at the communications station reported.

"Good, let me know as soon as they're gone," RJ instructed. She rubbed at her temples, wishing she'd managed more sleep.

* * *

A couple of hours later, RJ worked the communications console. A few moments later a voice boomed through the speakers. "Draper here."

"General Draper, this is RJ Anderson at the mountain." The last delivery has arrived. If you don't have anything else coming here, we're going to secure the facility."

"No RJ, we don't have anything else for you Proceed with securing the facility," Draper replied.

"I assume that means the efforts to alter its course haven't been successful?"

"No. For ten days in a row, we've detonated two twenty kiloton warheads, as close to the comet as we could, but they've had no effect.

The last pair detonated six hours ago. It's just moving too fast for us to get the blast close enough."

"Okay, I understand. We'll commence the locking down sequence now. We should be complete in about forty-eight hours, which will give us a good twenty-four hours before it arrives."

"Sounds good to me. General Fitch is here, and we've been discussing it. We want you online with us, two hours before the comet arrives."

"No problem. Are we still expecting arrival at 0930 eastern time?" RJ asked.

"Right about there," Draper agreed.

"Okay, we'll be online at 0730 your time, east coast."

"Good."

RJ disconnected the link and pushed an intercom button. "This is Anderson; we'll start securing the facility in ten minutes. All external personnel must leave immediately." RJ had several armed guards already waiting at the tunnel entrances, while others did a quick sweep of the facility, searching for anyone who might be trying to remain behind. She got up from her seat and headed for the elevator that would take her up to the central tunnel. When she arrived, she saw Amy and Brad had already made their way to the passageway and they too were watching proceedings.

The last of the external workers left the facility, and the word was passed confirming the sweep had successfully ensured everyone had gone.

Four front-end loaders were backed into the tunnel and positioned two at each end, facing outward. The drivers quickly jumped down from the vehicles and they too, exited the facility.

RJ pushed an intercom button on the wall and gave the order to close the doors. Less than a minute later the blast-proof doors at each end of the tunnel started to slowly close. It took almost five full minutes from the time the doors began moving until the time there was the loud metallic *thunk* as they locked into place.

Brad was suddenly overwhelmed by the sensation of being trapped in a tomb. He glanced at RJ and Amy. "What becomes of all those hundreds of people who were working on this place? It seems cruel just kicking them out, knowing they'll be dead in a few days."

RJ shook her head. "You don't need to worry about them. For maintaining secrecy regarding anything they saw here, they all get space for themselves and their families in a shelter about a hundred miles north of here," she explained turning away from the closed blast doors. "If we go to the command center we can at least watch them work."

"True. We aren't accomplishing much here," RJ agreed, as she headed for the elevator.

When the trio entered the command center, Brad activated the eight foot by five-foot LED monitor built into the wall and pulled up a view of the west entrance. He also brought up a view of the east entrance on one of the two smaller screens.

At least a dozen workers busied themselves at each entrance, moving heavy pressure-treated wooden beams into place. These beams would serve as a frame for the huge wall which was being constructed about a foot from the steel blast doors.

Nick a communications technician, was at one of the computer terminals and spoke up. "What's the purpose of the wall?"

RJ explained what was happening outside. "The team outside will collapse the end of the tunnel to disguise the entrance. The wall will keep the dirt and debris from getting into the door mechanism and causing any problem when we try to open them, after the sleep."

They continued to watch off and on throughout most of the day. When night fell, and the workers left, the walls were almost complete.

* * *

The next morning Amy walked into the command center after breakfast.

"What's the status of the sleepers?" RJ asked.

"The only ones awake beside the three of us, are Fitzpatrick in the reactor room, and Abby and Nick here in the command center," Amy answered.

"The reactor is going to run itself for possibly twenty years; two more days won't make a difference. Let's put Fitzpatrick into a capsule. I assume you're going to ride this out?"

"Yeah, I'm going to stick around until it's done. There's a part of me that's expecting to wake everyone up in a week and tell them this was a big false alarm."

"I've thought that too," Brad admitted.

"Amy, you get that guy snoozing, and I'll find us a deck of cards. There isn't much more for us to do. From here on out we're just observers," RJ instructed.

Amy went to the communications center and triggered the intercom. "Fitzpatrick, please report to your sleep capsule. It's bedtime."

As she headed for the door, Brad called out. "You need a hand?"

"Sure, it'll be quicker with two of us," Amy agreed.

* * *

RJ had just headed to the Mess Hall to grab a refill of coffee when she was interrupted by a radio call from the team outside. "Miss Anderson, the demolitions officer wants to talk to you," Abby announced from the communications console.

"Anderson here, what's up?

"I don't know how much this might affect you, but we're ready to blow the ends of the tunnels," the voice replied.

"Thanks for the warning, we're all set."

Brad and Amy returned to the command center and RJ glanced over at them. "They're about to blow the ends of the tunnels. What took so long getting in Fitzpatrick to sleep?".

"It was bad," Brad began. "As soon as he laid down in the capsule and saw the lid closing, he went crazy. I guess he's afraid of confined spaces, he ripped his IV out and was thrashing all over the place."

Amy continued. "We got him out and calmed him down, and I gave him a shot of Ativan. While we were waiting for it to take effect, we cleaned up the blood from where his IV ripped out. When the sedative took effect, we got him back the capsule and put him to sleep."

RJ nodded, wondering how she might react when it came time to sleep. She'd never liked confined spaces either.

They watched as the camera view of the tunnel entrance was instantly swathed in a cloud of dust. When the dust cleared, the tunnel entrance had disappeared.

Small loaders immediately went to work, smoothing out the debris to make it appear more natural. After a few storms and a bit of time, there wouldn't be any evidence that there was a tunnel entrance beyond the debris.

Chapter 33 – Day 0

RJ climbed out of bed and took a long shower. She felt terrible, probably because she'd tossed and turned all night. She dressed in a gray jumpsuit and walked to the mess hall, where Amy already had breakfast cooking. RJ was not hungry but forced herself to eat. They quickly ate and went back to the control room.

"Any news yet?" RJ asked when she entered.

"People all over the world are outside, searching for a place with a good view. Everyone wants to see the comet," Brad said.

"There was also a story a few minutes ago, regarding groups of people who have disappeared over the last few days. They're saying entire families are gone. There are a few unconfirmed reports of military troops showing up and taking people away from their homes. Fortunately, the media is so tied up with the comet story, they aren't paying it too much attention yet," Abby added.

Nick was busy establishing a secure link to Washington, and after a few seconds, General Fitch's face appeared on the screen.

"Good morning, General," RJ said.

"Morning guys. We're in the situation room at the White House. We have a makeshift shelter here, and we're going to remain here with the President through this."

"General, speaking of shelters, how many people are in the shelters now?" Amy asked.

"There are just over one hundred thousand people in shelters, spread across the country. They all have provisions which should last up to twenty years. There is other news. In the end, only one undersea shelter was built, but it's huge. They were expecting to house five thousand people. They were getting ready to start moving people into it when we lost contact two days ago. There's been a large amount of debris found in the area. We haven't had the chance to look further into it, but there is a Navy Deep Submergence Rescue Vehicle in the area. Not sure what we'll be able to do if there are any survivors, but there is a rescue effort underway." Matt Fitch explained solemnly.

Everyone was quiet for a minute as the tragic news sank in.

"Do we have an official countdown in operation?" RJ asked.

"Yes, it's precisely one hour fifty-seven minutes until we should start experiencing the effect, and the celebrations have been going on for hours already. The whole world is getting ready to view this once in a lifetime event. I saw a kid wearing a 'Welcome the Comet' T-shirt last night.

"People are treating this thing like it's the second coming. In fact, a few think it is. Very few are letting the talk of radiation keep them away. Everyone with a camera is awake and outside, ready to capture this glorious event. If only they knew that this thing was going to kill them all.

"The President made a speech an hour ago warning people that the possibility of radiation could be a little more serious than originally expected and suggesting they don't remain outside. Even if they listen, it won't matter unless they find a cave fast."

To RJ, the one hour and forty-seven minutes seemed to take weeks to pass. In the command center, Brad paced quietly the whole time. Amy disappeared and didn't return until there were only two minutes left.

On the large screen was an image of space being transmitted from a large ground-based telescope to Washington and relayed back to the mountain. "There it is," Fitch's voice came through the communications console. They all stared at the monitor and could clearly see the object getting larger by the second.

There were different views on each of the other screens. One of the cameras on the top of the mountain caught a fantastic sight. It was still dark in the Midwest, and as the comet came into view, it lit up the whole sky. Witnesses said that it was as bright as daylight for the few seconds that the comet itself was visible. Because of its massive length, the tail of the comet remained visible for several minutes. In the mountain, they stared at the different views. It was one of the most beautiful things Brad thought he'd ever seen. Then as quickly as it had appeared, it was gone.

On one of the TV monitors, the NBC anchor was showing scenes of massive celebrations occurring all over the world. In one European city, people were running through the streets, waving banners in an unrecognized language and shouting joyfully.

RJ pondered over the images she'd just witnessed. There was nothing remotely menacing about what she'd just seen. Yet she knew that soon, the whole world would stop talking about the beauty of the comet.

Twenty minutes passed quietly, and Amy remembered her earlier thoughts about this being a big false alarm. She wished it had been true.

There was sudden commotion on the monitor screen receiving a live feed from the situation room at the White House. After what seemed like an eternity, General Fitch came and spoke to the transmitter so they could hear him. "Did you hear any of that?"

"No Matt, what's going on?" RJ questioned.

"We received a call from Ramstein Air Force base in Germany. Their ground-based radiation detectors are squawking like crazy. Looks like radiation levels are steadily and rapidly rising over there. It makes sense, as the comet approached, Western Europe was one of the first places to have it travel directly overhead.

Over the next hour, radiation detectors across the United States, Europe, and Japan began sounding a warning. Tracking the radiation wasn't difficult, and it was clear it was spreading swiftly throughout the atmosphere.

World leaders were contacting Washington in a panic, demanding information. They were all provided with a standard response. *There is no indication that the radiation is the result of any kind of weapon activity. We suspect it's a result of the comet which passed Earth earlier today. We are investigating and will release our findings as soon as possible. At this time, we recommend seeking shelter in any Civil Defense Shelter or underground structure available.*

Six hours later, the first reports of people showing up at hospitals with radiation sickness began to filter through.

Ten hours after that, the first fatality related to radiation exposure was reported, when a seventy-six-year-old man, died in Madrid, Spain.

At the same time, it was reported that many hospitals were overflowing with victims suffering from radiation sickness.

Four days later, the radiation had spread throughout the atmosphere, and distress calls were being reported from an Antarctic research station where seven of their fourteen member team were sick.

The following day, it was confirmed that radiation poisoning was rapidly spreading through every nation on Earth.

A week later, there was no response to repeated attempts to contact the Antarctic research station.

It was estimated that seventy percent of the world population was sick, and there had been over six million fatalities. The Chinese and Russian Governments accused President Daniel Anson of knowingly hiding information regarding the comet's danger.

It was at this point RJ shut off the audio and video receivers and ordered her people to leave the command center. Watching the world slowly die was depressing and it was having a heavy impact on all of them.

They gathered in the mess hall, where Brad had prepared a large meal. There was music playing, and RJ intentionally made sure the topic of conversation revolved around memories of the work that had been done in preparing the mountain and the training they'd all endured. As the conversation continued, they found they could laugh a little despite what was happening outside the mountain.

RJ addressed the group. "We've all seen far more of what's happening outside than could be considered healthy. I know there's a part of each of us that wants to open the doors and take our chances. Being safe in here, while everything is collapsing around us makes me feel as if I'm hiding, behaving like a big chicken. But we need to remember the reason we're here - to help the survivors rebuild and to ensure that humanity survives this terrible event. I don't believe there's anything more to be gained from watching what's happening. It's time for all of us to sleep."

Brad thought over her words. Part of him desperately wanted to keep listening to the reports, to hear what was happening to his country and his planet. But RJ was right. There was nothing to gain by hearing another heart-wrenching report or more terrifying statistics. "Reluctantly, I agree with RJ," he said to the group. "It's time."

"I'll contact the White House and inform them of our decision; everyone else should clean up and get to your capsules."

"RJ, do you mind if I talk to Matt? I want to say goodbye," Amy asked.

"No problem. Let's go."

They returned to the command center and activated the communications equipment. It took only a few minutes for General Draper to appear on the screen.

"General, we've decided it's time. The last of us are heading for our sleep capsules," RJ said.

"Good decision. I was going to suggest it the other day, but I figured you'd decide when it was best for yourselves. Good luck RJ, you have a lot of work ahead of you."

"Thank you, General. Is Matt Fitch there? Amy wants to say goodbye."

"I'm sorry, Amy. Matt is ill and he's in with the physician. We don't know yet if it's radiation related. The radiation level is up a little in here, which we weren't expecting, but it's still fairly safe for now."

"I understand General; please tell him I asked for him," Amy asked, struggling to hide her disappointment.

"Will do, and good luck to all of you," Draper responded with a weak smile.

"Thank you, Good luck to all of you, too," RJ said and shut down the transmitter, and activated the recording computers. They would still receive status reports and regular updates, which would all be saved in the database and available when the team woke up.

RJ sat down at the computer terminal and input the command to begin shutting down non-essential systems. When the task was complete, she got to her feet and draped her arm across Amy's shoulders, and the two of them walked to where their capsules waited.

Amy and RJ assisted the others into their capsules and began the sleep process. They then undressed and assisted each other in preparing. They inserted the IV catheters, and the other tubing was hooked up. Each of them then went to their individual capsules, got in, and hooked up the IV, and urinary catheters to the internal systems of the capsule.

RJ hooked her facemask into place. The digital readout in the capsule indicated everything was ready. She glanced at the three buttons on the right. There was a small one that would start the flow of SF016 into her IV, and a larger one that would open and close the lid to the capsule. The largest of the three buttons would administer the drugs needed to help her wake up with fewer side effects. These drugs were supposed to be delivered automatically, but if the automatic delivery system didn't kick in, she could manually administer them herself.

She waited for the signal from Amy, indicating that she too was ready. After a minute, she heard Amy say 'ready', her voice muffled by the mask. She responded with her own 'ready' and heard the motor which operated the lid to Amy's capsule as it started to close. She pushed the button to close the lid to her own capsule.

RJ suffered a wave of panic as the lid to her own capsule closed. The dark transparent panel was only three inches from her face, and she felt trapped. It took all her willpower not to lash out. She closed her eyes and forced herself to take several slow, controlled breaths and calmed slightly. She was aware of the change in atmospheric pressure as the capsule pressurized. She waited until the lights for the lid and pressurization turned green and hesitantly pressed the button to start the flow of SF016 into her vein.

At first, she felt nothing; her anxiety at being confined was again increasing, and she started to consider pushing the button again when she suddenly felt the drugs taking effect. Her arms and legs grew heavy, and she was suddenly more tired than she'd ever been before. She tried to open her eyes but couldn't manage it.

Twenty minutes later, the computer turned off the lights inside the sleep chamber. With the exception of indicator lights on the equipment, everything in the whole mountain went dark.

Chapter 34

Consciousness was slowly returning. He was feeling foggy, and his head was clearing far more slowly than he would have expected. His mouth was extremely dry, his stomach was queasy, and his body ached. He struggled to open his eyes, but they were still too heavy. Worst of all was his breathing. With every breath he took, it seemed as if additional air was being forced into his mouth and nose. He couldn't remember where he was, but there was the soft hum of electrical equipment nearby.

He tried to stretch his arms, but something hard and metallic near his sides was significantly limiting his movement. He reached up to his face and discovered an object covering his mouth and nose. Instantly, panic started to build. Forcing his eyes open, he was briefly blinded by light he hadn't experienced in a long time.

He suddenly realized he was flat on his back, in a very small container. His immediate thought was that this was a coffin and he was in a grave. But there were glowing lights on the walls, and a partially transparent lid rested just inches above his face.

With each second, panic increased and his breathing was getting faster and more erratic.

He knew he needed to force himself to calm down, but the panic overtook any rational thoughts.

Suddenly the revelation of where he actually was hit him, and he remembered how to escape. He whipped his head to the right with so much force he struck his scalp on the console beside him, and blood started gushing from the jagged head wound. He touched his head and the sticky fluid ran down over his fingers. He knew one thing, once he escaped out of this thing, he would never lay in here again.

Ignoring the pain, he located the three green buttons and slammed his hand against the largest of them. For a moment he thought he heard a sound before the large green button began blinking red. The LED readout below the button now displayed three words; *Door Mechanism Failure.*

His sense of horror only increased when he saw that the curved, transparent lid hadn't opened as it should. He frantically started hitting the red button repeatedly, with increasing force, until the button cracked and got jammed inside the console.

He threw his legs up, hoping to push with his feet, but he didn't have the clearance needed in this confined space. Instead, his knee smashed into the lid and pain shot through him. Using his lower legs and knees, he pushed with all his strength, but nothing happened. He placed his palms on the transparency and pushed with both his arms and legs. His right hand left smeared bloody handprints on the clear surface. His last rational move was to press one of the other green buttons desperately hoping it would send him back to sleep. He heard a new sound and knew the sleeping drugs would end the nightmare he'd awakened to. The terror started to fade, but the respite was brief. Moments later, he heard the clear sound of an alarm beeping. He peered at the display, his terror returning when he saw the message *Check IV Flow.* He located the IV tubing where it attached to the wall of his chamber and followed it to the catheter in his arm. The problem was obvious. All his thrashing had mostly pulled the catheter out of his arm and the line was kinked and twisted. Frantically, he attempted to straighten the thin-walled catheter, but in the process pulled it out of his arm completely.

He grabbed the catheter and tried forcing the blood covered tube into the hole in his arm, but it crumpled into a ball when he tried to push it against his skin.

By now, his sense of horror had escalated, and his breathing rate had escalated over a hundred times a minute. He began screaming uncontrollably.

In a desperate effort, the man fought to turn over, thinking if he could just get his legs underneath him, he could push against the lid with his back. The space was much too small though, and he fought to turn his overweight, sweat-soaked frame, first to the side and then face down. Making this last movement, he collapsed face down onto the small mattress and found himself unable to breathe, as if someone was strangling him. Extremely nauseated and shaking uncontrollably, he clawed at his throat, his fingers finding the two hoses connected to the mask over his face. After rolling over, they'd become tightly wrapped around his neck, and he couldn't get them loose. The more he struggled, the more they tightened. Unable to move his head due to the python-like coils around his neck, he frantically kicked out in all directions. Almost immediately, he felt a tremendous pain in his left leg as it connected violently with an angled section of the wall. Despite the pain, he continued kicking uncontrollably until he realized his left leg wasn't striking anything and the pain grew tremendously with each kick. There was a part of his mind that knew he had to stop kicking because his fractured bones were rubbing together just above his ankle, but that part wasn't in any way in control. His head pounded from the lack of blood to his brain, and there was a growing pain in his chest which swiftly moved up into his shoulder. He tried to scream, but no sound came out. His strength faded as he fought to get his arms and legs underneath himself to push with his back, but he collapsed against the mattress again. He was facing the left wall, and he could see out of a small window situated at floor level. The view was filled with hundreds of identical containers, aligned in neat rows. Each of them, he knew, contained another member of his team. He hoped desperately to see just one of those containers open, as his should have done. As consciousness faded, he knew he would never see it happen.

Chapter 35

Her eyes opened slowly, but she couldn't focus. The light was extremely bright, and it was hurting her eyes. She fought to clear her head, but no matter how hard she tried, she couldn't remember where she was. She closed her eyes and rested.

She must have fallen back to sleep because when she woke again, the light was almost as painful as it had been before. She fought to remember. She was inside a container of some kind. It was familiar, but she couldn't remember why she was here.

She tried to open her mouth, but there was something over her face. She tried to take it off, and as she did, she remembered it was a mask. Her arms seemed extremely heavy, and her movements were clumsy and uncoordinated. After much effort, she managed to pull the mask off. She tried to open her mouth, but it was so dry her lips were stuck together. She finally pried them apart and attempted to call out, but no sound came from her throat.

Suddenly, she was aware that she was naked, and now she felt afraid.

The woman rested her head, and slowly the memories started coming. She fought to remember what she was supposed to do; it seemed as if she had to dig deeper and deeper into her own mind for answers that were buried long ago. She remembered the briefing on the effects she would experience. This wasn't at all how it had been described though, and she felt worse than she'd been told she would.

Finally, she remembered about the drugs that would help her feel better. She peered at the digital readout and saw they'd been administered automatically an hour ago, during the wake-up sequence. "Why do I feel so sick?" she thought.

Now all she wanted was to get out of the capsule. She located the large button and reached for it, her arm clumsy and weak, the movement painful. It finally made sense to her why this button was so much larger than the others were. She once had considered inquiring about its size but never got around to asking the question. She now realized that she probably would never have been able to hit the button, if it had been a smaller target for uncoordinated arms. It took several tries, but finally, she pushed it. The motor sprang to life, and the lid opened.

She experienced an immediate sense of relief when the lid was gone and started to move but quickly remembered the equipment she was still hooked to.

It took over twenty minutes to undo all the wires and tubes. The more she moved, the worse she felt. Her whole body was in pain, and she was getting dizzier by the minute.

She had attempted to sit up but grew increasingly nauseated, so she lay back and did what she could while moving as little as possible.

In training, she'd been able to undo all the equipment in less than two minutes. Now she'd needed to stop and rest four times.

Finally, she had all the equipment and tubes removed. She pulled herself up into a sitting position and tried to get out of the capsule. The nausea returned, much worse than before, but she struggled over the two-foot high side and collapsed to the floor of the chamber where she vomited repeatedly. Her well-aged stomach contents had a smell and taste that were completely overpowering.

Just before losing consciousness, RJ Anderson became aware of two things. First, she was lying naked on an extremely cold metal floor, with her face resting in a warm pool of her own foul vomit.

Second, something was very wrong.

Chapter 36

RJ's eyes opened slowly, and again she was confused. She was extremely cold, her face seemed to be stuck to the floor, and she hurt all over. For more than a minute she didn't move. Slowly, she remembered.

She peeled her face from the floor and noticed the vomit had mostly dried. She'd obviously been out for a long while. She sat up carefully, again experiencing some dizziness and nausea. Fortunately, it wasn't as intense this time.

She crawled to the capsule and opened the small built-in drawer underneath with trembling fingers, removing her undergarments and jumpsuit. While sitting on the freezing floor, she dressed as quickly as possible.

She fought to stand and found the dizziness and nausea returning. She fought them both back as best she could and attempted to walk. She quickly discovered she needed to hold onto the wall or some other object to keep from falling.

She kept trying to think of possible reasons why she felt this sick. Two things came to mind. There was a radiation leak in the reactor or a contaminant in the SF016. Either one would be disastrous for her mission.

She started out for the command center; questions flooding her mind. On the way, she stopped at a restroom taking a few minutes to clean as much vomit from her face and hair as she could. She rinsed her mouth out and then drank a little water. She could tell she was dehydrated and assumed much of her dizziness was related to this fact. She needed to go slowly, the nausea was still there, and she did not want to take a chance on it getting worse by drinking too fast.

She stumbled out of the restroom and crossed the hall to the health center. The pain in her joints was increasing with each movement. She located what she was looking for and quickly swallowed down 800mg of Ibuprofen, with a little more water.

She half stumbled from the health center and continued down the hall. Her balance was better, but she stayed close to the wall in case she needed it. She placed her palm on the scanner and heard the electronic voice. "Good Afternoon Miss Anderson." The computer voice seemed incredibly loud.

RJ walked unsteadily to a computer terminal and sat down with a thud. She rested for a moment then started activating the equipment. As she was working, she heard a faint noise by the door she'd entered through. She spun around so quickly she almost fell off the chair.

Someone was standing there.

It was an elderly man. His skin was sickly pale, and his hair was fastened in a long gray ponytail. His light blue shirt was stained and torn in several places, and there were holes in his pants at the knees. He stared at her for a second and then ran for the door.

"Stop!" RJ called as loudly as she could, but her voice came out as little more than a hoarse whisper. She got to her feet and attempted to run, but her balance and coordination weren't up to the task, and she landed face first on the floor.

She scrambled to her feet and went out into the corridor as quickly as she could. She surveyed the length of the hall, but there was no one there.

She hurried back to the computer terminal, punching in instructions to have the system seal and lock all doors within the facility. It meant all doors were now set to open to her hand access only and she also shut off all the lights except those in the command center.

She watched the system readouts carefully. A minute later, it revealed that someone had turned on the lights in the main corridor on the engineering level.

Now she knew where he was. She confirmed all the doors were secured on that level; whoever he was, he was trapped in the hall.

She sat back, confused and nervous. If this man had gotten into the facility, could there be others inside as well?

RJ struggled to her feet and went into her office. She opened the bottom desk drawer and took out the 9mm Beretta semi-automatic pistol she kept there. There was one round in the chamber, and she quickly grabbed the empty magazine from the same drawer and carefully loaded it. All weapons were stored with the magazines empty. Over time, the spring in the magazines will weaken if continually compressed Therefore they could fail to effectively push the rounds up into the chamber, causing the gun to jam.

This was one of the leading causes of a misfire so the emptying of all magazines was the standard procedure for weapon storage before the sleep.

She made sure the safety was on before placing the gun in the large leg pocket on her jumpsuit. She briefly considered going to her quarters for the shoulder holster but decided against it.

When she'd woken up, she'd assumed it was because the computers had determined the radiation levels outside had been safe for the required three-month period. She hadn't even considered the possibility that she might have been awakened for one of the four other possible reasons, one of which was intruder detection.

The computer indicated all doors were still securely closed. RJ activated the cameras in the central tunnel and saw the closed doors and the front-end loaders still in place. Next, she activated the external cameras, and the west camera showed that the giant steel doors were still completely covered with debris. She worked the camera that pointed at the east entrance but couldn't get it to activate. She switched to the backup camera and could see the door was still sealed, but exposed. Most of the dirt and debris, as well as the wooden wall was gone. She zoomed in on the door and could see dents and scratches on the door where someone had used tools in an unsuccessful attempt to gain entry. There were some objects on the ground by the sealed door, but from the camera's angle, she couldn't identify them.

She had to consider that someone might have gotten in through the maintenance passage that came in from the top of the mountain. The passage was used to access the cables which ran in conduits to the radar and antenna. There were several locked hatches to block access to the interior of their fortress though. She activated a camera on the top of the mountain and could see that the dome-shaped cover to the maintenance hatch was locked and in place.

RJ checked the systems readout and could see that the lights in the engineering corridor were still the only ones which had been turned on.

She pulled up the computer logs and reviewed what had initiated the sequence that awakened her. It clearly showed that her awakening had been an automatic response to safe radiation levels outside the mountain for three months.

So, who was the old man and why had the computers failed to respond to his presence?

RJ checked the computer's date and the color drained from her face. The dizziness came swarming back. Her hands flew over the keyboard as she rechecked the information, but the results remained constant. The computer said that the date was October 6, 2084.

The experts had told them radiation levels would return to safe levels in ten to twenty years. RJ reviewed the data three more times, and it became apparent that the radiation levels had only just reached the safe level.

The problem was that they had been asleep for fifty-four years.

Another thought crossed her mind, and she pulled up a list of EKG readings for all the sleepers in the facility. She realized she was holding her breath in fear of what she might find and deliberately took a deep breath, forcing herself into calm. She was greatly relieved to see that only nine units were showing no sign of cardiac activity. Nine out of over ten thousand seemed remarkably good odds. She pulled up a list of names of the possible fatalities and scanned through the data. Most recently added onto the list was her name. This made sense; the EKG electrodes were obviously recording no activity because she'd removed them well over an hour ago. There were two people listed in Main Sleep Chamber One and three in Main Sleep Chamber Two. The final three names on the list were Kelly Meyers, Dale Carter, and Joseph Fitzpatrick.

RJ's frustration increased, nothing was going the way it should have. She stared at the computer for a minute and then thought about Fitzpatrick. He was on the list of people to be awakened in the event of any problem arising. There were others too. Fifty-four years had passed, had anyone been woken to deal with complications during that time?

Again, she worked on the computer. She opened the log containing all information about computer generated wake-up sequences. There were three entries. First was today's event, for which she'd been awakened, and there were two other events listed. They had occurred twelve hours apart, almost thirty years ago when there'd been a failure in the reactor cooling system.

The computer had activated both the backup and reserve cooling systems, but the problem had remained. Consequently, an automatic wakeup sequence command was sent to the nuclear engineer on call which was Joseph Fitzpatrick. He'd been awakened thirty years ago and after twelve hours without Fitzpatrick logging into the system and responding to the alarm, the computer woke the second on-call person, Carter. By this time, the reactor problem was nearing critical.

RJ stared at the screen, trying to make sense of this information. If nothing else, it seemed as if the auto wake-up sequence had worked perfectly.

At some point, Carter and/or Fitzpatrick had apparently dealt with a problem, but now both of their EKGs were showing no cardiac activity in their capsules. Had there been a malfunction when they re-entered the sleep capsules?

Amy had once said they'd neglected to test re-sleeping a subject and had no idea of the effect of returning to sleep.

Then another thought crossed her mind. She got to her feet and quickly headed for the door, comforted by the presence of her weapon in her jumpsuit pocket. She rapidly returned to her sleep chamber and passed by her capsule, stepping around the mostly dry vomit on the floor. She continued toward the back of the room and saw two capsules which had no green indicator lights. One had a blinking standby light, and the other had a glowing red light. She slowly approached the one in standby mode and peered through the clear cover. Carter's capsule was empty.

Next, she went two rows over and stared into Fitzpatrick's capsule. She gasped, staring at the horrifying sight in front of her. There was dried blood smeared all over the inside glass of the capsule, including several bloody handprints. The skeletal remains of Fitzpatrick were lying face down. RJ could clearly see that one of his legs had been broken as were many of the electronics within the capsule. The hoses that connect from the port on the inside of the capsule to the mask on his face were wrapped around the neck. RJ accessed the individual capsule computer and saw the error message from almost thirty years before. DOOR MECHANISM FAILURE.

So that probably explained part of what was happening. The computers woke Fitzpatrick, and he couldn't get out of the capsule due to a mechanical failure. Fitzpatrick had obviously struggled and fought to free himself from the capsule but failed. When he didn't respond, the system woke Carter who had apparently handled the problem. She suspected that due to the nature of the emergency, by the time he discovered what had become of Fitzpatrick, it was too late to help him.

RJ walked two rows over and peeked into the capsule of Kelly Meyers. She remembered Kelly was a nurse who had seemed very friendly and vivacious the one time they'd spoken.

It was clear Kelly had died many years before. Accessing the computer, she confirmed the fatal failure was related to an inappropriate decompression of the capsule.

She was starting to get a picture of what had happened, but she needed more answers.

Chapter 37

RJ Anderson returned to the command center, considering her situation. The answers were being revealed, but the more answers she had, the more questions developed. She had to keep forcing the image of a frantic Fitzpatrick fighting to escape out of her mind.

RJ sat at the terminal and pulled up the status of the reactor. Everything was operational, and radiation levels were within normal limits. Next, she pulled up the communications logs and listened to all incoming transmissions which had come in since they'd gone to sleep.

Two weeks after the sleep began, Matt Fitch had posted a status report. RJ viewed the information and was shocked when she saw the General's face. His hair was thinning, and he looked fatigued. "Hello RJ, Amy, Brad. I must assume that you've successfully completed your sleep if you're hearing this message. The death toll is rising rapidly. The hospitals are virtually useless to the sick. The transportation system has collapsed. There's a lot of anger building up in the media that more wasn't done to help prevent this and provide more shelters. Before the media stops broadcasting, the President is going to announce that there is a group trained for the purpose of rebuilding and that they're housed in a special facility and will begin their work as soon as the radiation reaches normal levels. He won't disclose your location or any other pertinent details. There is a problem. Our experts have reviewed the data and have determined that there's much more radioactive debris in the atmosphere than we'd anticipated; in fact, there's five times as much as our worst-case scenarios had predicted. The radiation levels are much higher than we'd expected, and conditions won't be safe for your awakening for possibly as many as forty to sixty years instead of the anticipated ten to twenty. I linked to your computers and determined that technically, this shouldn't be a problem for you. It's just much longer than we'd calculated, and your equipment isn't designed for use for that period. The reserve supply of SF016 should be enough though, to allow you to make it all the way through. I'll update you as I get more information. Good luck."

The second message was dated one month later. General Draper's face appeared on the screen and RJ was shocked by what she saw. His hair was almost gone, and his face had a sickly gray pallor. "Hello RJ, I just wanted to give an update. I believe Matt explained that the President would be letting the country know you'd be around after the radiation levels stabilized to help in the rebuilding process. That message was sent out about two weeks ago. Since then, almost everything has ground to a halt. The last of the TV broadcasts went off the air a week ago. There's still some stuff circulating on shortwave radio but nothing official."

RJ noticed a drop of blood appear at the end of Draper's nose, and soon his nose was dripping. The General picked up a blood-covered cloth and held it under his nose. "Sorry about that. Many of us are experiencing this kind of thing. As I was saying, we still have contact with each of the emergency shelters. We've lost contact with all foreign governments. There are only two state governments we can still communicate with. To the best of our knowledge, all the hospitals are closed or abandoned. We've had to make brief trips out of the shelter to search for food and supplies, and consequently, we're all sick. Two nights ago, it was Matt Fitch's turn to go. He never returned.

"I know the original plan was for you to contact each of the shelters once you woke up; the problem is that they only had enough supplies for twenty years. It looks as if they're going to run out of supplies twenty to forty years before you wake up and start looking for them. They'll have had to leave their shelters many years before it was safe, so I don't know what you'll find. I wish you luck." With one last, regretful smile, Draper signed off.

There had been no other messages for almost twenty-two years. Then a face RJ had never seen before appeared on the viewscreen. The man appeared to be about fifty years old and had unnaturally pale skin. "I'm Greg Daniels, site leader of Shelter Seventeen located in the White Mountains in New Hampshire. Over the past twenty years, we've lost twenty percent of our shelter's inhabitants to deaths from miscellaneous causes, or because they left the shelter of their own volition. In two instances, it was because the Senate voted to banish them because of crimes committed inside the shelter. These occurrences allowed us to stretch out our food reserves for about another eighteen months. Despite this, we're down to a two-day food supply. In three days, we'll have to head outside and take our chances. Our instruments show the radiation levels were much higher than expected and they've been decreasing at a much slower rate than we were expecting. When we leave here, we'll all be exposed to radiation levels that are still in the red zone. Good luck to you."

There were messages from fourteen other shelters, all with similar stories. All had found ways to extend their food supplies for a period between two to ten years. Most were sending out foraging parties to look for food and bring it back. The more RJ listened, the more depressed she became.

Eventually, she stopped listening to the messages and closed her eyes, resting her head back against the chair.

Several important questions needed to be answered immediately. Why was she so sick, and would the others also be as sick as she was? Was the old man actually Carter, and if so, why did he stay awake? What had he been doing? Most importantly, was anyone alive outside of the mountain?

She decided to try something; reaching for the intercom switch she depressed the button to broadcast on the entire engineering level. "Dale, this is RJ, can you hear me? I want to talk to you."

RJ waited thirty seconds and tried again. "Dale, it seems as if everything here in the mountain is really good, but I need some information. Please talk to me." This time she opened the transmitter on the intercom in the engineering hall. She heard movement, but Dale didn't speak.

"Dale, I don't want to leave you trapped in that hall. I don't think you've done anything wrong, but before I let you out, I need to talk to you."

Now she could hear a muttered voice, which seemed to be speaking, but not clearly.

"Can you speak up Dale? I can't hear you."

There was more movement but then nothing but silence.

She huffed out a frustrated breath. "Okay, Dale, I've got some things to do. I'll be back in a while."

It had reached the point where she'd need assistance, but there were a few things she needed to take care of first.

She walked to the mess hall, heated up a frozen meal, and made some lemonade from concentrate powder and water. After eating her first meal in over half a century, she went to her quarters and took a long hot shower, then put on a clean jumpsuit. She transferred the weapon to the leg pocket on the new outfit and headed to the health center, locating a narrow gurney and some other supplies. She accessed the medical databases and reviewed the drug information she'd learned during her in-depth orientation to the sleep process.

Finally, she rolled the gurney out of the health center and into the sleep chamber where she'd been woken.

Their original plan had been for her to wake Brad Warren after determining they were going to end the sleep. Now things had changed, and she wanted someone who was more familiar with the sleep process to wake up first. She parked the gurney next to Amy Travers' capsule, went to the head of the controls and started inputting commands. Immediately the computer stopped the flow of SF016 into Amy's veins and infused the three drugs designed to ease the wake-up sequence.

Next, the system shut off the special gasses she was breathing so she was now getting pure oxygen from the mask.

RJ watched the display and saw Amy's heart rate and breathing increase. When they'd reached the recommended levels, RJ decompressed the capsule and activated the mechanism that would open the cover. As soon as the capsule was open, RJ removed the urinary catheter and unplugged the EKG wires. Next, she lifted her friend onto the narrow gurney. She switched the mask for a standard oxygen mask and connected it to the oxygen tank clamped to the underside of the gurney.

RJ disconnected the IV tubing which came from inside the capsule at the point where it connected to the catheter in Amy's arm, and plugged in the IV she'd set up and hung on the pole attached to the gurney. She secured the tubing with tape and opened the flow all the way, infusing .9% saline and she intended to run in the whole liter, to help combat the dehydration she suspected Amy would be suffering. She also injected some anti-nausea medication into the line. The medication was one of the three drugs that were automatically infused during the wake-up sequence, but clearly, a second dose was needed to aid in the recovery process.

RJ closed the capsule lid and rolled the gurney with her friend into the health center. Once there, she parked in the Triage area and plugged the oxygen into the wall port to conserve what was in the portable tank.

She found a chair and pulled it up next to the gurney. Within a few minutes, Amy's eyes were starting to flutter.

"Amy, wake up."

It took a few minutes before Amy could open her eyes and focus clearly on her commander.

"I feel awful," Amy finally said. She tried to sit up and quickly fell back onto the gurney as a wave of nausea and dizziness struck her. "I shouldn't be feeling like this."

"Just lay still and rest, it'll take some time to pass. You're dehydrated, I'm giving you fluids, and I also gave you something extra for the nausea," RJ explained with a smile. "You should've seen me, I didn't have any extra fluids or meds, and no one was there to help me through this. I passed out naked on the floor with my face in a pool of my own barf. You're getting it easy."

"But we shouldn't feel this sick. Something went wrong," Amy said, with fear in her voice.

RJ had to strain to hear her. "Yeah, something went wrong. We slept much longer than planned. You once told me that the longer someone slept, the worse they would feel."

RJ stepped away and returned with a paper cup, half full of water. "Just drink a little; I don't want to deal with you puking."

"Thanks, I feel as if I slept two hundred years. How long was it?"

RJ noticed the dramatic improvement in her voice following the few sips of water.

"We were out for fifty-four years," RJ announced bleakly. "There are still many unanswered questions, but it seems the radiation was more intense than estimated."

Amy's eyes widened. "I can't believe the equipment is still functional after this much time. How many sleepers did we lose?"

"It seems we lost six or seven," RJ said.

"Wow, I expected to lose more than that with the twenty-years. I know that sounds awful, but really it's very good statistics. How did the animals do?"

"I haven't checked on them yet," RJ admitted.

The bag of IV fluids was almost empty so RJ shut off the flow and got the tape and gauze pads so she could remove the IV catheter from her friend's arm.

Once the catheter was out and the small bandage in place Amy tried to sit up again. She suffered some mild dizziness and nausea, but it seemed bearable.

RJ helped her to her feet, and Amy immediately grabbed the side of the gurney for support. They worked together to get Amy dressed, and then she sat on the side of the gurney for a minute or two before attempting to stand again, this time with more success.

"It will take you a few minutes to start feeling better. The more I've moved around, the quicker things have improved," RJ explained.

"Where's Brad?"

"Considering the problems with waking up from the sleep, I figured it would be best to change plans and wake you first."

"Makes sense."

Amy moved to the wall and using it for support, she made her way to the sink, where she splashed cold water on her face a few times and rinsed her mouth out, spitting the water into the sink.

"Feel better?" RJ asked.

"A little, but still sick."

"Yeah, it took me over an hour before I didn't feel like I needed to barf. Think you can walk?"

"Yeah. Where to?"

"Let's go to the command center. You can sit for a while, and we can go over some stuff," RJ suggested.

Using RJ's arm for support, the two women walked to the control room. Once they got there, she slumped at a terminal and closed her eyes for several minutes.

"You okay?" RJ asked, leaning against the console.

"Yeah, it's getting better." Amy noticed the weapon in RJ's leg pocket. "Why the gun?"

"When I first woke up and stumbled in here, there was someone already in here."

"No way! Who was it?" Amy asked, sounding a little nervous.

"It was an old man, he looked terrible. I only got a brief look at him. I suspect it's Carter."

"Dale Carter?"

"Yeah, there was a reactor issue twenty-nine years ago, and he was woken by the computers since Fitzpatrick couldn't open his capsule. From what I can figure, Carter never returned to his capsule. I've checked, and there's no sign that anyone has gained access to the mountain," RJ explained.

"Where is he now?" Amy asked as she started punching commands into the computer keyboard.

"I've got him trapped in the engineering hall. All the doors are locked. He won't answer the intercom, but I can hear him moving around."

"What about Fitzpatrick?"

"Dead in his capsule. Looks like he fought to get out, but there was some kind of door failure," RJ explained.

"As freaked out as he was when we put him in there, if he was trapped he probably had a heart attack," Amy surmised.

"I wouldn't be surprised."

"What's our next step?"

"As soon as you're feeling up to it, we need to wake a few more people so we can get started. Do you have any ideas about anything that will help ease the effects of the wake-up?" RJ inquired.

"Yeah, I've already changed the global settings in all the sleep chambers for fluid administration. Gradually over the next twenty-four hours, all sleepers will get an extra liter of fluid, except for those on the command center staff. They're getting theirs much quicker, they should be rehydrated in an hour, and the medication doses for the wake-up sequence have been modified to hopefully keep everyone from feeling as poorly as we did," Amy said, as she continued her work at the keyboard.

"Good, I want Brad and the command center staff awake first, followed by a few people from security and our final reactor engineer. We need to find out what Carter has been doing for thirty years."

"Okay RJ, but I'll be waking one of the physicians next. I don't want to be bringing anyone out and running into problems I can't handle. Is that okay with you?" Amy asked.

RJ thought about it for a moment. "Yeah, but I want to get moving on this. I'll get you some food. That made me feel better quickly, and as soon as you're up to it, we'll wake up your doctor."

Chapter 38

Two hours later RJ and Amy had successfully awakened Doctor Frank Cross, and while Amy was helping him get functional, RJ returned to the command center where she started testing and retesting electronic and mechanical systems. While there, she also reviewed computer logs.

As she was reading a maintenance report, the doors opened and Brad Warren stumbled in.

"Good morning, Brad, you look like crap," RJ said with a smile.

"That's exactly how I feel, but at least I wasn't passed out face first in my own puke," he responded with a wink.

"I can't believe Amy told you that! What else has she told you?" RJ asked.

"Let's see, fifty-four years, seven deaths, Fitzpatrick trapped, good chance there will be no one alive, and Carter is an old man locked in a hallway," Brad said with a smile.

"That's most of it, but I just learned something interesting. I looked at the equipment status, and almost everything is operating on primary systems. Very few things are on backup, and nothing is running on emergency reserve. I thought it was interesting especially when you consider Fitzpatrick and Carter were awakened for a critical failure in a cooling system that Carter repaired. At the time when Carter was awakened, many primary systems had failed over to their backup systems and a few nonessential systems had gone offline. All of those are fully functional now and operating on primary systems. For the last thirty years, it would seem Carter has been maintaining all the systems."

"That might explain why he stayed awake," Brad said. "We need to talk to him."

"That might be a problem. For the first twelve years or so that he was awake, he kept meticulous repair notes. For seven or eight years after that, the notes were there, but much less complete. This change seems to have happened gradually over several years. Then all his notes started appearing in a language that I don't recognize, but I think it might be German. For the past three years, there are almost none and what notes there are, make no sense at all."

"Do you think he went nuts?" Brad asked.

"I think so, but nobody would be surprised; trapped alone for thirty years with no one to talk to and you can't even go outside. The disturbing part is that just before the change in his record keeping stopped, there's a comment in the notes. It says, 'I'm sorry, I didn't mean to kill her, I just needed someone to talk to'."

"Do you think he's talking about Kelly Meyers?" Brad asked.

"I suspect so – if you don't know what you're doing and you depressurize a capsule too quickly, you'll kill the occupant. After years alone, he became so desperate he was willing to wake someone, and he accidentally killed her. I suspect that finally pushed him over the edge." As RJ spoke the two technicians, Abby and Nick entered the command center, using each other for support.

"Good morning," RJ said cheerfully. "The good news is I've been awake for six hours and I'm feeling almost normal. The bad news is that the first two hours are terrible."

"Thanks," they responded, almost in unison.

"Take a seat and relax for a little while. When you're feeling up to it, I need one of you to finish checking all the internal systems. I've completed all the sleep chambers except for the animal chamber, and I need the other of you to begin checking all external sensors. Learn everything you can about outside conditions and graph out what the computers have been tracking outside while we've been asleep. Also, start monitoring for radio communications and see if you can hit any of the five satellites they put up there for us. I'm not too optimistic about them but see what happens."

The satellites had been designed for the sleepers and built with exceptional radiation shielding. They were to use minimal power and orbit, waiting for a signal from the sleepers, at which time they would jettison the heavy radiation shielding and fully power up. They would be available for observation and communications. They were launched just 1 week before the comet passed the Earth.

"While you're doing that, we'll head down to the engineering level. Are you ready to move yet?" she asked Brad.

"Yeah, I should be okay."

She helped him up, and they slowly left the room. At the health center, they acquired the same gurney they'd been using to remove sleepers from the capsules, as well as Dr. Stephen Cross.

They took the elevator to the lower level and saw that the door between the elevator and the rest of the corridor was closed.

"Good Afternoon, Miss Anderson," the computerized voice said, and the door slid open.

Standing in the middle of the corridor, staring at them, was Dale Carter. His hair was long and gray, and his skin had an almost deathly pale look to it. He was so thin RJ almost wondered if he'd eaten anything during the past thirty years. His eyes were wild, and he seemed utterly terrified. As soon as he saw them, he ran to the far end of the corridor and curled into a ball in the corner.

Brad slowly approached with the other two a pace or two behind him. "Dale, it's me, Brad Warren."

Carter started whimpering, but wouldn't look at them.

Brad spoke again. "I bet it was lonely being here all by yourself for such a long time. I understand you've been busy, taking care of everything while we were sleeping."

All three saw Dale slowly nod his head.

"Why don't you come upstairs with us, we want to thank you for everything you did," RJ commented softly.

Dale started shaking his head almost violently. The three of them moved closer, and they saw the elderly man's body grow rigid. Without warning he leapt to his feet and charged the group, an almost animal-like growl coming from his throat as he ran.

Brad and RJ grabbed him as he tried to force his way past them. It was clear to all three of them that Carter was not trying to hurt them, but instead to get away from them.

As they struggled in the hall, Dr. Cross rammed a needle into Carter's leg and quickly pushed the plunger on the 3cc syringe attached to it. Carter yelled, and the three of them succeeded in pushing him back against the far wall before retreating down the corridor. Carter seemed satisfied that they were leaving and didn't pursue his attempts to get past them. They exited the corridor and closed the door behind them, all breathing heavily after the confrontation.

Brad spoke first. "What did you give him, Doc?"

"It was a dose of Ativan. Now we wait fifteen minutes, and he'll be more cooperative."

"Fine with me," RJ agreed.

Fifteen minutes later, they re-entered the corridor and found Dale sitting in the corner. He didn't react as they approached and put up minimal resistance as they moved him onto the gurney. They wheeled him to the health center and placed him in a standard bed in the triage area, applying leather restraints to keep him subdued.

RJ and Brad returned to the command center, where the staff was still busy completing their tasks. "What have you got so far?" RJ questioned.

"So far, I can tell you that animal losses are significantly higher than human. It looks like we lost ten percent of the chickens and three percent of the pigs. On a good note, we lost less than one percent of the cows. All the systems down there are working okay. Actually, it seems like all the systems in the whole mountain are doing well," Abby explained.

There was a beep from the internal communications system. Nick responded and listened to a message through his headset.

"Miss Anderson, reactor room on the intercom for you."

RJ spoke up. "This is Anderson."

"RJ, this is Dan Waterman in the reactor room. I don't know exactly what Carter has done, but there have been some unusual repairs made. I'm not saying he did the wrong thing; I haven't had an opportunity to review his notes yet. At this point, we're doing fine here, but it's going to take a while to understand what's been done."

"Thanks for the report, Dan. One of your trainees will be awoken later tonight, or at latest, in the morning. Let me know what else you find."

"Thanks, RJ. Is there a chance of my talking to Carter? It might make things here easier to understand."

"He's heavily sedated right now. I tried to talk to him earlier, but he didn't seem to be capable of conversing. I'll let medical know you need some time with him, as soon as he's ready."

"Thanks."

Waterman clicked off, and RJ turned Brad. "I need you to get one or two people to help you and conduct a room by room visual inspection of the entire facility. Who knows what else Carter has done over the last thirty years."

"Good idea. I'll let you know what I find," Brad agreed, heading for the door.

"Okay, what else have you two found?" RJ asked the team at the consoles.

"Outside temperature is seventy-nine degrees, which is within normal parameters for this time of year. Humidity is thirty-four percent; sun position matches up with the date and time the computers are displaying. Radiation is still present, currently sitting at about seventy-five roentgens. Not great, but just within our safety limits. Looking back over the past fifty years of data, there are no signs of significant climatic changes. Radiation levels apparently peaked around twenty-five hundred roentgens, which is fifty percent more than anticipated.

That happened roughly six months after the comet passed, and they've been slowly, but steadily decreasing ever since," Nick reported.

"Sixty percent of the external cameras are operational, but there's a large blind spot along the northern perimeter where five cameras are down. It looks like the external buildings are in fairly good shape; they need some work, but they're not too bad considering how much time has passed." Abby added. "Also, Miss Anderson, all radio frequencies are a negative. We're continuing to scan the entire spectrum, but there's nothing out there. We aren't transmitting currently, just listening. Oh, and I've sent the wake-up code to the satellites repeatedly, and so far I'm not getting much. Number Four sent the expected response, but it was weak and since then we've had nothing else."

"Okay, keep monitoring and working on those satellites. Start transmitting our pre-planned message first thing in the morning," RJ instructed.

"One other thing; I was reviewing computer logs from during the sleep period. Things were very quiet for the first twenty-five years, which is to be expected, and then there was a sudden increase in activity. It seems Mr. Carter made heavy use of the computers for many years. I don't have all the details yet, but he used them to learn how to repair everything from the facilities computers, to the air conditioning system. It also seems as if he taught himself the basics of medicine and he studied six foreign languages. During the past six years or so his computer usage significantly declined, and he hasn't touched them at all in the last year."

"Good, that helps. Please get me a complete breakdown of what he worked on during those years," RJ instructed.

Brad entered the command center again, pulling up a chair and dropping into it. "All I did was take a leisurely walk around this place, and I feel like I ran ten miles. I hope this clears up soon."

RJ smiled and wheeled her chair across to him. "Find anything interesting?"

"The whole place smells a bit musty, but structurally we're in great shape. In most places, it seems as if nothing's been disturbed. Carter obviously spent some time down in the pit. I could see where he opened containers to get tools and spare parts for his maintenance work. He obviously got bored, too. He didn't do much damage, but he got into some stuff, I'm not sure what yet. The strangest thing is, there's a Humvee down there which has been completely disassembled. Not beaten up, just neatly taken apart."

"That's weird!" RJ commented. "But I guess if you've got thirty years to kill, you have to entertain yourself somehow. Did he mess with anything else?"

"Two of the pigs and five chickens have been removed from the animal chamber. I also found bloodstains in the main kitchen by the mess hall, so I think he butchered and ate them. Other than that, not much else was disturbed. It seems as if he got into stuff, but put it back later."

"What's left of our food supply?"

"It looks like he was trying to be careful regarding how much he ate. He made a dent in the food supplies, but it's a small dent," Brad explained.

"Good. From what I can tell, if Carter hadn't stayed awake and dealt with the issues he did, many of us would've repeatedly been awakened – or worse. He's really made a big difference to how everything came together," RJ admitted. "Considering what a pain he was fifty-four years ago, it seems we owe him a great debt."

"Yeah. He worked for thirty years to make sure we made it through and now when we finally wake-up, he's completely out of his mind," Brad commented quietly.

Chapter 39

Brad and Amy walked into the command center looking much better the following morning. They'd both slept well the night before, a fact that seemed somewhat ironic considering they'd just awakened from a fifty-four-year slumber.

Brad was feeling completely normal; the effects of the extended sleep all but gone. He'd enjoyed harassing Amy at breakfast, telling her she looked good for someone who'd been born eighty-six years earlier. The comment had earned him a sizeable bruise on his upper arm.

RJ was already in her office, studying reports regarding the mountain's status.

"What's new, RJ?" Brad asked cheerfully.

"Not much. I tried talking to Carter this morning, but he's still out of it. Doc says he was malnourished and hasn't been taking good care of himself. He was awake, but he didn't seem to know who I was." RJ glanced up from her reports. "We started broadcasting a greeting about twenty minutes ago. It's transmitting on all frequencies once every three minutes."

"Is there anything new on the satellites? Amy Travers asked.

"Nothing yet. What's going on in your areas?"

"All two hundred members of the primary team are awake, and work has begun on dismantling the two chambers on this floor. We'll have those rooms refurbished as personal quarters as soon as possible," Amy explained.

"All personnel are checking out their specific areas of responsibility and making sure everything's in order. There are teams in the pit, prepping for us to re-join the world," Brad added.

"Good, let's get this going then." RJ reached out and depressed the intercom button. "All personnel, this is Anderson. Prepare to open outer doors." RJ got up from her seat. "Let's go watch," she suggested, and the others followed her out to the central tunnel.

Upon reaching the central tunnel, crews were already sitting in the two loaders, waiting for the orders to start up the engines. Eight Humvees were being removed from the pit on the elevator, four facing one end of the tunnel, the other four facing the other. Half a dozen heavily armed soldiers in full combat gear sat in each vehicle.

Once everyone was in position, RJ contacted the command center and gave the order for the large west doors to be opened. In moments, a grinding sound erupted in the tunnel as the massive doors started to part. Once the doors were moving, the engines of the two front-end loaders facing west roared to life.

As the door moved, the wooden wall became visible a few inches beyond. It was bulging inwards, and many of the support beams appeared to have partially rotted through. The wall had been intended to last thirty years less than it had, and its condition confirmed this. The two loaders approached the wall, lifting their buckets high in the air. Once the buckets rested on the upper supports, the operators slowly increased pressure as they lowered them. The weakened supports quickly gave way, and the old wall caved inwards under a heavy load of dirt. Both machines swiftly went to work, removing the dirt, stone, and broken wood.

The same effort was underway at the smaller east tunnel entrance, but when the doors opened the loaders had a much easier time, as the wall, and much of the dirt was already gone.

When the loaders had cleared a large enough opening, they moved out of the way and the Humvees raced past them, exiting the tunnel. Once the vehicles had cleared the tunnel entrance, the loaders returned to their task, pushing all the debris out of the tunnel entrance, and into a large, neat pile.

The exiting Humvees split off, going in different directions and dropping off soldiers every two hundred yards along the perimeter fence. These men and women would inspect the grounds and the fence, making notes of any issues which needed immediate attention. As soon as this mission was complete, they would remain on guard until the intrusion detection system was operational again and all repairs had been made. The next step was for two Humvees to head out for the residential quarters outside the west entrance, where their crews would ensure the buildings were unoccupied. They had also been tasked with making preliminary reports regarding the structural integrity of the buildings to help determine what would be needed to make them habitable again.

The last two Humvees and their occupants were tasked with guarding the east and west gates. Immediately after they'd secured the gates, the guards retrieved collapsible poles from inside the Humvees and extended them to their full ten-foot length. The poles were clamped securely to the side of each gatehouse, and an American flag was raised on each.

Technically, there wasn't a US government anymore, and the act of raising the flag was strictly symbolic, but RJ had insisted on it, certain it would boost her team's morale.

Two hours later, Brad appeared at the door to RJ's office. "I got the report for you."

"Good. What have they found?"

"There's minor damage to the perimeter fence which will be repaired by tonight. The intrusion detection system is functional, but it's been turned back off so the fence repairs can be made. I've got a team working on the perimeter cameras, they'll be online again tomorrow. We have communications with both guard posts, the one on the east end is in rough shape and needs some work. We can't get any power out there yet, but we'll move a small generator out there temporarily. Westside is in good shape, they've got phone and radio communications."

"Sounds good. Actually, it's much better than I'd feared," RJ admitted.

"I agree. I suspected it would be much worse. It looks like someone tried to gain access through the East tunnel doors after we were asleep. They dug their way in, to the doors and then tried to cut through."

"Did they do much damage?"

"No. Only minor damage, nothing we need to worry about immediately. They were using saws to try to cut their way in, there was also the remains of an acetylene torch."

"How about the residential quarters?" RJ asked.

"It looks like there has been no human or animal habitation. They'll need some work, preliminary reports estimate only ten percent of the rooms are habitable," Brad explained. "I have a repair team on the way out to see what will be needed and estimate a time frame."

"Excellent. When will we be ready to move beyond the perimeter?"

"Hopefully, after lunch. We're getting the equipment checked out now. Have you gotten anything from communications yet?"

"Nope. We're still transmitting on all frequencies, but nothing," RJ explained.

"RJ, I've asked everyone who's been to the perimeter, and there's been no sign of animal life; a few insects, but nothing else." Brad's voice had taken on a concerned tone.

RJ nodded but remained mute on the subject, and Brad could read the concern in her eyes.

Finally, RJ spoke. "Let's see if we can get anything out of Carter, by then it'll be time for lunch."

They entered the health center and strode into the triage area. The first person they discovered was Abby, lying on a hospital bed and trying to look relaxed. A needle in her arm was attached to blood-filled tubing which was slowly filling a donation bag.

"I see you're doing your duty," Brad announced with a bright smile. All the sleepers were required to immediately begin donating blood, to build up a ready supply in their blood bank.

"Since I hate needles so much, I figured it would be better to be one of the first, that way I wouldn't spend the next few days thinking about it," Abby explained.

After some good-natured teasing, Brad followed RJ over to where Carter was resting.

He was lying in a standard hospital bed, an IV in his right hand. He'd been cleaned up and shaven, but he still had an unhealthy pallor.

A nurse approached. "He's awake, but I wouldn't be too hopeful. You can talk to him but if he gets agitated, I'll have to ask you to leave."

They thanked her and slowly approached the bed. "Hey Dale, how are you feeling?" Brad asked in a quiet voice.

Dale whipped his head around at the sound; his eyes wild with fear.

RJ reached out and took hold of his hand. At first, he tried to pull away, but then he relaxed. The fear slowly receded from his expression and was replaced with sorrow. "Ich abwarten lange," Dale said sadly.

Brad and RJ glanced at each other. "I'm sorry Dale, I don't understand. Can you say that in English?" RJ said.

Confusion crossed Dale's face and there was a long pause before he spoke again. "I waited for so long. Long, long time."

"I know Dale. You waited by yourself for a very long time."

"I waited. I was lonely, but I waited," Dale said.

"You took care of all of us while we slept," RJ responded.

"I waited and waited and waited, but you never came."

"We're here now."

"I was so lonely."

"Dale, do you remember my name?" RJ asked.

"I waited and waited, and I was so lonely." Tears welled in Dale's eyes as he spoke.

"Dale, do you remember my name?" RJ repeated.

Dale didn't react.

Chapter 40

RJ returned to the central tunnel after lunch to find Amy, Jill Warren and Jill's Weapons Officer, Steve Perk going over the plans for the afternoon's scouting mission. Perk and another man who'd joined the group were both dressed in flight suits.

Two UH-60L Black Hawk helicopters were in the process of being towed through the tunnel to the landing pad and Jill's AH-64D Apache Helicopter gunship was riding the elevator up out of the pit.

Eight Humvees were lined up outside, four at each gate. They would split into teams of two, each containing six heavily armed soldiers and this afternoon's mission was to proceed to any nearby towns within a forty-mile radius and commence reconnaissance.

The Black Hawks had two functions. They too would be scouting the area, going out as far as one hundred mile radius, seeking signs of life. They'd been armed with miniguns and rockets and would provide support to the ground teams if they ran into trouble.

The Apache Gunship was backup in case any teams got into trouble. Heavily armed with its 30MM M230 chaingun cannon and 70 Hydra (2.75 inch) folding-fin rockets, as well as air-to-ground Hell Fire missiles, it would be a comfort to those going into the unknown. With luck, RJ thought, the only thing the Apache would do today was a brief test flight to ensure all systems were operational.

Forty minutes later, the Humvees passed out through the gates, and the rotors of the Black Hawks started turning. The Humvees rapidly drove towards the highway, although there were several occasions where they needed to go off-road due to obstructions and damage to the road.

Just knowing that there were ten extra people available aboard the armed helicopter was very reassuring for the ground force.

To a casual observer, these newcomers would look like an aggressor force, but the reality was that they were there to make initial contact and scout out the area. The goal was to befriend any survivors and work with them, to learn and rebuild a modern society.

One fact was simple, only fools would wander into the unknown without the means to defend themselves, and these teams were more than ready to protect themselves if needed. The reinforcements aboard the Black Hawks were more heavily armed, just in case everyone's expectations were wrong.

Alpha Team, led by Sergeant Davis, entered the town of Merrillville, comforted by hearing the sound of the Black Hawk's twin T700-GE-701C turboshaft engines overhead. The town that had once had a population of close to five thousand was now a ghost town. Most of the buildings were in terrible condition after more than fifty years without maintenance. Many had collapsed, and most of the others were missing parts of their roofs. The rusted hulks of cars were everywhere; the Humvees had to push several out of the way because they were blocking the streets.

Sargent Davis was surprised by how many of the cars had bodies in them. It seemed that in the final days of the disaster, many people had been trying to escape to anywhere, running from a death which was inevitable. Most of the bodies strapped into the cars were nothing more than clothing-covered skeletons. In a heavily rusted Ford Windstar minivan, the team saw a tiny skeleton still strapped into a car seat. A faded bonnet rested on the top of the baby's head.

Sergeant Davis led them into the first building they reached, the town's hardware store. The front door was locked, so they went around to the rear of the building and forced the back door open. Afterward, Davis couldn't explain why he'd chosen to go through the back, other than to say it just seemed wrong to smash in the front entrance. They entered the building and looked around, discovering a thick layer of dust on every surface. Tools still filled the shelves and hung on the walls. Davis picked up a DeWalt cordless drill, recalling how he'd considered buying one identical to this... fifty-four years before. He put it back down, unable to think of a single thing he could do with it now.

There was some damage overhead, where water had leaked in through holes that had developed in the roof, otherwise, the place was in excellent condition. With a couple of days of effort and a new roof, the store could easily reopen for business. After several minutes recording the condition of the store, Davis determined there were no signs of life and ordered his team to leave through the same door they'd entered.

Next door to the hardware store was Jack's Pizza, the name still clearly legible on the large front glass window. There was a wood framed door beside the window and the store hours were printed in marker on a small red and white plastic sign attached to the glass. The rest of the front wall was in fair shape, but beyond that the roof had caved in at some point, pushing the sidewalls out and partially collapsing the back wall.

The next building was a medium-sized ranch house, with white seamless vinyl siding and the rusted remains of a Ford Explorer in the driveway. When Davis reached for the doorknob, he experienced a ridiculous urge to knock before entering. Knowing the rest of his team would give him grief, he resisted the urge and grasping the doorknob, used his shoulder to push against the partially rotted wooden door. He met with a small amount of resistance and when Davis had pushed his way through, the team saw that the obstruction had been caused by a small skeleton. There was a moment of confusion regarding the shape and size of the skeleton until they saw tufts of fur and a red nylon collar around its neck. Three identification tags were attached to the collar. One of his team member's slowly crouched down and checked the tags. "His name was Guido," he announced.

Davis surveyed the area. They had entered a kitchen, which at first glance seemed to have held up well over the years. On the counter by the window, a man's watch rested. Davis picked up the watch and recognized it as one identical to what his brother wore. It had a titanium finish, and its battery could be recharged by any light source. His brother had once told him that as long as it got some regular exposure to everyday light, it would keep going forever. Davis checked and saw that even with the light coating of dust, it was indeed still running, and the time was very close to being accurate, even after fifty-four years. He reverently placed the watch back, exactly where he'd found it.

The team moved further into the house. Several of the windows had been broken, and there was extensive damage from the weather after so many years. Davis inhaled, and a musty, unpleasant odor got caught in his nostrils, worsening as they went deeper inside. In the living room, there was a faded portrait on the wall of a happy couple, who appeared to be in their sixties. In the photo, they were formally dressed, and there was a handsome German Sheppard sitting obediently at their feet.

Davis moved slowly, and in places could feel the floor was spongy beneath his feet. "Why don't the rest of you head back out, I'm not too comfortable with the strength of this floor. Daniels, come with me. We'll take a quick look around the rest of the house and be right out," Davis instructed.

The two men continued working their way through the house and came across a bedroom. It was dark in the room, but Davis could still make out the scene before him. There were two people in the bed, and he suspected the one on the right was female, judging by the remains of her nightshirt. There was nothing left of either body, other than clothing, bones, and some hair. The one on the right was shirtless, and his right arm was bent upwards, resting on the pillow next to his head. Still clutched in the remains of his hand was a small caliber handgun. There was a hole in the side of the skull, just above the right ear.

Daniels gently peeled back the covers from the woman's body and pointed out how stained the sheets were from the fluids which had no doubt leaked from the body as it decomposed. He carefully examined the head and then the torso, but there weren't any signs of bullet wounds or any other kind trauma.

For the next two hours, Davis and his team investigated buildings in the small town, visiting perhaps fifteen more home and twice as many businesses. In almost every building they encountered skeletons, but no living people. It appeared there hadn't been anyone around for many, many years.

Sergeant Davis was getting ready to head back to their rendezvous point at the town square when he decided to check out one last building. His team entered the Baptist Church which was situated on the south side of the town.

Entering the wooden structure, Davis was stunned by what they discovered. Across the top of every pew was sheets of plywood, laid out as makeshift beds. There was a skeleton on every single board. A count by Daniels confirmed there were at least a hundred skeletons in the old church. At first, the sight seemed incomprehensible, but quickly the picture came into focus. When the local hospital had gotten overloaded, many of the townsfolk had brought the sick and dying here, either because this was the only other organized group trying to help them, or because they knew that divine intervention was the only possible hope in what was a hopeless situation.

His men were staring in shocked silence at the spectacle before them when there was a sudden clatter from the back of the sanctuary. They all looked up in time to see a brief movement. Not sure what was going on, several of his team members raced forward while the rest ran outside to cut off any escape route.

Davis was hurrying around the side of the church when he saw what had to be the world's ugliest cat. It slipped out through a hole in a window and disappeared into some overgrown hedges. The rest of his team raced out a side door in pursuit of the hideous-looking feline but after five minutes of searching, it was clear the cat was gone and wouldn't be back anytime soon.

Later in his report, Davis admitted this was the first animal life they'd seen that day, and as much as he disliked them, for the first time in his life he was actually glad to have seen a cat.

Chapter 41

As the day wore on, the teams all provided similar reports – no human sightings. There had been some insects seen though, and one group had apparently seen some birds.

Amy Travers was circling above Delta team when there was a sudden rush of radio traffic. The team reported that they'd found something… or someone. After several minutes it became clear there were fresh human footprints in the town visible in some fine sand which had blown in from the desert. The team was certain the tracks couldn't be more than a day or two old.

Amy could hear the excitement growing in the men's voices on the ground, but for the next two hours they'd searched and come up with nothing. Now it was time for the ground teams to return to the mountain. Darkness was closing in, and RJ had given clear orders that all ground teams needed to be in by dark.

The aircraft had a little time to themselves now, since they wouldn't be needed to cover the ground forces. While they also had orders to return by dark, they could afford to spend some time searching the area before turning back due to their swifter speed.

As Amy flew, she used the thermal imaging scanners to try and locate any heat sources on the ground which might indicate there were people in the area. If she located anything, it would make a good starting point for tomorrow's search efforts.

Amy had been watching a large storm building on the radar for the past hour or so. Suddenly there was lots of lightning in the immediate vicinity, and the wind speed increased dramatically. Controlling the aircraft was becoming more challenging. Like it or not Amy knew it was time to head back, so she increased her altitude and speed and started back toward the mountain.

Flying on, something on the instrument panel caught her eye. On the ground below, was a thermal image, much hotter than the surrounding area. She stared at the image for a moment or two; it almost seemed as if there were two hot objects down there and they were in motion.

Despite the storm battering the chopper, Amy was holding her own against it and she decided to risk a quick look. She dropped altitude rapidly, quickly coming into visual range of the objects.

It took her a minute to figure what was going on. Two motorcycles were being ridden in circles around a group of three people. The bikers were striking at the group with pipes or clubs, and the group was huddled together, trying to protect each other. The heat from the engines of the bikes is what she had seen on her screen.

Amy suspected the noise of the bikes and the wind and rain of the storm had prevented anyone on the ground hearing the helicopter's approach. Now though, Amy dropped low to the ground and rapidly approached the group. One of the bikers suddenly noticed the approaching helicopter and signaled to his partner. The two bikes sped off toward the west.

Amy dropped the HU-60 to about twenty-five feet above the ground. She kept the nose of the aircraft pointed towards the two bikers, who'd come to a stop about fifty yards away and were watching her movements curiously.

Four ropes dropped down from the helicopter, and in seconds, eight men rappelled to the ground. When they reached the wet sand below, six of the men spread out and formed a perimeter around the three people who had been attacked. They dropped to the ground in a prone position, automatic weapons pointed outward and fingers on triggers.

The other two approached the three in the middle of the circle and began assessing their injuries.

While this was transpiring, the two figures on motorcycles stared on with expressions of amazement. Having seen the two viciously attacking the unarmed people, Amy almost wanted them to draw a gun and start shooting. If they did, she would be justified in pressing the trigger button her finger rested on. The action would release a pair of high explosive rockets, which would easily obliterate both the men and the machines they were sitting on.

The two bikes accelerated abruptly and turned away, moving out into the desert swiftly. "Ground 1, targets are gone. Report your status," Amy requested.

"We're prepping three civilians for transport. We'll be ready in three."

"Acknowledging three minutes, I'll sweep the area once to make sure there are no more of them. Be quick, the weather is getting worse."

Amy flew a quick circle several hundred meters out from the people on the ground. When she was comfortable that there were no additional threats, she landed the aircraft, and the men came aboard with their three patients. All three were lying on portable stretchers and quickly secured inside the helicopter. Less than a minute after touching down, they were back in the air.

As the aircraft rose, Amy could feel the forces of the storm pushing them down and toward a steep wall of rock. She fought the machine and kept it under control, gaining speed and altitude. As they moved faster and higher, the threat from the storm diminished, and Amy was able to get her airspeed up closer to the 160mph maximum cruising speed. When she had the chance, Amy glanced back and the men working on the injured people they'd rescued.

"Give me a report on their condition, and I'll pass on the information to the mountain," Amy instructed over her headset. Once the team leader reported the information back, Amy radioed the information through. "Mountain Base this is Air Two" she called into the radio.

"Air Two, this Mountain Base, go ahead."

"Inbound with three civilian casualties, ETA twenty minutes. We need priority clearance on the landing pad. Stand by to copy patient's conditions for medical."

"Go ahead when ready Air Two," Nick's voice responded.

"Patient one is approximately a thirty-year-old female, who was being attacked with clubs when we found her. She's unresponsive with a head injury and multiple arm fractures. She's intubated, we're ventilating her, and we have an IV in place. Patient two is also female and about the same age, also beaten with clubs. She has a right-sided chest wall deformity and is having significant trouble breathing. The abdomen is rigid, and internal hemorrhage is suspected. They're working on IVs and will sedate her, then place a chest tube. They'll paralyze her and intubate if needed. Patient three is a twelve-year-old male, conscious and alert with an arm fracture. So far, no other injuries found."

"Information received Air Two. Air One is landing now, and we'll have it towed out of the way immediately. Medical teams will meet you on the pad."

During the remainder of the flight, Amy was concerned about her new passengers but also thankful. They had found survivors. Their mission could continue.

As Amy approached the mountain, she could see three hospital stretchers and a group of people lined up at the entrance to the tunnel. As soon as the wheels touched the ground, her team started unloading the injured.

By the time she got out of the UH-60, the tow vehicle was already hooking to the front of the aircraft to pull it into the tunnel and out of harm's way as the fierce storm drew closer.

She hurried to the health center and into the triage area. There was a nurse and a medic working on the young boy, while RJ gently tried to ask him some questions. Amy learned that the other two were already being prepared for surgery.

Seeing that there was little more that she could do, she headed for the mess hall. Having spent all afternoon in the cockpit of the Black

Hawk had made her quite hungry. Grabbing a generous helping of spaghetti with Italian sausage, a Caesar salad, and some iced tea, she took a seat at the back of the room.

Only a couple of minutes passed before RJ entered and settled into a chair across from her. "What happened out there? How did you find them? Who beat them?" She sounded flustered.

"If you stop asking questions for a minute, I'll tell you the whole story, RJ," Amy announced. She popped a slice of Italian sausage into her mouth and groaned in appreciation.

RJ smiled weakly. "Okay, tell me the story."

When Amy finished her rundown of the events, RJ nodded in appreciation. "Sounds like you did a great job."

"Did you learn anything from the kid?"

"Not yet. He's a bit of a mess right now. He's in pain and he's been given morphine, which makes it trickier to get any useful information from him. He's never seen an aircraft, let alone ridden in one, and he's terrified the two women will die. Unfortunately, there's a good chance one of them will die. Only thing we know for sure is that one of them is his mother. One of the med techs is primarily a child psychologist. She'll be staying with him for now. As soon as his arm is fixed, she'll give him a short tour of the facility. Hopefully, that will loosen him up a bit."

"You know, we just found five people. There must be more. I think this will make everyone feel a whole lot better."

Chapter 42

Mike and Wade had experienced better evenings. They'd been busy all day on a foraging trip, and now they were being sent out to the generator shed. Neither of them particularly minded working in the generator shed, but the storm was intensifying and at least one of them would have to sit by the ancient machine and fight to keep it running for as long as it was needed.

The crazy part about this whole situation was that the generator was usually started every Saturday morning and they kept it running for twelve hours, once every week. It was a schedule which had been in place ever since they'd arrived here almost a year before. The schedule never changed, and while several other generators were used in the town, this one was used for a special purpose.

Now, they were about to go out into some of the nastiest weather imaginable to start the blasted thing on a Thursday evening. It made no sense. But from what they'd heard, these orders had come directly from the old man. No one would consider arguing with him, not after all he'd done for them. If it weren't for the old man, most of them wouldn't be alive.

His efforts over the past years hadn't just brought the group to this town but had enabled them to grow in numbers. There were twice as many of them now as there'd been before.

Mike could still remember sitting with the old man in the shelter, asking him questions about what things were like before the comet came.

The old man could describe the old days with such great detail, a younger Mike had been able to envision living back in those times. Even better were the promises that in the future they would all be able to leave the shelters and return to that life. The old man even told of his dreams in which people from the days before the comet would be waiting for them outside and help them start over.

Drawn back from his thoughts, Mike nodded his head to confirm he was ready, and Wade forced the door open. The two teens raced out into the storm.

Wade stopped just long enough to make sure the door was tightly shut before he ran after his friend. By the time the two of them had run the twenty yards to the generator shed, they were thoroughly soaked.

Since it was night and they couldn't leave the door open for moonlight to light the shed, they used matches and lit a kerosene lantern which was easily more than a century old. The dim light it gave off was just enough for the boys to do their work.

It took less than ten minutes to get the generator running at full power. As soon as the generator spluttered to life, the two overhead light bulbs lit up brightly, and Wade extinguished the old lantern.

Mike leaned over and pressed the talk button on the intercom mounted on the wall. "Generator on," he called.

Mike thought this final act was rather ridiculous; the lights in the offices of the main building would have come on as soon as the generator started, and if the lights were on, obviously the generator must be working. Nevertheless, it was the required procedure.

"Thanks, boys," came the friendly reply.

"Was that him?" Wade asked, sounding shocked.

"Sure was. You almost never see him in the admin building at this time of night."

The boys picked up a deck of worn playing cards that they kept stashed in the shed and were just a few hands into their game when the sound of screaming and yelling erupted from the administration building. The storm was loud and fierce overhead, but the boys still heard it.

Without any thought for the rules requiring at least one of them to stay with the generator at all times when that it was running, they both took off at a dead run. Mike reached down and ran his fingers over the revolver that was always on his hip. The only explanation for the sudden eruption of screams was desert raiders.

The raiders refused to join the community but were more than willing to slip in and attempt to steal whatever they wanted. Usually, they rode in on motorcycles, and on one occasion they had a small pickup truck which they'd managed to get running. There were times when community members tried to resist them, but someone always got hurt or killed, and most of the time it wasn't the raiders.

Wade had fallen in the slippery mud and Mike managed to jump over his body, racing on with his hand on his holster. A mud-covered Wade was right behind him. The noise had settled down some, as Mike entered the main room, he could see that his initial assessment was wrong.

Everyone seemed to be in one of the most joyous moods Mike had ever seen. Almost as happy as the day when the old man declared it was safe to leave the shelter.

The sound of the door slamming had caught the group's attention, and they turned and stared at the boys and saw the confused expressions on their faces.

"We heard screaming, thought something must be wrong," Wade explained.

Focusing more closely on the mud-covered teen, the group, started laughing.

Mike removed his hand from the gun and hurried across to the other members of the group. "What's going on?"

"Quiet! It's starting again," a man standing at the equipment console demanded.

"Turn it up louder!" Someone shouted back.

Over the old speakers hanging on the wall, a female voice rang out. "Greetings, this is the commanding officer of a team of specialists who were prepared before the comet devastated our civilization. We have a team of over ten thousand men and women, specifically trained for rebuilding our once great nation. We have the technology, tools and knowledge of the past with us and will be helping to rebuild. Please contact us on this frequency, and we'll send a team to meet with you to start the long project which lies ahead of us all. Thank you."

The cheering started up all over again.

"The message repeats every three minutes on all frequencies," the man at the console explained.

"What do we do now?" a woman somewhere in the crowd asked.

"I'll answer them," a deep voice responded. A tall strong-looking man started moving through the crowd, walking slowly and with confidence. The silver-gray hair was the only visible feature which would allow anyone to realize he was as old as he truly was.

With respect, bordering on awe, the crowd quickly parted for the old man. He walked to the console, turned, and faced the group. "For years, I've been telling you the stories about the past. Many of you as children heard me speak of how one day we would rebuild. I said that I envisioned people waiting to help us as we fought to turn things back to where they were. These are the people I spoke of."

Chapter 43

Amy had finished her meal, and the two women were still discussing the discovery of living people nearby. RJ admitted she was worried about the two men on motorbikes, who'd been attacking them, but until they got a clearer picture, she couldn't imagine what they could do about it. "Tomorrow, why don't you head back to where you found them and start searching for anything which might give us an idea about where they were going. We'll see if the boy can help. Maybe an offer of a helicopter ride might make him more cooperative," RJ suggested.

"Sounds good. I'm almost finished here. Wanna stop back at the medical center and see if there are any updates on the two women?"

Before RJ could answer, a voice echoed through the intercom. "Miss Anderson, please report to the command center," Abby requested, sounding excited.

"Wonder what that's all about," RJ questioned.

"She sure seems worked up about something," Amy agreed.

Amy dropped off her tray, and they hurried towards the command center. Brad Warren met up with them, coming out of the health center. "What's got Abby all excited?" he asked.

"Don't know yet," RJ responded.

"Good evening Miss Anderson," The computer said when RJ placed her hand on the wall pad. The doors slid open, and RJ caught sight of her two technicians. They were on their feet and Nick was anxiously waving the group over.

"What's going on?" RJ demanded.

"We got a message! Someone responded to the radio transmission!" Nick shouted.

"What did they say?" Brad asked.

"Sounded like an older guy, says his name is David. He's the leader of a local town, says he's been waiting for us. He even asked for you by name."

"He asked for me? That doesn't make any sense. Is he still there?" RJ asked.

"Should be, I asked him to stand by while we located you."

RJ made her way to one of the consoles and sat down, surprised by how nervous she felt.

"David, this is RJ Anderson. Are you still there?"

"Miss Anderson, I'm so glad to hear your voice. We've been listening for your message every week for the past year. We anxiously want to meet with you."

"We're looking forward to meeting with you, too. I can send someone to meet with you tomorrow. Will that work?"

"Excellent. We're excited to begin working with your people."

"I understand that when you contacted us, you asked for me by name. My name isn't mentioned in the broadcast we transmitted. How do you know me?"

"That's a long story, but I'll give you all the details when we meet. I suspect there's lots of information we can share," David explained.

RJ was none too pleased with the obtuse answer but decided not to push the point. "What can you tell me about your group?" she asked.

"There's about forty of us, we're trying to attract more people all the time. People are scattered in small groups all over the country. We wanted to bring them all here, close to your mountain, so we can begin rebuilding."

RJ shared a pointed glance with Brad and Amy. It was obvious they were all thinking the same thing. How could this old guy know about the mountain? That information was supposed to remain strictly protected. “We can definitely help with that. It sounds like your goals are exactly in line with our mission. I need to know one thing, are you missing a small group of people from your community? We found two women and a boy in the desert about thirty miles north of our location. The women are in bad shape, one may well die. They were being beaten up by a couple of guys on motorcycles when we found them.”

“No Miss Anderson, we aren’t missing anyone from our group. I suspect they were probably on their way to join up with us because where you found them is close to our location. We have a problem with raiders, they ride around on their motorcycles often attacking people who can’t defend themselves” David explained.

“I suspect we can help in that regard, too,” RJ answered.

“What became of the raiders who attacked this group you mentioned?”

“They escaped into the desert.”

“That’s unfortunate. I’ll look forward to meeting with your people tomorrow.”

“Good night David.”

“Good night.”

RJ locked gazes with Brad. “This doesn’t make sense. How can they know so much about us?”

“I guess we’ll find out in the morning,” was Brad’s only response.

Chapter 44

Bud lay face down in the mud, fighting to keep himself as low to the ground as possible. He'd been waiting here for almost an hour now. Tam was somewhere up ahead, but he couldn't see her. The storm was still raging, and while it should keep the mountain people from seeing her, it made him uneasy not knowing where she was.

He'd objected to her being chosen to crawl up close to their perimeter; she was young and less experienced. Not to mention the fact that they were lovers and he was worried about her because of their close relationship.

In truth he understood why she'd been chosen, her small build increased her chances of success and she made a smaller target for their weapons if she was seen. The fact that she was new to the group meant she had less information she could reveal if she was captured. Bud didn't like thinking of her as expendable, but in the eyes of the others, that's what she was.

Tam had been captured when he and the other raiders broke into an underground bunker a year before. Tam was the only member of her family, and one of the only inhabitants of the bunker to survive the attack. After many months of resistance, she'd agreed to become one of them, instead of remaining their servant and prisoner.

Now she was out ahead of the raiding party, scouting out this new group. If the things they'd heard were even partially correct, this could be a fantastic opportunity. Some of the other raiders claimed to have seen some of these mountain people enter a deserted town, and their weapons were in excellent condition. They'd even reported that these newcomers were using radio communications. They had followed them back to this mountain and alerted the rest of the raiders.

Rumors were circulating throughout the raiders though, rumors which suggested someone had seen a helo flying overhead.

Personally, Bud found this impossible to believe. As far as he knew, there hadn't been any helos flying for years. Bud had seen a few at airports and military bases, but they were usually in really bad shape.

A few years ago, a raiding party had found one in good condition, and the raiders had worked for over a month to get it working. Eventually, they did get it running, and the engine had sounded quite smooth. Unfortunately, as soon as they got it into the air, the flying machine had gotten out of control, and the body started spinning almost as fast as the rotors. It had only climbed about thirty feet into the air when it suddenly dropped.

Bud had once seen a combat scene on an old video disk where a helo had hit the ground and immediately exploded. When their helo dropped that day, everyone on the ground had run for their lives. After several minutes without an explosion, they carefully approached the helo to discover the two people aboard had died in the crash. It was the closest Bud had gotten to seeing a real helo flying.

The raiders had a base camp in the mountains, and there were about fifty in their group. They'd come from all over the area and joined together because there was strength in numbers.

Bud joined the raiders years before, after his parents had been killed. His mother was suspected to have died from cancer, and Bud and his father had gone on with living the best they could. They foraged for food and stayed in sheltered areas as much as possible.

One cold evening, Bud's father was trying to get an old kerosene heater working when the heater fell off a rickety table and covered him with burning fuel. Bud had tried desperately to help his father, but the fire quickly spread through the small house they'd been staying in and Bud had to flee, leaving his dying father thrashing around on the floor.

Bud had met up with the raiders shortly after and they'd welcomed him. Initially, he'd been bothered by the violence the raiders used against others, but over time Bud had become desensitized to it, and it seldom concerned him anymore.

Most of the raiders were in their late teens or twenties, the offspring of parents who had originally been in shelters. Some had been born to parents who'd survived the radiation, due to luck, skill and more than a little ingenuity. Numerous stories had circulated about those few who survived, even though they took no precautions and made no effort to avoid the deadly radiation. There were no answers as to why they'd survived when so many others had not, but the simple fact was that somehow, they had made it.

Today the raiders had selected twenty-five of their best fighters and set out for the mountain. Their leader had agreed that any caves in the mountain couldn't possibly hold more than a couple of dozen men. Since they were sneaking up under cover of darkness, the element of surprise would be on their side. The raiders had the advantage, and they could quickly overtake a few dozen men. They'd formed up into two squads and Bud led one, while a young raider named Owen led the second. Bud was in overall command.

The longer he waited, the more his concern for Tam had increased. The fact that there were twenty-three other raiders all around them did nothing to ease his fears.

His team had left their motorcycles about a mile back and crept to this point on foot. As soon as Tam reached them with a report, they would sneak in as close as possible and attack without warning.

Bud's concern only increased when he noticed the storm was subsiding and the additional cover it had provided would soon disappear.

It took another ten minutes, but he finally saw a lone figure, crouched down and running out of the darkness. He brought his old M-16 assault rifle up and centered the sight on the chest of the individual. Bud knew there would be over twenty other weapons trained on the runner and until positive identification was made, they would remain pointed and ready to fire.

When Tam was only ten feet away, her young face became visible and Bud's right arm shot up into the air, signaling the others that her identity was confirmed.

As a group, they retreated about twenty yards back and concealed themselves behind a large collection of rocks.

"What did you see?" Bud demanded.

"Yeah, how close did you get?" another voice called.

"There's a gatehouse at the entrance, with two guards. One of them was asleep. There's a large pile of rocks about twenty-five yards from the gatehouse, I watched them for about fifteen minutes with the binoculars, and the only activity I saw was when the guard who was awake stepped out to pee. They have a vehicle, it's a military Hummer. I couldn't tell what kind of condition it's in. The best part is that they have power and I could hear a small generator running."

Bud was more excited than he'd been in a long time by this news. Generators were always in short supply and bringing another one back to camp would elevate him to hero status with the other raiders.

"Did you see any weapons?" Owen asked.

"I couldn't see inside the gatehouse, but the one who stepped out appeared to be carrying an M-16, or maybe an M-4. The light wasn't good; I only got a glimpse of it. I think we should be able to get close enough to take them both out without shooting and waking the rest of their people."

"All right," Bud said. "We'll move back up. Tam will lead us to the rocks she hid behind. From there, we'll try to take them quick and quiet. Any questions?"

It took the raiders over twenty minutes to move back into position. The first half of the journey was easy, everyone moving at a crouched run, but the rest of the way the raiders crawled on their bellies through the wet dirt and mud.

Once they reached the rocks, Bud lifted the binoculars he carried and studied the scene in front of him. The only difference that Bud could see from what Tam had said was that there was no sign of the guards. The guards' vehicle was just as Tam described, but they were nowhere in sight.

They waited another ten minutes, but nothing changed. While they waited, Bud listened to the sound of the generator, certain he could hear another mechanical noise coming from much further up. If that was another generator, this was already the most significant find for the raiders in a very long time.

Bud decided he'd had enough; the two guards must be in the gatehouse, sleeping and out of view. He signaled his men and he and Owen led their squads toward the gatehouse. As they approached, Bud was aware that the sound of the second, distant generator almost seemed to be getting louder.

He and four of his men burst through the entrance to the ten foot by ten foot gatehouse with their weapons ready and quickly swept the room. It was empty. No sooner had this registered in Bud's mind, than the generator quit and all the lights went out.

Bud stopped in his tracks, trying to make sense of what was happening when Owen started yelling for him to come outside. Bud did as Owen said, and noticed that the other generator was still running and seemed even louder than it had only moments ago.

Racing outside he saw four vehicles rushing toward them out of the darkness, Owen was pointing up, and Bud's blood ran cold. The sound he'd been hearing wasn't another generator, it was coming from the helo which was hovering just in front of his group. Even in the darkness, Bud could make out the deadly rockets and massive cannon pointed directly at him. He dived to the ground and noticed that the four Humvees had formed a half circle, preventing them from advancing any further.

When he looked at the rest of the raiding party on the ground, he could see at least a dozen bright red dots of light moving back and forth over them. He assumed these must be from laser scopes mounted on the rifles of troops, waiting unseen out in the darkness.

Bud could just make out a man standing in the back of the nearest Humvee, manning the mounted machine gun. He was wearing a helmet and wore a bizarre set of goggles which gave him a bug-like appearance.

Bud had never seen anything like it, but he'd heard about bizarre goggles that allowed the wearer to see in the dark as clearly as if it was daylight. It meant that he could see one of them, but they could see him and his entire team.

Until these last two revelations crossed Bud's mind, the option of fighting had been on the table. Now it was run, and hopefully not get shot in the back – or surrender.

Bud had come to the conclusion that retreating would be the best option when suddenly, one of his men who lay four feet away jumped up and opened fire on the helo with a shotgun. The other raiders hurriedly got to their feet, some running for the gate and others beginning to shoot. Bud turned to run, knowing there was no way they could win this fight.

He'd taken little more than a couple of steps when he glanced back over his shoulder and saw flames shooting from the helo's cannon. Something smashed into him at waist level and he was thrown in the air before crashing back onto the ground. The sounds of weapon fire quickly came to a halt.

Bud was surprised by how little pain he experienced. He twisted his head to one side and realized all the raiders near him were down, several clearly dead. Owen lay twenty feet away, alive but wounded.

Lying next to Bud's head was a severed leg. It took him a minute to recognize the boot, and he vomited when he realized the leg he was staring at was his own.

He heard the generator by the guardhouse startup, and three large floodlights lit up the entire area.

His teeth began to chatter, cold seeping through his bones, and he knew he was losing too much blood. He found himself hoping Tam had escaped with the others who'd run. He wished he'd turned around and run the second things went wrong.

Bud suddenly noticed something strange; none of the raiders were being pursued by the soldiers. He was baffled as to why these troops weren't hunting down and eliminating his friends. That's what he would have ordered them to do.

He reached down and gingerly touched his wounds. His hand jerked back when he realized what he was touching was a large loop of his own intestines.

He heard a whistling sound, and then soldiers rushed toward his team with their weapons at the ready, night vision devices removed. They started collecting weapons from the dead and dying.

He caught an unexpected movement in his peripheral vision and forced his head around to see what it was. Bud watched as Tam climbed out of a shallow hole behind the gatehouse which looked freshly dug. Without a backward glance, she walked over to a woman wearing a gray jumpsuit and shook her offered hand. Tam was still carrying her weapon and his heart twisted with agony matching the excruciating pain slowly building in his body. His fury built, but he was powerless to do anything.

His vision started to fade, but he was able to make out the image of Owen slowly bringing his AK-47 assault rifle up and pointing it directly at Tam. Part of Bud wanted to warn her, but another part was enraged that he wouldn't be the one to pull the trigger.

A single shot rang out, and the last image Bud saw was Owen's head disappearing in a red mist.

* * *

As soon as the weapons had been collected, Jill Warren increased power to the AH-64 Apache and increased altitude. Her co-pilot gunner (CPG) Steve activated the thermal imaging systems which instantly revealed the scene below in a whole different manner. The heat of the people's bodies glowed brightly, but not as bright as the heat radiating from the generator and the Humvees engines. Lower heat readings were coming from the body parts scattered around and the dead, whose bodies had started cooling off.

Jill was disappointed; it had appeared they'd be able to capture the raiders without firing a single shot, until someone did something stupid and started shooting, and the rest of the fools joined in.

Jill estimated close to fifty rounds had been fired at her aircraft during the brief battle, though only one round had made contact, and it ricocheted harmlessly off the armored fuselage.

She rose to a thousand feet altitude and slowly advanced. It took less than a minute to start picking up the heat signatures from the fleeing raiders. Jill followed them, confirming her external lights were off. She was a lot higher than she would usually have flown while trying to follow someone, but her orders were explicit; she was not to be detected.

The Apache's crew watched as the raiders reached their motorcycles and sped off into the night. Jill was no longer worried about being heard, so she dropped down and started following the bright heat signatures of the motorcycles.

At one point, she considered how easily she could eliminate the whole group with a few well-placed rockets, but there had already been far more deaths tonight than they'd hoped for. This part of her mission, if all went well, wouldn't involve any weapons at all.

Chapter 45

"As most of you know, things have started getting interesting around here," RJ began, addressing the people who'd gathered around the large conference table. "Last night we were contacted by radio by the leader of a group of survivors who've apparently taken up residence in a town about twenty-five miles from here. Brad will be leading a team later this morning to meet up with the survivors for a face-to-face meeting. While this sounds wonderful, there are some genuine concerns regarding this group. The information they have about the mountain is troubling. In just the few minutes of contact we had last night, it became apparent they knew several vital pieces of information about us, our location, and our mission. In of itself, it's no major problem, but it is something we'll have to investigate further."

"While I was talking to their leader last night, he told us there are groups of raiders in the area. They attack with violence and don't hesitate to kill if they think you've got something they want. We've confirmed the injured civilians found yesterday evening had been attacked by a group of these raiders. They're usually on motorcycles and in some cases, apparently, have access to other vehicles. Last night a group of twenty-five of these raiders attacked the south gate here at the mountain. They were apparently planning on discovering what we had that could be of use to them."

There was a smattering of laughs at this statement. Most everyone had heard about the outcome of the battle and some almost felt sorry for the raiders, who'd had no idea what they were coming up against.

RJ continued. "This is Tam," she announced, placing her hand on the shoulder of the girl sitting by her side at the table. "She had been sent by the raiders as a forward scout, but when she realized what she'd come across, she offered us information about the coming attack in exchange for safety from the raider group and she wants to work with us. The intelligence she's already provided has proven invaluable. We intentionally allowed several of the raiders to escape last night and an Apache followed them back to what appears to be a semi-permanent encampment just southeast of here. Air One is currently on its way back here from dropping off a ten-man recon team. Their instructions are to remain undetected and monitor all activity at the camp. We'll have air support on twenty-four-hour standby, just in case the team gets into trouble, which means we're already going to be running short of manpower. After this meeting, we're going to wake another forty sleepers. Specifically combat troops, pilots, and medical personnel. Our limited medical personnel were overwhelmed twice yesterday, first with the three civilian casualties and later with the five wounded raiders we recovered, so we'll get that problem taken care of. There will also be a few construction people woken up to get the external personnel quarters back into shape because we'll need them soon. We'll also be getting four more Humvees and two more UH-60 Black Hawks up and running. We'll make a determination regarding another gunship after today's meeting."

As the meeting broke up, RJ got Brad's attention, and the two of them took a walk. "I want to make sure you watch your back at that meeting," RJ said. "I'll be uneasy until there's an explanation as to how they know what they do. I'm sure there's a reasonable explanation, but this just isn't the way it was supposed to work."

Chapter 46

Brad Warren sat in the front seat of the UH-60 designated Air Two as it flew rapidly across the barren terrain. They'd followed the Colorado River north for ten minutes before changing course, heading west. Dr. Stephen Cross and a security team sat in the back of the Black Hawk. Dr. Cross had been brought along to assess the general health of the community and provide medical help to anyone who needed it.

Members of the security team had undergone disaster relief training, so they could assist in making an initial survey of the town and assess what needed to be done.

They were also present because they didn't know exactly what they were heading into and needed to be prepared in case this David wasn't as friendly as he initially seemed. Backing up Brad's team was a fully armed team aboard Air One who were currently heading toward the site where Travers found the injured group the night before. They would investigate the scene and see if any more information could be learned as to the origin of the victims of the attack. If needed they could be over Brad Warren's location in less than ten minutes.

The AH-64 Apache gunship, Air Three, was also in the air, its function to be available if either of the aircrews or any ground crews needed air support.

Amy brought the helicopter in for a landing, a short distance from a large group which had gathered in what appeared to be the center of town. She'd chosen the position specifically, wanting lots of open space around the aircraft. Safety was a factor, but she was just as concerned with making sure no one could approach the aircraft without being seen.

The first two soldiers to leave the helicopter took up sentry positions on either side of the aircraft. Amy and Brad climbed out next, quickly followed by Dr. Cross and the rest of the security team.

As Brad was in command of this mission, Amy held back, prepared to assist him if necessary they approached the group, aware of the obvious looks of pleasure and awe they garnered. Twenty feet away from the group, Brad was stunned when the crowd broke into spontaneous applause and people ran forward, hugging the team. It was unexpected and even a bit disconcerting; Amy looked to Brad for guidance but saw he was looking back at her with a confused expression.

The noise died down and the crowd parted, making way for a man who was approaching Brad and his team. He looked to be about seventy-five years old; perhaps six foot three, he was dressed in a clean white dress shirt and light tan pants. A well-worn fedora was on his head. He had a short, neat beard and walked with the aid of a hand-carved walking stick. "My name is David; I'm the leader of these people," the old man said, holding out his hand.

"I'm Brad Warren. I'm second in command of our team." The two men shook hands.

"Mr. Warren, we've been anxiously waiting for your awakening. I knew you were out here somewhere, but I didn't know the exact location of the mountain."

"You knew we were sleeping? The whole sleep project was classified, that was never supposed to get out," Brad commented, his confusion apparent.

"When we came out of the shelter, I led these people here. I didn't know your exact location, but I knew it had to be in this general area. Plus, I wanted a town that we could use as a good starting point for rebuilding. This town is perfectly situated, we even have an airport. We don't have any planes, obviously, but I knew you did. For the past year, I've been working everyone here pretty hard, getting as much work done as possible to prepare it for your arrival."

He gestured with his right hand toward the area around them. The description of dilapidated buildings the previous day's teams had reported certainly didn't pertain to this little town. New construction was readily apparent, and everything was neat and clean. There were flowers in places and some grass which looked recently mowed.

"Sir, I think it's great that you've gotten all this done and you're ready to work with us, but I need to understand how you know so much about us," Brad said, the tone of his voice a little firmer.

David smiled. "I understand your concerns. Everything I know about you and your team, I learned from my mother. Do you have someone named Amy Travers on your team?"

Brad glanced behind him and nodded. Amy stepped forward. With a noticeable hesitation in her voice, she spoke. "I'm Amy Travers."

The old man's face lit up. "My parents always spoke so highly of you! Other than my mother, you were my father's closest friend."

Amy shook her head. "I'm sorry. Who are you?" she asked nervously.

The old man smiled when he answered. "My name is David Cowan; my father's name was James."

Epilogue – 6 Months Later

Brad Warren drove the Humvee down the gravel road leading out to the airport. It was an exciting day because RJ was on her way back from Massachusetts with what they hoped would be the first group of survivors who wanted to join to them. In the passenger seat beside him was an eager David Cowan. David appeared in better health than he had six months before. The day to day stress of leading his people had taken a heavy toll on the man. Now that the sleepers were here, and even though things were more exciting than ever, he finally thought he could slow his pace a little.

During the drive, Brad reminisced about everything that had been accomplished in the short period of time since the awakening.

After the initial meeting between Brad and David, relations and interaction between the former sleepers and David's people proceeded better than anyone had hoped. Long ago plans were modified and put into motion and there'd been massive amounts of building construction and road repair.

Over eight thousand sleepers had been awakened and were contributing to close to a hundred different projects.

The local power generating facilities along the Colorado River was partially back online, and relatively reliable electricity was flowing.

Cellular phone service was available in the three adjoining towns, which were now designated as stage one of the rebuilding project.

The local hospital was still in need of further repairs, but it was open and operational. Advanced medical care was now available to people, many of whom had never seen a physician before.

The raiders were no longer a threat in the Tri-town area. Shortly after that first encounter with the raiders, armed helicopters and ground troops swarmed in on the raider's camp while they slept. Without a single shot being fired, every raider was rounded up and their weapons and equipment confiscated. They were given two options. Behave and join in the rebuilding efforts or leave the area. Most chose to leave, but some joined the growing community.

Within a month of the initial awakening, the local airport had reopened, and many of the sleepers' aircraft were moved there permanently. The rest would be moved once more hanger space was available. Soon reconnaissance flights began, using F-15E fighter jets. Instead of missiles, these aircraft carried sophisticated cameras which were used to look for evidence of other groups who were rebuilding.

Night flights were equipped with thermal imaging cameras, and groups of survivors were located by heat signatures given off by equipment and cooking fires.

Before long several dozen groups had been located. The decision was made to focus first on a collection of groups in the New England area. As soon as they'd been located and charted, the F-15s took off again. This time they 'bombed' the sites. Several thousand printed leaflets were dropped over each location describing what the sleeper mission had been, rebuilding efforts, and giving the radio frequency which could be used to establish contact.

For those who didn't wish to relocate to the tri-town area, efforts would be made to maintain regular communication for the purposes of information exchange. Experts on farming, engineering and medicine would make regular visits to any friendly settlements wanting to participate.

The Humvee entered the airport boundaries, and Brad saw two old school buses pull in behind him. The buses had been stored inside a garage which had mostly survived the last fifty-four years, and it had only taken a couple of weeks to get them back on the road. Now, Brad hoped they wouldn't be leaving the airport empty.

David and Brad exited the Humvee and hurried into the terminal, where a temporary control center had been set up while the control tower was rebuilt.

"Do you have an ETA on them?" David asked.

"About ten minutes, sir. We had them on the radar a while ago, and then the radar went down again. It's been quite unreliable. I have someone looking into it now."

David inclined his head in acknowledgment. "Okay, thanks."

The two men walked out towards the old observation area. There was construction going on all around them, but they didn't seem to notice.

"So, how many are you guessing will be on board, Brad?" David wondered.

"If we get twenty, I'll be happy," Brad answered.

David started to respond, but he was cut off by Brad's shout. "There they are!"

Brad pointed to the north, and it took only a few seconds for David to focus on the spot in the sky that was growing rapidly.

Eight minutes later a C-141 transport plane rolled up, and the doors opened a few minutes later. As soon as the stairs were in place RJ emerged, looking tired as she descended the stairs.

Both David and Brad watched with growing concern as seconds passed and no one else appeared at the doors. Finally, a young girl cautiously stepped out, followed by an older man. Brad counted thirty people before his cell phone rang and he lost count. He quickly answered, his gaze firmly focused on watching more and more people get off the plane.

"Brad, it's me," said a familiar voice.

"RJ, how did everything go?" Brad looked around, saw her standing below his window, watching him as the line of people walked past her.

"We only had room for a hundred of them; we'll go and pick up the other half in a few days. Some of them have chosen to stay there to work to build their own community, but they want our help."

"Sounds fantastic, we'll be right down," Brad exclaimed.

He turned to David and told him the news and saw the single tear which formed in the old man's eye, just before he turned and ran off, anxious to meet the new arrivals.

The End

If you enjoyed THE ARK by Christopher Coates, please log onto Amazon and give it a great review.

Thank You!

About the Author

Christopher Coates grew up on Cape Cod Massachusetts, and moved to Michigan for college.

He currently lives in Kent City, Michigan with his wife-Jerri, daughter-Nicole and son-Jared.

Christopher is a retired Firefighter/Paramedic who works full time in Information Systems for a major West Michigan company.

Printed in Great Britain
by Amazon

34307335R00156